THE BEST OF THE WEST

THE BEST OF THE WEST

NEW SHORT STORIES FROM THE WIDE SIDE OF THE MISSOURI

Edited by James Thomas
With Tom Hazuka, Jonathan Maney,
and Denise Thomas

Peregrine Smith Books
Salt Lake City

89 88 3 2

Acknowledgments of previous publication and permissions to reprint the stories in this book may be found on page ix and x.

Published by Gibbs Smith, Publisher
P.O. Box 667
Layton, Utah 84041

Design by J. Scott Knudsen

Printed and bound in the United States of America

Library of Congress Cataloging-in-Publication Data

Best of the West : new short stories from the wide side of the Missouri / edited by James Thomas with Tom Hazuka, Jonathan Maney, and Denise Thomas.
p. cm.
ISBN 0-87905-332-1
1. Western stories. 2. American fiction—20th century. 3. Short stories, American—West (U.S.) I. Thomas, James, 1946- .
PS648.W4B47 1988 88-9932
813'.0874'08—dc19 CIP

Where West Is

Long before we were born
the people who lived in the world
had their way of finding west
without the use of delicate instruments.

One of them whose duty it was
to find west would begin to walk
in the direction of the setting sun
while chanting the tale of the world
in his head.

When he was finished
he would bend down and
draw a line in the dirt
with his finger.

Beyond this line
everything was west.

Thom Tammaro

CONTENTS

ACKNOWLEDGMENTS

"Where West Is" by Thom Tammaro. Appeared in *Quarterly West.* Copyright © 1974, 1988 by Thom Tammaro. Reprinted by permission of the author.

"A Hunk of Burning Love" by François Camoin. First appeared in *Missouri Review.* Published in *Why Men Are Afraid of Women,* University of Georgia Press. Copyright © 1984, 1988 by François Camoin. Reprinted with permission of the author and the University of Georgia Press.

"The Man Who Knew Belle Starr" by Richard Bausch. Appeared in *The Atlantic.* Published in *Spirits and Other Stories,* Linden Books, a division of Simon & Schuster, Inc. Copyright © 1979, 1983, 1985, 1986, 1987, 1988 by Richard Bausch. Reprinted by permission of Linden Books.

"Yellow Woman" by Leslie Marmon Silko. Published in *Storyteller* by Leslie Marmon Silko, Seaver Books, New York, New York. Copyright © 1981, 1988 by Leslie Marmon Silko. Reprinted with permission of Seaver Books.

"Phenomena" by Ron Carlson. First appeared in *Writer's Forum.* Published in THE NEWS OF THE WORLD, Stories by Ron Carlson, W. W. Norton & Company, Inc. Reprinted by permission of the author and W. W. Norton & Company, Inc. Copyright © 1987 by Ron Carlson.

"Desert Owls" by Bill Ripley. Appeared in *Quarterly West.* Copyright © 1988 by Bill Ripley. Reprinted by permission of the author.

"Bob and The Other Man" by Allen Wier. First appeared in *Sandlapper.* Published in *Things About To Disappear,* Louisiana State University Press. Copyright © 1978, 1988 by Allen Wier. Reprinted by permission of the author and Louisiana State University Press.

"True Romance" by Ron Hansen. First appeared in *Esquire,* From the forthcoming *Nebraska* by Ron Hansen, Atlantic Monthly Books. Reprinted by permission of the author. Copyright © 1984, 1988 by Ron Hansen.

"Great Falls" by Richard Ford. First appeared in *Esquire.* Published in *Rock Springs* by Richard Ford, Atlantic Monthly Books. Copyright © 1987, 1988 by Richard Ford. Reprinted by permission of The Atlantic Monthly Books.

"No One's A Mystery" by Elizabeth Tallent. First appeared in *Harpers.* Published in *Time With Children,* Alfred A. Knopf, Inc. Copyright © 1984, 1987, 1988 by Elizabeth Tallent. Reprinted with permission of the author and the P.E.N. Syndicated Fiction Project.

INTRODUCTION

What we care about in the best stories we read are the people living through them, not where the stories are set. Yet it is true that the American West has affected the character of those who have made it their home, shaped in fact the stories which are their lives—as well as influenced the behavior of those simply passing through it—in a way no other geographical region of this country could. To be in the vast openness of the West is to become immediately sensitized to the landscape: to be constantly aware of it when not in awe of it, engaged or endangered by it, conditioned if not controlled by it.

Of course there are also cities ringed with freeways and throbbing with industry, and in them and around them communities with close neighborhoods. There is the combustion and confusion and warm comfort that can be found anywhere in the country where people have knotted themselves together. But in the West these concentrations of human togetherness are highly self-conscious, set as they are against a backdrop of empty desert and vertiginous mountains, dense forest and rapacious rivers, a wideness and an openness and an emptiness so large that in its midst an entire sea has evaporated, atomic bombs are tested, and an Indian nation as large in area as Vermont, New Hampshire and Connecticut combined has survived. In the West, between its occasional cities, it is possible to drive at the speed limit for an hour and not meet another vehicle; and to wander off the road on foot can mean, as it has for many, being lost forever.

Not only does the wildly beautiful but indifferent terrain of the West affect the long and short vision of the individual, it also affects human relationships, the interpersonal dynamics which are at the center of all our best stories, whether fiction or fact. It is not clear why this is so. But the reasons, I believe, can be found or *felt* in the collective truth of the stories in this anthology. Each story is a case study of a tenuous human relationship, and in each one the West itself can be sensed and understood as a major factor in why things happen as they do. Take the West *out* of the story and somehow everything is different; we realize that what happened to the characters, and between them, would and could not have happened anywhere else. And that is an awfully large thing to say about a geographical area—indeed, an almost ominous thing.

In the West it is—at least technically—never hard to get away from people, although it often seems quite difficult to get *to* people. Physical distance is a factor, but only one. There is also a kind of social distancing, usually friendly but not always, and not to be confused with any societal stratification we associate with the East, with money, or with both. This is the distancing we recognize, and with which we can often identify, behind the eyes that say, Look, I *came* here to be alone. Individualism is nowhere more noticeable than it is in the West, a kind of individualism that is in part a product of the region's relative isolation; and it is further defined in these stories where, because of it, we find a certain wariness, an uneasiness that is only occasionally comforted in any of the conventional ways.

Good fiction—the fiction that moves us—is itself wary. Simply put, it is aware of us long before we are aware of it. It is anticipatory—like the snake which, if we see it at all, is already eyeing us and prepared to surprise. The best fiction always surprises us, often enough it startles us, and at times it frightens us. These stories surprise, and some of them will make you more than uneasy.

The West has, of course, been the subject or setting of serious fiction since it was discovered. Stephen Crane, Bret Harte, Jack London, Willa Cather, and Mark Twain, among others, helped keep the rest of America posted on what frontier life was like. But in this century, and up until quite recently, fiction *about* the West did not progress with the years. Instead, the Old West was canonized and recanonized—and continues to be today by superb writers including E. L. Doctorow and Larry McMurtry. In the past twenty years, however, and especially in the last ten, the present-day West has emerged as the setting, if not the subject matter, of a new wealth of fiction.

This first volume of *Best of the West* brings together twenty recently published stories which, taken together, provide us with a powerful and penetrating vision of life in today's West, as well as a premier showcase of literary talent. It was not difficult arriving at twenty; it *was* difficult making final decisions. Many fine writers and many good stories could not be included. Fortunately, there is every likelihood that the writers who were edged out of this collection will be heard from again under this title, since we are already scouring the 150 or so periodicals which take short fiction seriously for the next volume of *Best of the West.*

What, exactly, is the West? That is, what has been our criterion for inclusion of a story in this anthology? The answer is that, finally, we have felt it essential to remain subjective. Thus you will find no catalogue of states here, no argument about how Texas is or isn't of the West, no mention of sagebrush. What is the West? If anything it is a state of mind, well represented by these stories. Rather than belabor the question, let me tell you instead where this book, and book series, originated. It was over a beer, with Nat Sobel of Sobel Weber Associates, Inc., New York City, in what was his second visit to Park City, Utah, a silver-mining town turned ski resort and host to the occasional film festival or writers' conference.

Said Nat, "How about . . . ," and concluded with the title of this book. I said yes and yes, but—and here we go—but how exactly do we define 'the West'? "The West," said Nat, only a bit incredulous with the question, "the West? Look, kid, you know. You *know. The West!*"

You know. I'm sure you do, we do. But if there is any question, let's again read the stories—the best of the West.

James Thomas
Salt Lake City

FRANÇOIS CAMOIN

A HUNK OF BURNING LOVE

Gene is already there when I come through the door of the New Deal Cafe and Bar. There's a sausage speared on the end of his fork and he's waving it in Rita's face. Gene's a fat man but a long way from jolly; he can in fact be mean as a snake if you give him half a chance. His hat is on the stool beside him, upside down with his work gloves folded in it. This morning we'll be digging post holes for a new fence in old man Hazzard's pasture.

"This sausage looks more like a dog turd," he says.

I like Rita. We have been to bed together now and then, after a hard Saturday night, in her little trailer out back of the cafe.

"Ease up, Gene," I tell him.

He turns around on the stool and gives me his Monday morning stare, cold and nasty, as if I was some Dallas-Fort Worth traveling salesman cutting in on his time, instead of the man he has been working alongside of, off and on, for the past three years since I came down from Chicago.

"Can I have the number three?" I ask Rita. "And lots of coffee?"

Gene is still giving me the stare. "I know what you've been doing," he says.

"What's that?"

"Never mind," he says. "I know, that's all."

"Eat your breakfast," I tell him. "It's going to be a hard day. Mellow out, buddy."

He looks after Rita, who is jiggling her way into the kitchen with my order. "Yeah?" he says.

His eyes show white all around like a spooky horse. I'm watching him carefully, ready to slide off my stool and give him room, but he blinks and heaves a big sigh. "One of these times they are by pure accident going to get somebody back there that knows how to cook and then I am going to have to start eating my breakfast in some other cafe because my stomach couldn't stand the surprise. Dog turds," he says, shoving the sausage in his mouth and chewing loud enough to make the salesmen at the table behind us turn around and look.

Gene looks back at them and smiles his best affable smile; they have the good sense to smile back.

Rita puts my breakfast down in front of me and swipes at the counter with a wet cloth. "Don't mind him," she says.

As soon as we get settled in the truck Gene slips the same old eight-track in the stereo; we ride the fifteen miles out to Hazzard's property listening to "Hound Dog" and "Blue Suede Shoes" and the rest of this tormented music that Gene likes so well.

He lights up a joint big as a dollar cigar and passes it across to me. In no time we are driving along in a cloud so thick it's a wonder he can find the road through the windshield.

"It was all them drugs give him by Jewish doctors," Gene says. "That killed him, I mean."

"How do you know they were Jewish?"

"I read about it," he says. "You telling me they weren't?"

"I don't know."

"You don't know much," he says.

His truck is an old four-wheel-drive Ford with balloon tires and a worn-out suspension; every little bump sends us swooping across the highway almost into the ditch on the far side.

"You think I'm some kind of bigot, don't you?" he says.

"No."

"Yeah you do."

"Watch the road," I tell him. "It's all right."

"No it ain't all right." He takes a deep drag, adds to the cloud. The truck bounces; Elvis sings. The heater is on and I feel dopey and too warm.

"The King," Gene says finally. "Being from Chicago you wouldn't know what that means."

"Why not? I watched Elvis the first time he was ever on TV, on the Ed Sullivan Show. I know the songs."

"Nope," Gene says. His voice is final. It reminds me of the bumper sticker on his tailgate. GOD SAID IT. I BELIEVE IT. THAT SETTLES IT. In blue and yellow. Not that I've ever heard of him going to church; he's religious in a patriotic, formal kind of way. It goes with the Confederate flag on the other side of the tailgate. I kidded him about fighting losing battles once, until he got mad, but it seems to me that's what the South is all about—how to get beaten and somehow come out on top morally.

"You been living down here with real folks three years now," Gene says. "You wear Dingo boots and a big buckle on your belt, and I taught you to drink Lone Star, but that don't mean you *know*."

Somebody coming the other way in a station wagon honks his horn and flashes the lights to tell us to get back on our own side of the road. Gene gives them the finger without letting himself get worked up about it. The King sings about the child born in the ghet-to. Gene turns him down.

"Hey, Lawrence," he says.

"Larry," I tell him for the hundredth time.

"Law-rence," he says. "You ever think what it's all about? Life, I mean. You ever stop to think how we're all going to die?"

"Monday's always bad," I tell him. "We'll be there in a minute and we'll work up a good sweat. You'll feel better."

"No," he says. "I don't think I will."

The tape is hung up between tracks and I give it a kick to get it started again, and turn up the volume; I'd rather listen to Elvis than to Gene getting himself spooked by life.

"I ought to be running fence around my own place instead of old man Hazzard's," he says. "Have some kids. You ever have kids, Lawrence?"

"Two."

"Where they at?"

"Chicago."

"You just left them there?" He shakes his head as if he can't believe a man could do such a thing.

By lunchtime we are down to just pants and boots. It's January and not much above freezing but we have worked up a fine sweat putting up half a dozen lengths of new split rail. Hazzard's pasture is mostly what they call *caliche,* hard as good Chicago cement. Here and there a little bit of bunch grass rises out of it, barely alive. It's a pasture the same way the New Deal Cafe is a restaurant.

Gene stretches out on the ground and uncaps a Lone Star. He hasn't said anything for the past couple of hours, but I can tell it's still Blue Monday.

"You and Rita," he says.

"What about me and Rita?"

He rubs his thumb and forefinger together and grins. "I know what you've been doing."

"It's no secret."

"I guess not," he says. We both stare at the sky, which is, like most always, enormous and blue. Now and then down here there is some sort of weather, usually violent. The rest of the time the sky is like a TV screen when the station is off the air, a blank waiting to be filled in.

"Not that I give a damn," Gene says.

"About Rita and me?"

"That's right," he says. He sits up and drinks the rest of the bottle in one gulp and throws the empty carefully into the back of the pickup, with the fenceposts, the rusty tools, the other empties.

With his shirt off Gene looks pretty bad, though I can see how strong he still is. But everything is beginning to slump and settle and dry out and crack. His chest looks like the fields out there after a hard rain and a couple of days of sun.

"Gene?"

"You son of a bitch," he says.

About four o'clock I am taking a turn with the digging bar, a piece of wrought iron six feet long and as big around as an axe handle, which we use to break up the caliche before we can dig it out. Gene is leaning on the two- handled scoop waiting for me to to get done.

"Indians," he says.

"What about Indians?"

"There used to be Indians all around here," he says.

I take another shot at the caliche. The bar feels like it weighs a hundred pounds. "What happened to them?"

Gene looks at me like I've asked a dumb question. "They died out," he says. "Or they went someplace else. See any Indians in Chicago?"

"I guess so."

"That's what I should do," he says. "Go someplace else."

"And do what?" I ask him. If I could only talk to Gene I think something important might happen. But it's a dream: I can't talk to him.

"I can't tell until I got there, Lawrence," he says.

We dig for a while. He takes a turn; I take a turn. Over our heads the sky is like a page from a book that hasn't been written.

"Sometimes you can find old bones out here. I found a tooth once," Gene says. He fumbles in his pocket and brings out a little piece of yellow ivory; it looks like a tooth from a six-year-old. "Indian," he says, holding it out to me cupped in his hand.

It feels so light it has no consequence at all. "Probably a thousand years old," he says. "I was going to have it made into a ring but I never did."

I hand it back to him, but he shakes his head. "Keep it," he says. "Give it to Rita, she likes stuff like that."

"You're sore about me and Rita, aren't you?"

"No," he says.

He's standing in front of me with the bar raised, ready to take another lick at the hole. With his arms up like this, his chest looks like a young man's: not so devastated. We're out here about fifteen miles from nowhere, just Gene and me alone. The muscles are like blow-up balloons. Put a pipe in his mouth and he'd look like Popeye. He could kill me without thinking about it, and your average Texas jury would let him off with a year or two.

"I lost her fair and square," he says. "Before you ever come down here from Chicago. She don't believe in love." His face is both sad and puzzled; the whites of his eyes are showing. There might be a tear in his eye, or it might be only the wind, which is blowing cold and mean, coming from that part of the world Gene doesn't believe in.

"Well, Law-rence," he says. "It's about time to quit for the day. Let's go home."

In the truck we listen to Elvis some more but Gene doesn't talk. He drives it slow and easy, listening to the King, nodding his head now and then as if he's just said something to himself that he agrees with. The stereo is going bad and sometimes Elvis comes out from the left speaker, or the right, or quits altogether until I kick the dashboard and get him singing again. I get my feet as close to the heater as I can; now that I'm just sitting I'm cold and a little puzzled and sad myself. I wish we had this day over again, so we could do it different.

"You're a dumbass, Law-rence," Gene says.

It's like a judgment; he might be right. I'm not feeling any better about the day. We're sitting in the New Deal Cafe and Bar; it's two in the morning and all but a couple of really serious drinkers have gone home for the night.

"A real dumbass," he says.

One of the drunks puts a half dollar in the jukebox and picks out a tune.

"Seems like that's all anybody plays any more since he died," Rita says.

Gene looks up at her. "We could still get ourselves married," he says.

"Time for you to go on home when you start talking like that." She puts a hand over his. "Go get yourself some sleep," she says. We have been taking turns explaining this day to her, and it's clear she doesn't like the sound of it any more than we do.

"Love," Gene says. He waves his free hand at the jukebox: the drunk is leaning on it, staring at the record going round and round, caught up in some kind of personal tragedy.

"Don't you care about love?" Gene says.

"No." Rita says.

"I can't believe that," he says.

"Go home, Gene," she tells him.

The King is singing "Jailhouse Rock" and Gene does a clumsy little dance step on his way out of the New Deal; he stops at the door and waves goodbye to us, then he stops grinning and gives me a narrow look.

"Chicago," he says. He rubs his thumb and forefinger together and nods at Rita without taking his eyes off me. It's his Monday morning stare.

Rita's trailer is about fifteen feet long, and set up like one room, with a bed smack up against the back wall and a little kitchen up front. There's a tiny toilet, but if she wants to take a shower she has to go into the cafe, where there's a tin stall behind the kitchen that the help can use. It isn't much of a place to live, but I've been in there with her one or two times when it was pouring rain and lightning and thundering, and it's the coziest thing you can imagine, lying in the bed listening to the water and the wind beating on the sheet metal six inches away from your head while you're warm and safe under the covers.

"It was just a lousy day," I tell her.

"Let me see the tooth," she says. "Is it really a thousand years old?"

I have to reach out and fumble around on the floor until I find my Levi's, and there it is in the back pocket. She holds it up to the light.

"That's so goddamned sad," she says.

I put my arm around her; there's plenty of flesh there, too much, some people might say, but tonight I wish there was more, so much I couldn't get my arms around it all. She's a giving woman, but tonight I maybe want more than she can give.

"I like it when you hold me like that," she says.

"Yeah?" My nose is buried in her hair, which smells like cigarette smoke.

"Don't you go thinking about love," she says.

"That's Gene," I tell her. "Not me."

"Let it sell the songs," she says. "I don't want any of it in my personal life."

"You don't have to worry about me."

"That's what I hope," she says.

After a while she gets up and turns off the overhead light, leaving the little lamp on over the kitchen sink, and we make love, very slow and sweet, driving it easy, and go to sleep tangled up with each other. One of her legs is over mine, my arm is under her head, and with my free hand I'm holding her breast, which is a comfort.

What wakes me up is at first not clear. The trailer is rocking a little but I figure it's in my head, a hangover from the dream I was having in which every one of old man Hazzard's fence posts was rising slowly out of the ground. In the dream I didn't want to know what was pushing them up. Rita is already sitting up, looking around wild-eyed, still more than half in a dream herself.

"It's Gene," she says.

"We were just dreaming," I tell her. "Come on down here and go back to sleep."

I hear footsteps outside and a fist begins to beat slowly on the trailer door; the glasses in the kitchen rattle like dry bones, and something in the sink falls over.

"Rita," Gene's voice says, very drunk and very loud. "Rita, honey, it's me."

He begins to pound on the door again, pulls on the handle, rocks our little trailer. It's a big one-man storm going on out there.

"I love you," he shouts. "I know that son of a bitch Lawrence is in there with you, but it don't matter. We'll have kids; I'll build you a regular house. I'll be tender with you. Love me, goddamn it."

He runs around to the other side of the trailer and bangs on the metal wall; it sounds like thunder. Rita puts her hands over her ears. "Oh God," she says. "I can't stand it."

There's a little window just over the bed. I pull the curtain back and look out, but it's too dark—the only thing I can make out is my own face staring back at me with a peculiar lost expression.

"He's going to keep it up. I just know it," Rita says.

The footsteps are coming back around; they stop just under the window. Gene knows where the bed is. He says something but his voice is funny and I can't understand the words.

"What's he doing?" Rita says. She takes her hands away from her ears so she can hear better.

"I think he's singing."

It gets louder and I can start to make it out. I can see him out there, standing on his toes to get his mouth up to the window, one hand pressed on each side of it to keep his balance, hugging our trailer.

"I'm just a hunk, a hunk-a burning love," he sings.

I pull Rita down in the bed beside me and lay the covers over our heads. I put my arms around her. It's the coziest thing you can imagine.

RICHARD BAUSCH

THE MAN WHO KNEW BELLE STARR

On his way west McRae picked up a hitcher, a young woman carrying a paper bag and a leather purse, wearing jeans and a shawl—which she didn't take off, though it was more than ninety degrees out and McRae had no air conditioning. He was driving an old Dodge Charger with a bad exhaust system and one long crack in the wrap-around windshield. He pulled over for her, and she got right in, put the leather purse on the seat between them, and settled herself with the paper bag on her lap between her hands. He had just crossed into Texas from Oklahoma. This was the third day of the trip.

"Where you headed?" he asked.

She said, "What about you?"

"Nevada, maybe."

"Why maybe?"

And that fast he was answering *her* questions. "I just got out of the Air Force," he told her, though this wasn't exactly true. The Air Force had given him a dishonorable discharge, after four years at Leavenworth for assaulting a staff sergeant. He was a bad character. He had a bad temper that had got him into a load of trouble already, and he just wanted to get out West, out to the wide open spaces. Just to see it, really. He had the feeling that people didn't require as much from a person way out where there was that kind of room. He didn't have any family now. He had five thousand dollars from his father's insurance policy, and he was going to make the money last a while. He said, "I'm sort of undecided about a lot of things."

"Not me," she said.

"You figured out where you're going?"

"You could say that."

"So where might that be?"

She made a fist and then extended her thumb, and turned it over. "Under," she said. "Down."

"Excuse me?"

"Does the radio work?" she asked, reaching for it.

"It's on the blink," he said.

She turned the knob anyway. Then she sat back and folded her arms over the paper bag.

He took a glance at her. She was skinny and long-necked, and her hair was the color of water in a metal pail. She looked just old enough for high school.

"What's in the bag?" he said.

She sat up a little. "Nothing. Another blouse."

"Well, so what did you mean back there?"

"Back where?"

"Look," he said, "we don't have to do any talking if you don't want to."

"Then what will we do?"

"Anything you want," he said.

"What if I just want to sit here and let you drive me all the way to Nevada?"

"That's fine," he said. "That's just fine."

"Well, I won't do that. We can talk."

"Are you going to Nevada?" he asked.

She gave a little shrug of her shoulders. "Why not?"

"All right," he said, and for some reason he offered her his hand. She looked at it and then smiled at him, and he put his hand back on the wheel.

It got a little awkward almost right away. The heat was awful, and she sat there sweating, not saying much. He never thought he was very smooth or anything, and he had been in prison; it had been a long time since he had found himself in the company of a woman. Finally she fell asleep, and for a few miles he could look at her without worrying about anything but staying on the road. He decided that she was kind of good-looking around the eyes and mouth. If she ever filled out, she might be something. He caught himself wondering what might happen, thinking of sex. A girl who traveled alone like this was probably pretty loose. Without quite realizing it, he began to daydream about her, and when he got aroused by the daydream he tried to concentrate on figuring his chances, playing his cards right, not messing up any opportunities—but being gentlemanly, too. He was not the sort of man who forced himself on young women. She slept very quietly, not breathing loudly or sighing or moving much; and then she simply sat up and folded her arms over the bag again and stared out at the road.

"God," she said. "I went out."

"You hungry?" he asked.

"No."

"What's your name? I never got your name."

"Belle Starr," she said, and, winking at him, she made a clicking sound out of the side of her mouth.

"Belle Starr," he said.

"Don't you know who Belle Starr was?"

All he knew was that it was a familiar-sounding name. "Belle Starr."

She put her index finger to the side of his head and said, "Bang."

"Belle Starr," he said.

"Come on," she said. "Annie Oakley. Wild Bill Hickok."

"Oh," McRae said. "Okay."

"That's me," she said, sliding down in the seat. "Belle Starr."

"That's not your real name."

"It's the only one I go by these days."

They rode on in silence for a time.

"What's *your* name?" she asked.

He told her.

"Irish?"

"I never thought about it."

"Where you from, McRae?"

"Washington, D.C."

"Long way from home."

"I haven't been there in years."

"Where *have* you been?'

"Prison," he said. He hadn't known he would say it, and now that he had, he kept his eyes on the road. He might as well have been posing for her; he had an image of himself as he must look from the side, and he shifted his weight a little, sucked in his belly. When he stole a glance at her, he saw that she was simply gazing out at the Panhandle, one hand up like a visor to shade her eyes.

"What about you?" he asked, and felt like somebody in a movie—two people with a past come together on the open road. He wondered how he could get the talk around to the subject of love.

"What *about* me?"

"Where you from?"

"I don't want to bore you with all the facts," she said.

"I don't mind," McRae said. "I got nothing else to do."

"I'm from way up north."

"Okay," he said, "you want me to guess?"

"Maine," she said. "Land of moose and lobster."

He said, "Maine. Well, now."

"See?" she said. "The facts are just a lot of things that don't change."

"Unless you change them," McRae said.

She reached down and, with elaborate care, as if it were fragile, put the paper bag on the floor. Then she leaned back and put her feet up on the dash. She was wearing low-cut tennis shoes.

"You going to sleep?" he asked.

"Just relaxing," she said. But a moment later, when he asked if she wanted to stop and eat, she didn't answer. He looked over and saw that she was sound asleep.

His father had died while he was at Leavenworth. The last time McRae saw him, he was lying on a gurney in one of the bays of D.C. General's emergency ward, a plastic tube in his mouth, an IV set into an ugly yellow-blue bruise on his wrist. McRae had come home on leave from the Air Force—which he had joined on the suggestion of a juvenile judge—to find his father on the floor in the living room, in a pile of old newspapers and bottles, wearing his good suit, with no socks or shoes and no shirt. He looked like he was dead. But the ambulance drivers found a pulse and rushed him off to the hospital. McRae cleaned the house up a little and then followed in the Charger. The old man had been going steadily downhill from the time McRae was a boy, so this latest trouble wasn't new. In the hospital they got the tube in his mouth and hooked him to the IV, and then left him there on the gurney. McRae stood at his side, still in uniform, and when the old man opened his eyes and looked at him, it was clear that he didn't know who he was. The old man blinked, stared, and then sat up, took the tube out of his mouth, and spit something terrible-looking into a small metal dish that was suspended from the complicated apparatus of the room, which made a continual water-dropping sound, like a leaking sink. He looked at McRae again, and then he looked at the tube. "Jesus Christ," he said.

"Hey," McRae said.

"What."

"It's me."

The old man put the tube back in his mouth and looked away.

"Pops," McRae said. He didn't feel anything.

The tube came out. "Don't look at me, boy. You got yourself into it. Getting into trouble, stealing and running around. You got yourself into it."

"I don't mind it, Pops. It's three meals a day and a place to sleep."

"Yeah," the old man said, and then seemed to gargle something. He spit into the little metal dish again.

"I got thirty days of leave, Pops."

"Eh?"

"I don't have to go back for a month."

"Where you going?"

"Around," McRae said.

The truth was that he hated the Air Force, and he was thinking of taking the Charger and driving to Canada or someplace like that, and hiding out for the rest of his life. The Air Force felt like punishment—it *was* punishment— and he had already been in trouble for his quick temper and his attitude. That afternoon he left his father to whatever would happen, got in the Charger, and started north. But he didn't make it. He lost heart a few miles south of New York City, and he turned around and came back. The old man had been moved to a room in the alcoholic ward, but McRae didn't go to see him. He stayed in the house, watching television and drinking beer, and when old high school buddies came by he went around with them a little. Mostly he stayed home, though, and at the end of his leave he locked the place and drove back to

Chanute, in Illinois, where he was stationed. He hadn't been there two months before he got into the scrape that landed him in prison. A staff sergeant caught him drinking beer in the day-room of one of the training barracks and asked for his name. McRae walked over to him, said, "My name is trouble," and, at the word *trouble,* struck the other man in the face. He'd had a lot of beer, and he had been sitting there in the dark, going over everything in his mind, and the staff sergeant, a baby-faced man with a spare tire of flesh around his waist and an attitude about the stripes on his sleeves, had just walked into it. McRae didn't even know him. Yet he stood over the sergeant where he had fallen and started kicking him. The poor man wound up in the hospital with a broken jaw (the first punch had done it), a few cracked ribs, and multiple lacerations and bruises. The court-martial was swift. The sentence was four years at hard labor, along with a dishonorable discharge. He'd had less than a month on the sentence when he got the news about his father. He felt no surprise, nor, really, any grief, yet there was a little thrill of something like fear; he was in his cell, and for an instant some part of him actually wanted to remain there, inside walls, where things were certain and no decisions had to be made. A week later he learned of the money from the insurance, which would have been more than the five thousand except that his father had been a few months behind on the rent and on other payments. McRae settled what he had to of those things, and kept the rest. He had started to feel like a happy man, out of Leavenworth and the Air Force. And now he was on his way to Nevada or someplace like that—and he had picked up a girl.

He drove on until dusk, stopping only for gas, and the girl slept right through. Just past the line into New Mexico he pulled off the interstate and went north for a mile or so, looking for some place other than a chain restaurant to eat. She sat up straight and pushed the hair back from her face. "Where are we?"

"New Mexico," he said. "I'm looking for a place to eat."

"I'm not hungry."

"Well," he said, "you might be able to go all day without eating, but I got a three-meal-a-day habit to support."

She brought the paper bag up from the floor and held it in her lap.

"You got food in there?"

"No."

"You're very pretty—childlike, sort of, when you sleep."

"I didn't snore?"

"You were quiet as a mouse."

"And you think I'm pretty."

"I guess you know a thing like that. I hope I didn't offend you."

"I don't like dirty remarks," she said. "But I guess you don't mean to be dirty."

"Dirty."

"Sometimes people can say a thing like that and mean it very dirty, but I could tell you didn't."

He pulled in at a roadside diner and turned the ignition off. "Well?" he said.

She sat there with the bag on her lap. "I don't think I'll go in with you."

"You can have a cold drink or something," he said.

"You go in. I'll wait out here."

"Come on in there with me and have a cold drink," McRae said. "I'll buy it for you. I'll buy you dinner, if you want."

"I don't want to," she said.

He got out and started for the entrance, and before he reached it, he heard her door open and close, and turned to watch her come toward him, thin and waiflike in the shawl, which hid her arms and hands.

The diner was empty. A long, low counter ran along one side, with soda fountains and glass cases in which pies and cakes were set. There were booths along one wall. Everything seemed in order, except that no one was around. McRae and the girl stood in the doorway for a moment and waited, and finally she stepped in and took a seat in the first booth. "I guess we're supposed to seat ourselves," she said.

"This is weird," McRae said.

"Hey," she said, rising. "A jukebox." She strode over to it and leaned on it, crossing one leg behind the other at the ankle, her hair falling down to hide her face.

"Hello?" McRae said. "Anybody here?"

"Got any change?" the girl asked.

He gave her a quarter and then sat at the counter. A door at the far end of the diner swung in and a big, red- faced man entered, wearing a white cook's apron over a sweat-stained baby-blue shirt, the sleeves of which he had rolled up past the meaty curve of his elbows. "Yeah?" he said.

"You open?" McRae asked.

"That jukebox don't work, honey," the man said.

"You open?" McRae said, as the girl came and sat down beside him.

"I guess maybe I am."

"Place is kind of empty."

"What do you want to eat?"

"You got a menu?"

"You want a menu?"

"Sure," McRae said. "Why not."

"Truth is," the big man said, "I'm selling this place. I don't have menus anymore. I make hamburgers and breakfast stuff. Some french fries and cold drinks. A hot dog, maybe. I'm not keeping track."

"Let's go somewhere else," the girl said.

"Yeah," the big man said, "why don't you do that."

"Look," McRae said, "what's the story here?"

The other man shrugged. "You came in at the end of the run, you know what I mean? I'm going out of business. Sit down and I'll make you a hamburger, on the house."

McRae looked at the girl.

"Okay," she said, in a tone that made it clear that she would've been happier to leave.

The big man put his hands on the bar and learned toward her. "Miss, if I were you, I wouldn't look a gift horse in the mouth."

"I don't like hamburger," she said.

"You want a hot dog?" the man said. "I got a hot dog for you. Guaranteed to please."

"I'll have some french fries," she said.

The big man turned to the grill and opened the metal drawer under it. He was very wide at the hips, and his legs were like tree trunks. "I get out of the Army after twenty years," he said, "and I got a little money put aside. The wife and I decide we want to get into the restaurant business. The government's going to be paying me a nice pension, and we got the savings, so we sink it all in this goddamn diner. Six and a half miles from the interstate. You get the picture? The guy's selling us this diner at a great price, you know? A terrific price. For a song, I'm in the restaurant business. The wife will cook the food and I'll wait tables, you know, until we start to make a little extra, and then we'll hire somebody—a high school kid, or somebody like that. We might even open another restaurant, if the going gets good enough. But, of course, this is New Mexico. This is six and a half miles from the interstate. You know what's up the road? Nothing." He had put the hamburger on, and a basket of frozen french fries. "Now the wife decides she's had enough of life on the border, and off she goes to Seattle to sit in the rain with her mother, and here I am trying to sell a place nobody else is dumb enough to buy. You know what I mean?"

"That's rough," McRae said.

"You're the second customer I've had all *week,* bub."

The girl said, "I guess that cash register's empty, then, huh."

"It ain't full, honey."

She got up and wandered across the room. For a while she stood gazing out the windows over the booths, her hands invisible under the woolen shawl. When she came back to sit next to McRae again, the hamburger and french fries were ready.

"On the house," the big man said.

And the girl brought a gun out from under the shawl—a pistol that looked like a toy. "Suppose you open up that register, Mr. Poor Mouth," she said.

The big man looked at her, then at McRae, who had taken a large bite of his hamburger and had it bulging in his cheeks.

"This thing is loaded, and I'll use it."

"Well, for Christ's sake," the big man said.

McRae started to get off the stool. "Hold on a minute," he said to them both, his words garbled by the mouthful of food, and then everything started happening at once. The girl aimed the pistol. There was a popping sound—a single small pop, not much louder than the sound of a cap gun—and the big man took a step back, into the dishes and pans. He stared at the girl, wide-eyed, for what seemed like a long time, and then went down, pulling dishes with him in a tremendous shattering.

"Jesus Christ," McRae said, swallowing, standing back far from her, raising his hands.

She put the pistol back in her jeans, under the shawl, and then went around the counter and opened the cash register. "Damn," she said.

McRae said, low, "Jesus Christ."

And now she looked at him; it was as if she had forgotten he was there. "What're you standing there with your hands up like that?"

"God," he said, "oh, God."

"Stop it," she said. "Put your hands down."

He did so.

"Cash register's empty." She sat down on one of the stools and gazed over at the body of the man where it had fallen. "Damn."

"Look," McRae said, "take my car. You can have my car."

She seemed puzzled. "I don't want your car. What do I want your car for?"

"You—" he said. He couldn't talk, couldn't focus clearly, or think. He looked at the man, who lay very still, and then he began to cry.

"Will you stop it?" she said, coming off the stool, reaching under the shawl and bringing out the pistol again.

"Jesus," he said. "Good Jesus."

She pointed the pistol at his forehead. "Bang," she said. "What's my name?"

"Your—name?"

"My name."

"Belle—" he managed.

"Come on," she said. "The whole thing. You remember."

"Belle—Belle Starr."

"Right," She let the gun hand drop to her side, into one of the folds of the shawl. "I like that so much better than Annie Oakley."

"Please," McRae said.

She took a few steps away from him and then whirled and aimed the gun. "I think we better get out of here. What do you think?"

"Take the car," he said, almost with exasperation; he was frightened to hear it in his voice.

"I can't drive," she said simply. "Never learned."

"Jesus," he said. It went out of him like a sigh.

"Lordy," she said, gesturing with the pistol for him to move to the door, "it's hard to believe you were ever in *prison.*"

The interstate went on into the dark, beyond the glow of the headlights. He lost track of miles, road signs, other traffic, time; trucks came by and surprised him, and other cars seemed to materialize as they started the lane change that would bring them over in front of him. He saw their taillights grow small in the distance, and all the while the girl sat watching him, her hands somewhere under the shawl. For a long time he heard only the sound of the rushing night air at the windows, and then she moved a little, shifted her weight, bringing one leg up on the seat.

"What were you in prison for, anyway?"

Her voice startled him, and for a moment he couldn't think of an answer.

"Come on," she said. "I'm getting bored with all this quiet. What were you in prison for?"

"I—beat up a guy."

"That's all?"

"Yes, that's all." He couldn't keep the irritation out of his voice.

"Tell me about it."

"It was just—I just beat up a guy. It wasn't anything."

"I didn't shoot that man for money, you know."

McRae said nothing.

"I shot him because he made a nasty remark to me about the hot dog."

"I didn't hear any nasty remark."

"If he hadn't said it, he'd still be alive."

McRae held tight to the wheel.

"Don't you wish it was the Wild West?" she said.

"Wild West," he said. "Yeah." He could barely speak for the dryness in his mouth and the deep ache of his own breathing.

"You know," she said, "I'm not really from Maine."

He nodded.

"I'm from Florida."

"Florida," he managed.

"Yes, only I don't have a southern accent, so people think I'm not from there. Do you hear any trace of a southern accent at all when I talk?"

"No," he said.

"Now you—you've got an accent. A definite southern accent."

He was silent.

"Talk to me," she said.

"What do you want me to say?" he said. "Jesus."

"You could ask me things."

"Ask you things—"

"Ask me what my name is."

Without hesitating, McRae said, "What's your name?"

"You know."

"No, really," he said, trying to play along.

"It's Belle Starr."

"Belle Starr," he said.

"Nobody *but,*" she said.

"Good," he said.

"And I don't care about money, either," she said. "That's not what I'm after."

"No," McRae said.

"What I'm after is adventure."

"Right," McRae said.

"Fast living."

"Fast living, right."

"A good time."

"Good," he said.

"I'm going to live a ton before I die."

"A ton, yes."

"What about you?"

"Yes," he said. "Me too."

"Want to join up with me?"

"Join up," he said. "Right." He was watching the road.

She leaned toward him a little. "Do you think I'm lying about my name?"

"No."

"Good," she said.

He had begun to feel as though he might start throwing up what he'd had of the hamburger. His stomach was cramping on him, and he was dizzy. He might even be having a heart attack.

"Your eyes are as big as saucers," she said.

He tried to narrow them a little. His whole body was shaking now.

"You know how old I am, McRae? I'm nineteen."

He nodded, glanced at her and then at the road again.

"How old are you?"

"Twenty-three."

"Do you believe people go to heaven when they die?"

"Oh, God," he said.

"Look, I'm not going to shoot you while you're driving the car. We'd crash if I did that."

"Oh," he said. "Oh, Jesus, please—look, I never saw anybody shot before—"

"Will you *stop it?*"

He put one hand to his mouth. He was soaked: he felt the sweat on his upper lip, and then he felt the dampness all through his clothes.

She said, "I don't kill everybody I meet, you know."

"No," he said. "Of course not." The absurdity of this exchange almost brought a laugh up out of him. How astonishing, that a laugh could be anywhere in him at such a time, but here it was, rising up in this throat like some loosened part of his anatomy. He held on with his whole mind, and a moment passed before he realized that *she* was laughing.

"Actually," she said, "I haven't killed all that many people."

"How—" he began. Then he had to stop to breathe. "How many?"

"Take a guess."

"I don't have any idea," he said.

"Well," she said, "you'll just have to guess. And you'll notice that I haven't spent any time in prison."

He was quiet.

"*Guess,*" she said.

McRae said, "Ten?"

"No."

He waited.

"Come on, keep guessing."

"More than ten?"

"Maybe."

"More than ten," he said.

"Well, all right. Less than ten."

"Less than ten," he said.

"Guess," she said.

"Nine."

"No."

"Eight."

"No, not eight."

"Six?"

"Not six."

"Five?"

"Five and a half people," she said. "You almost hit it right on the button."

"Five and a half people," McRae said.

"Right. A kid who was hitchhiking, like me; a guy at a gas station; a dog that must've got lost—I count him as the half; another guy at a gas station; a guy that took me to a motel and made an obscene gesture to me; and the guy at the diner. That makes five and a half."

"Five and a half," McRae said.

"You keep repeating everything I say. I wish you'd quit that."

He wiped his hand across his mouth and then feigned a cough to keep from having to speak.

"Five and a half people," she said, turning a little in the seat, putting her knees up on the dash. "Have you ever met anybody like me? Tell the truth."

"No," McRae said, "nobody."

"Just think about it, McRae. You can say you rode with Belle Starr. You can tell your grandchildren."

He was afraid to say anything to this, for fear of changing the delicate balance of the thought. Yet he knew the worst mistake would be to say nothing at all. He was beginning to sense something of the cunning that he would need to survive, even as he knew that the slightest miscalculation might mean the end of him. He said, with fake wonder, "I knew Belle Starr."

She said, "Think of it."

"Something," he said.

And she sat farther down in the seat. "Amazing."

He kept to fifty-five miles an hour, and everyone else was

speeding. The girl sat straight up now, nearly facing him on the seat. For long periods she had been quiet, simply watching him drive. Soon they were going to need gas; they had less than half a tank.

"Look at those people speeding," she said. "We're the only ones obeying the speed limit. Look at them."

"Do you want me to speed up?"

"I think they ought to get tickets for speeding, that's what I think. Sometimes I wish I were a policeman."

"Look," McRae said, "we're going to need gas pretty soon."

"No, let's just run it until it quits. We can always hitch a ride with somebody."

"This car's got a great engine," McRae said. "We might have to outrun the police, and I wouldn't want to do that in any other car."

"This old thing? It's got a crack in the windshield. The radio doesn't work."

"Right. But it's a fast car. It'll outrun a police car."

She put one arm over the seat back and looked out the rear window. "You really think the police are chasing us?"

"They might be," he said.

She stared at him a moment. "No. There's no reason. Nobody saw us."

"But if somebody did—this car, I mean, it'll go like crazy."

"I'm afraid of speeding, though," she said. "Besides, you know what I found out? If you run slow enough, the cops go right past you. Right on past you, looking for somebody who's in a hurry. No, I think it's best if we just let it run until it quits and then get out and hitch."

McRae thought he knew what might happen when the gas ran out: she would make him push the car to the side of the road, and then she would walk him back into the cactus and brush there, and when they were far enough from the road, she would shoot him. He knew this as if she had spelled it all out, and he began again to try for the cunning he would need. "Belle," he said. "Why don't we lay low for a few days in Albuquerque?"

"Is that an obscene gesture?" she asked.

"No!" he said, almost shouted. "No! That's—it's outlaw talk. You know. Hide out from the cops—lay low. It's—it's prison talk."

"Well, I've never been in prison."

"That's all I meant."

"You want to hide out."

"Right," he said.

"You and me?"

"You—you asked if I wanted to join up with you."

"Did I?" She seemed puzzled by this.

"Yes," he said, feeling himself press it a little. "Don't you remember?"

"I guess I do."

"You did," he said.

"I don't know."

"Belle Starr had a gang," he said.

"She did?"

"I could be the first member of your gang."

She sat there thinking this over. McRae's blood moved at the thought that she was deciding whether or not he would live.

"Well," she said, "maybe."

"You've got to have a gang, Belle."

"We'll see," she said.

A moment later she said, "How much money do you have?"

"I have enough to start a gang."

"It takes money to start a gang?"

"Well—" He was at a loss.

"How much do you have?"

He said, "A few hundred."

"Really?" she said. "That much?"

"Just enough to—just enough to get to Nevada."

"Can I have it?"

He said, "Sure." He was holding the wheel and looking out into the night.

"And we'll be a gang?"

"Right," he said.

"I like the idea. Belle Starr and her gang."

McRae started talking about what the gang could do, making it up as he went along, trying to sound like all the gangster movies he'd seen. He heard himself talking about things like robbery and getaway cars and not getting nabbed and staying out of prison, and then, as she sat there staring at him, he started talking about being at Leavenworth, what it was like. He went on about it, the hours of forced work and the time alone, the harsh day-to-day routines, the bad food. Before he was through, feeling the necessity of deepening her sense of him as her new accomplice—and feeling strangely as though in some way he had indeed become exactly that—he was telling her everything, all the bad times he'd had: his father's alcoholism, and growing up wanting to hit something for the anger that was in him; the years of getting into trouble; the fighting and the kicking and what it had got him. He embellished it all, made it sound worse than it really was, because she seemed to be going for it and because, telling it to her, he felt oddly sorry for himself; a version of this story of pain and neglect and lonely rage was true. He had been through a lot. And as he finished describing for her the scene at the hospital the last time he saw his father, he was almost certain he had struck a chord in her. He thought he saw it in the rapt expression on her face.

"Anyway," he said, and smiled at her.

"McRae?" she said.

"Yeah?"

"Can you pull over?"

"Well," he said, his voice shaking, "why don't we wait until it runs out of gas?"

She was silent.

"We'll be that much farther down the road," he said.

"I don't really want a gang," she said. "I don't like dealing with other people that much. I mean, I don't think I'm a leader."

"Oh, yes," McRae said. "No—you're a leader. You're definitely a leader. I was in the Air Force and I know leaders, and you are definitely what I'd call a leader."

"Really?"

"Absolutely. You are leadership material all the way."

"I wouldn't have thought so."

"Definitely," he said. "Definitely a leader."

"But I don't really like people around, you know."

"That's a leadership quality. Not wanting people around. It is definitely a leadership quality."

"Boy," she said, "the things you learn."

He waited. If he could only think himself through to the way out. If he could get her to trust him, get the car stopped—be there when she turned her back.

"You want to be in my gang, huh?"

"I sure do," he said.

"Well, I guess I'll have to think about it."

"I'm surprised nobody's mentioned it to you before."

"You're just saying that."

"No, really."

"Were you ever married?" she asked.

"Married?" he said, and then stammered over the answer. "Ah—uh, no."

"You ever been in a gang before?"

"A couple times, but—they never had good leadership."

"You're giving me a line, huh."

"No," he said, "it's true. No good leadership. It was always a problem."

"I'm tired," she said, shifting toward him a little. "I'm tired of talking."

The steering wheel was hurting the insides of his hands. He held tight, looking at the coming-on of the white stripes in the road. There were no other cars now, and not a glimmer of light anywhere beyond the headlights.

"Don't you ever get tired of talking?"

"I never was much of a talker," he said.

"I guess I don't mind talking as much as I mind listening," she said.

He made a sound in his throat which he hoped she took for agreement.

"That's just when I'm tired, though."

"Why don't you take a nap?" he said.

She leaned back against the door and regarded him. "There's plenty of time for that later."

"So," he wanted to say, "you're not going to kill me— we're a gang?"

They had gone for a long time without speaking, an excruciating hour of minutes, during which the gas gauge had sunk to just above empty, and finally she had begun talking about herself, mostly in the third person. It was hard to make sense of most of it, yet he listened as if to instructions concerning how to extricate himself. She talked about growing up in Florida, in the country, and owning a horse; she remembered when she was taught to swim by somebody she called Bill, as if McRae would know who that was; and then she told him how when her father ran away with her mother's sister, her mother started having men friends over all the time. "There was a lot of obscene things going on," she said, and her voice tightened a little.

"Some people don't care what happens to their kids," McRae said.

"Isn't it the truth?" she said. Then she took the pistol out of the shawl. "Take this exit."

He pulled onto the ramp and up an incline to a two-lane road that went off through the desert, toward a glow that burned on the horizon. For perhaps five miles the road was straight as a plumb line, and then it curved into long, low undulations of sand and mesquite and cactus.

"My mother's men friends used to do whatever they wanted to me," she said. "It went on all the time. All sorts of obscene goings-on."

McRae said, "I'm sorry that happened to you, Belle." And for an instant he was surprised by the sincerity of his feeling: it was as if he couldn't feel sorry enough. Yet it was genuine: it had to do with his own unhappy story. The whole world seemed very, very sad to him. "I'm really very sorry," he said.

She was quiet a moment, as if thinking about this. Then she said, "Let's pull over now. I'm tired of riding."

"It's almost out of gas," he said.

"I know, but pull it over anyway."

"You sure you want to do that?"

"See?" she said. "That's what I mean—I wouldn't like being told what I should do all the time, or asked if I was sure of what I wanted or not."

He pulled the car over and slowed to a stop. "You're right," he said. "See? Leadership. I'm just not used to somebody with leadership qualities."

She held the gun a little toward him. He was looking at the small, dark, perfect circle at the end of the barrel. "I guess we should get out," she said.

"I guess so," he said.

"Do you have any relatives left anywhere?"

"No."

"Your folks are both dead?"

"Right, yes."

"Which one died first?"

"I told you," he said. "Didn't I? My mother, my mother died first."

"Do you feel like an orphan?"

He sighed. "Sometimes." The whole thing was slipping away from him.

"I guess I do too." She reached back and opened her door. "Let's get out now."

And when he reached for the door handle, she aimed the gun at his head. "Get out slow."

"Aw, Jesus," he said. "Look, you're not going to do this, are you? I mean, I thought we were friends and all."

"Just get out real slow, like I said to."

"Okay," he said. "I'm getting out." He opened his door, and the ceiling light surprised and frightened him. Some wordless part of him understood that this was it, and all his talk had come to nothing: all the questions she had asked him, and everything he had told her—it was all completely useless. This was going to happen to him, and it wouldn't mean anything; it would just be what happened.

"Real slow," she said. "Come on."

"Why are you doing this?" he asked. "You've got to tell me that before you do it."

"Will you please get out of the car now?"

He just stared at her.

"All right, I'll shoot you where you sit."

"Okay," he said. "Don't shoot."

She said in an irritable voice, as though she were talking to a recalcitrant child, "You're just putting it off."

He was backing himself out, keeping his eyes on the little barrel of the gun, and he could hear something coming, seemed to notice it in the same instant that she said, "Wait." He stood half in and half out of the car, doing as she said, and a truck came over the hill ahead of them, a tractor trailer, all white light and roaring.

"Stay still," she said, crouching, aiming the gun at him.

The truck came fast, was only fifty yards away, and without having to decide about it, without even knowing that he would do it, McRae bolted into the road. He was running; he heard the exhausted sound of his own breath, the truck horn blaring, coming on, louder, the thing bearing down on him, something buzzing past his head. Time slowed. His legs faltered under him, were heavy, all the nerves gone out of them. In the light of the oncoming truck he saw his own white hands outstretched as if to grasp something in the air before him, and then the truck was past him, the blast of air from it propelling him over the side of the road and down an embankment, in high, dry grass, which pricked his skin and crackled like hay.

He was alive. He lay very still. Above him was the long shape of the road, curving off in the distance, the light of the truck going on. The noise faded and was nothing. A little wind stirred. He heard the car door close. Carefully he got to all fours and crawled a few yards away from where he had fallen. He couldn't be sure of which direction—he only knew he couldn't stay where he was. Then he heard what he thought were her footsteps in the road, and he froze. He lay on his side, facing the embankment. When she appeared there he almost cried out.

"McRae?" she said. "Did I get you?" She was looking right at where he was in the dark, and he stopped breathing. "McRae?"

He watched her move along the edge of the embankment. "McRae?" She put one hand over her eyes and stared at a place a few feet over from him, and then she turned and went back out of sight. He heard the car door again, and again he began to crawl farther away. The ground was cold and rough, sandy.

He heard her put the key in the trunk. He stood up, tried to run, but something went wrong in his leg, something sent him sprawling, and a sound came out of him that seemed to echo, to stay on the air, as if to call her to him. He tried to be perfectly still, tried not to breathe, hearing now the small pop of the gun. He counted the reports: one, two, three. She was standing there at the edge of the road, firing into the dark, toward where she must have thought she heard the sound. Then she was rattling the paper bag. She was reloading—he could hear the click of the gun. He tried to get up and couldn't. He had sprained his ankle, had done something very bad to it. Now he was crawling wildly, blindly, through the tall grass, hearing again the small report of the pistol. At last he rolled into a shallow gully. He lay there with his face down, breathing the dust, his own voice leaving him in a whimpering, animal-like sound that he couldn't stop, even as he held both shaking hands over his mouth.

"McRae?" She sounded so close. "Hey," she said. "McRae?"

He didn't move. He lay there perfectly still, trying to stop himself from crying. He was sorry for everything he had ever done. He didn't care about the money, or the car, or going out west, or anything. When he lifted his head to peer over the lip of the gully and saw that she had started down the embankment with his flashlight, moving like someone with time and the patience to use it, he lost his sense of himself as McRae; he was just something crippled and breathing in the dark, lying flat in a little winding gully of weeds and sand. McRae was gone, was someone far, far away, from ages ago—a man fresh out of prison, with the whole country to wander in and insurance money in his pocket, who had headed west with the idea that maybe his luck, at long last, had changed.

LESLIE MARMON SILKO

YELLOW WOMAN

My thigh clung to his with dampness, and I watched the sun rising up through the tamaracks and willows. The small brown water birds came to the river and hopped across the mud, leaving brown scratches in the alkali-white crust. They bathed in the river silently. I could hear the water, almost at our feet where the narrow fast channel bubbled and washed green ragged moss and fern leaves. I looked at him beside me, rolled in the red blanket on the white river sand. I cleaned the sand out of the cracks between my toes, squinting because the sun was above the willow trees. I looked at him for the last time, sleeping on the white river sand.

I felt hungry and followed the river south the way we had come the afternoon before, following our footprints that were already blurred by lizard tracks and bug trails. The horses were still lying down, and the black one whinnied when he saw me but he did not get up—maybe it was because the corral was made out of thick cedar branches and the horses had not yet felt the sun like I had. I tried to look beyond the pale red mesas to the pueblo. I knew it was there, even if I could not see it, on the sandrock hill above the river, the same river that moved past me now and had reflected the moon last night.

The horse felt warm underneath me. He shook his head and pawed the sand. The bay whinnied and leaned against the gate trying to follow, and I remembered him asleep in the red blanket beside the river. I slid off the horse and tied him close to the other horse, I walked north with the river again, and the white sand broke loose in footprints over footprints.

"Wake up."

He moved in the blanket and turned his face to me with his eyes still closed. I knelt down to touch him.

"I'm leaving."

He smiled now, eyes still closed. "You are coming with me, remember?" He sat up now with his bare dark chest and belly in the sun.

"Where?"

"To my place."

"And will I come back?"

He pulled his pants on. I walked away from him, feeling him behind me and smelling the willows.

"Yellow Woman," he said.

I turned to face him. "Who are you?" I asked.

He laughed and knelt on the low, sandy bank, washing his face in the river. "Last night you guessed my name, and you knew why I had come."

I stared past him at the shallow moving water and tried to remember the night, but I could only see the moon in the water and remember his warmth around me.

"But I only said that you were him and that I was Yellow Woman—I'm not really her—I have my own name and I come from the pueblo on the other side of the mesa. Your name is Silva and you are a stranger I met by the river yesterday afternoon."

He laughed softly. "What happened yesterday has nothing to do with what you will do today, Yellow Woman."

"I know—that's what I'm saying—the old stories about the ka'tsina spirit and Yellow Woman can't mean us."

My old grandpa liked to tell those stories best. There is one about Badger and Coyote who went hunting and were gone all day, and when the sun was going down they found a house. There was a girl living there alone, and she had light hair and eyes and she told them that they could sleep with her. Coyote wanted to be with her all night so he sent Badger into a prairie-dog hole, telling him he thought he saw something in it. As soon as Badger crawled in, Coyote blocked up the entrance with rocks and hurried back to Yellow Woman.

"Come here," he said gently.

He touched my neck and I moved close to him to feel his breathing and to hear his heart. I was wondering if Yellow

Woman had known who she was—if she knew that she would become part of the stories. Maybe she'd had another name that her husband and relatives called her so that only the ka'tsina from the north and the storytellers would know her as Yellow Woman. But I didn't go on; I felt him all around me, pushing me down into the white river sand.

Yellow Woman went away with the spirit from the north and lived with him and his relatives. She was gone for a long time, but then one day she came back and she brought twin boys.

"Do you know the story?"

"What story?" He smiled and pulled me close to him as he said this. I was afraid lying there on the red blanket. All I could know was the way he felt, warm, damp, his body beside me. This is the way it happens in the stories, I was thinking, with no thought beyond the moment she meets the ka'tsina spirit and they go.

"I don't have to go. What they tell in stories was real only then, back in time immemorial, like they say."

He stood up and pointed at my clothes tangled in the blanket. "Let's go," he said.

I walked beside him, breathing hard because he walked fast, his hand around my wrist. I had stopped trying to pull away from him, because his hand felt cool and the sun was high, drying the river bed into alkali. I will see someone, eventually I will see someone, and then I will be certain that he is only a man—some man from nearby—and I will be sure that I am not Yellow Woman. Because she is from out of time past and I live now and I've been to school and there are highways and pickup trucks that Yellow Woman never saw.

It was an easy ride north on horseback. I watched the change from the cottonwood trees along the river to the junipers that brushed past us in the foothills, and finally there were only piñons, and when I looked up at the rim of the mountain plateau I could see pine trees growing on the edge. Once I stopped to look down, but the pale sandstone had disappeared and the river was gone and the dark lava hills were all around. He touched my hand, not speaking, but always singing softly a mountain song and looking into my eyes.

I felt hungry and wondered what they were doing at home now—my mother, my grandmother, my husband, and the baby. Cooking breakfast, saying, "Where did she go?—maybe kidnapped." And Al going to the tribal police with the details: "She went walking along the river."

The house was made with black lava rock and red mud. It was high above the spreading miles of arroyos and long mesas. I smelled a mountain smell of pitch and buck brush. I stood there beside the black horse, looking down on the small, dim country we had passed, and I shivered.

"Yellow Woman, come inside where it's warm."

He lit a fire in the stove. It was an old stove with a round belly and an enamel coffeepot on top. There was only the stove, some faded Navajo blankets, and a bedroll and cardboard box. The floor was made of smooth adobeplaster, and there was one small window facing east. He pointed at the box.

"There's some potatoes and the frying pan." He sat on the floor with his arms around his knees pulling them close to his chest and he watched me fry the potatoes. I didn't mind him watching me because he was always watching me—he had been watching me since I came upon him sitting on the river bank trimming leaves from a willow twig with his knife. We ate from the pan and he wiped the grease from his fingers on his Levi's.

"Have you brought women here before?" He smiled and kept chewing, so I said, "Do you always use the same tricks?"

"What tricks?" He looked at me like he didn't understand.

"The story about being a ka'tsina from the mountains. The story about Yellow Woman."

Silva was silent; his face was calm.

"I don't believe it. Those stories couldn't happen now," I said.

He shook his head and said softly, "But someday they will talk about us, and they will say, 'Those two lived long ago when things like that happened.' "

He stood up and went out. I ate the rest of the potatoes and thought about things—about the noise the stove was making and the sound of the mountain wind outside. I remembered yesterday and the day before, and then I went outside.

I walked past the corral to the edge where the narrow trail cut through the black rim rock. I was standing in the sky with nothing around me but the wind that came down from the blue mountain peak behind me. I could see faint mountain images in the distance, miles across the vast spread of mesas and valleys and plains. I wondered who was over there to feel the mountain wind on those sheer blue edges—who walks on the pine needles in those blue mountains.

"Can you see the pueblo?" Silva was standing behind me.

I shook my head. "We're too far away."

"From here I can see the world." He stepped out on the edge. "The Navajo reservation begins over there." He pointed to the east. "The Pueblo boundaries are over here." He looked below us to the south, where the narrow trail seemed to come from. "The Texans have their ranches over there, starting with that valley, the Concho Valley. The Mexicans run some cattle over there, too."

"Do you ever work for them?"

"I steal from them," Silva answered. The sun was dropping behind us and the shadows were filling the land below. I turned away from the edge that dropped forever into the valleys below.

"I'm cold," I said, "I'm going inside." I started wondering about this man who could speak the Pueblo language so well but who lived on a mountain and rustled cattle. I decided that this man Silva must be Navajo, because Pueblo men didn't do things like that.

"You must be a Navajo."

Silva shook his head gently. "Little Yellow Woman," he said, "you never give up, do you? I have told you who I am. The Navajo people know me, too." He knelt down and unrolled the bedroll and spread the extra blankets out on a piece of canvas. The sun was down, and the only light in the house came from outside—the dim orange light from sundown.

I stood there and waited for him to crawl under the blankets.

"What are you waiting for?" he said, and I lay down beside him. He undressed me slowly like the night before beside the river—kissing my face gently and running his hands up and down my belly and legs. He took off my pants and then he laughed.

"Why are you laughing?"

"You are breathing so hard."

I pulled away from him and turned my back to him.

He pulled me around and pinned me down with his arms and chest. "You don't understand, do you, little Yellow Woman? You will do what I want."

And again he was all around me with his skin slippery against mine, and I was afraid because I understood that his strength could hurt me. I lay underneath him and I knew that he could destroy me. But later, while he slept beside me, I touched his face and I had a feeling—the kind of feeling for him that overcame me that morning along the river. I kissed him on the forehead and he reached out for me.

When I woke up in the morning he was gone. It gave me a strange feeling because for a long time I sat there on the blankets and looked around the little house for some object of his—some proof that he had been there or maybe that he was coming back. Only the blankets and the cardboard box remained. The .30-30 that had been leaning in the corner was gone, and so was the knife that I had used the night before. He was gone, and I had my chance to go now. But first I had to eat, because I knew it would be a long walk home.

I found some dried apricots in the cardboard box, and I sat down on a rock at the edge of the plateau rim. There was no wind and the sun warmed me. I was surrounded by silence. I drowsed with apricots in my mouth, and I didn't believe that there were highways or railroads or cattle to steal.

When I woke up, I stared down at my feet in the black mountain dirt. Little black ants were swarming over the pine needles around my foot. They must have smelled the apricots. I thought about my family far below me. They would be wondering about me, because this had never happened to me before. The tribal police would file a report. But if old Grandpa weren't dead he would tell them what happened—he would laugh and say, "Stolen by a ka'tsina, a mountain spirit. She'll come home—they usually do." There are enough of them to handle things. My mother and grandmother will raise the baby like they raised me. Al will find someone else, and they will go on like before except that there will be a story about the day I disappeared while I was walking along the river. Silva had come for me; he said he had. I did not decide to go. I just went. Moonflowers blossom in the sand hills before dawn, just as I followed him. That's what I was thinking as I wandered along the trail through the pine trees.

It was noon when I got back. When I saw the stone house I remembered that I had meant to go home. But that didn't seem important any more, maybe because there were little blue flowers growing in the meadow behind the stone house and the gray squirrels were playing in the pines next to the house. The horses were standing in the corral, and there was a beef carcass hanging on the shady side of a big pine in front of the house. Flies buzzed around the clotted blood that hung from the carcass. Silva was washing his hands in a bucket full of water. He must have heard me coming because he spoke to me without turning to face me.

"I've been waiting for you."

"I went walking in the big pine trees."

I looked into the bucket full of bloody water with brown-and-white animals hairs floating in it. Silva stood there letting his hand drip, examining me intently.

"Are you coming with me?"

"Where?" I asked him.

"To sell the meat in Marquez."

"If you're sure it's O.K."

"I wouldn't ask you if it wasn't," he answered.

He sloshed the water around in the bucket before he dumped it out and set the bucket upside down near the door. I followed him to the corral and watched him saddle the horses. Even beside the horses he looked tall, and I asked him again if he wasn't Navajo. He didn't say anything; he just shook his head and kept cinching up the saddle.

"But Navajos are tall."

"Get on the horse," he said, "and let's go."

The last thing he did before we started down the steep trail was to grab the .30-30 from the corner. He slid the rifle into the scabbard that hung from his saddle.

"Do they ever try to catch you?" I asked.

"They don't know who I am."

"Then why did you bring the rifle?"

"Because we are going to Marquez where the Mexicans live."

The trail leveled out on a narrow ridge that was steep on both sides like an animal spine. On one side I could see where the trail went around the rocky gray hills and disappeared into the southeast where the pale sandrock mesas stood in the distance near my home. On the other side was a trail that went west, and as I looked far into the distance I thought I saw the little town. But Silva said no, that I was looking in the wrong place, that I just thought I saw houses. After that I quit looking off into the distance; it was hot and the wildflowers were closing up their deep-yellow petals. Only the waxy cactus flowers bloomed in the bright sun, and I saw every color that a cactus blossom can be; the white ones and the red ones were still buds, but the purple and the yellow were blossoms, open full and the most beautiful of all.

Silva saw him before I did. The white man was riding a big gray horse, coming up the trail toward us. He was traveling fast and the gray horse's feet sent rocks rolling off the trail into the dry tumbleweeds. Silva motioned for me to stop and we watched the white man. He didn't see us right away, but finally his horse whinnied at our horses and he stopped. He looked at us briefly before he lapped the gray horse across the three hundred yards that separated us. He stopped his horse in front of Silva, and his young fat face was shadowed by the brim of his hat. He didn't look mad, but his small, pale eyes moved from the blood-soaked gunny sacks hanging from my saddle to Silva's face and then back to my face.

"Where did you get the fresh meat?" the white man asked.

"I've been hunting," Silva said, and when he shifted his weight in the saddle the leather creaked.

"The hell you have, Indian. You've been rustling cattle. We've been looking for the thief for a long time."

The rancher was fat, and sweat began to soak through his white cowboy shirt and the wet cloth stuck to the thick rolls of belly fat. He almost seemed to be panting from the exertion of talking, and he smelled rancid, maybe because Silva scared him.

Silva turned to me and smiled. "Go back up the mountain, Yellow Woman."

The white man got angry when he heard Silva speak in a language he couldn't understand. "Don't try anything, Indian. Just keep riding to Marquez. We'll call the state police from there."

The rancher must have been unarmed because he was very frightened and if he had a gun he would have pulled it out then.

I turned my horse around and the rancher yelled, "Stop!" I looked at Silva for an instant and there was something ancient and dark—something I could feel in my stomach—in his eyes, and when I glanced at his hand I saw his finger on the trigger of the .30-30 that was still in the saddle scabbard. I slapped my horse across the flank and the sacks of raw meat swung against my knees as the horse leaped up the trail. It was hard to keep my balance, and once I thought I felt the saddle slipping backward; it was because of this that I could not look back.

I didn't stop until I reached the ridge where the trail forked. The horse was breathing deep gasps and there was a dark film of sweat on its neck. I looked down in the direction I had come from, but I couldn't see the place. I waited. The wind came up and pushed warm air past me. I looked up at the sky, pale blue and full of thin clouds and fading vapor trails left by jets.

I think four shots were fired—I remember hearing four hollow explosions that reminded me of deer hunting. There could have been more shots after that, but I couldn't have heard them because my horse was running again and the loose rocks were making too much noise as they scattered around his feet.

Horses have a hard time running downhill, but I went that way instead of uphill to the mountain because I thought it was safer. I felt better with the horse running southeast past the round gray hills that were covered with cedar trees and black lava rock. When I got to the plain in the distance I could see the dark green patches of tamaracks that grew along the river; and beyond the river I could see the beginning of the pale sandrock mesas. I stopped the horse and looked back to see if anyone was coming; then I got off the horse and turned the horse around, wondering if it would go back to its corral under the pines on the mountain. It looked back at me for a moment and then plucked a mouthful of green tumbleweeds before it trotted back up the trail with its ears pointed forward, carrying its head daintily to one side to avoid stepping on the dragging reins. When the horse disappeared over the last hill, the gunny sacks full of meat were still swinging and bouncing.

I walked toward the river on a wood-hauler's road that I knew would eventually lead to the paved road. I was thinking about waiting beside the road for someone to drive by, but by the time I got to the pavement I had decided it wasn't very far to walk if I followed the river back the way Silva and I had come.

The river water tasted good, and I sat in the shade under a cluster of silvery willows. I thought about Silva, and I felt sad at leaving him; still, there was something strange about him, and I tried to figure it out all the way back home.

I came back to the place on the river bank where he had been sitting the first time I saw him. The green willow leaves that he had trimmed from the branch were still lying there, wilted in the sand. I saw the leaves and I wanted to go back to him—to kiss him and to touch him—but the mountains were too far away now. And I told myself, because I believe it, he will come back sometime and be waiting again by the river.

I followed the path up from the river into the village. The sun was getting low, and I could smell supper cooking when I got to the screen door of my house. I could hear their voices inside—my mother was telling my grandmother how to fix the Jell-O and my husband, Al, was playing with the baby. I decided to tell them that some Navajo had kidnapped me, but I was sorry that old Grandpa wasn't alive to hear my story because it was the Yellow Woman stories he liked to tell best.

RON CARLSON

PHENOMENA

First of all, I'm not one of these people who ever wanted to see a U.F.O., an unidentified flying object. I have never wanted to see an unidentified anything. The things in my life, I identify; that's good with me. I'm not one of these people who is strange or weirded-out over unexplainable phenomena. I don't want any phenomena at all, and we're lucky in Cooper, because there isn't much phenomena. About the time there is a little phenomena, like Chaney and Gibbs sawing through the roof of the K-Mart, I identify the phenomena and throw them in jail.

I'm the sheriff.

So I'm not a weirdo. Things happen sometimes and I do my best. My name is Derec Ferris, and I've traced the Ferrises back all the way to Journey City, near the border, and there isn't a weirdo in the whole bunch. Now, I'm the sheriff; you notice I didn't say I'm the law around here. Whitney used to say he was the law around here. That was when he was sheriff. I can tell you exactly when he stopped saying that. Four years ago in September. We were together in his car late one night after coffee at The World, and we nailed this speeder right down from the high school. A rented Firebird, gunmetal gray. Actually we flashed him on the curve of Quibbel's Junk Yard and it took us the whole mile of town to slow down. We pulled him over in front of Cooper Regional, where Whitney and I had been Cougars for four years together. It was about two in the morning. Whitney put his hand on my arm and went up to the Pontiac. I could see he was working up his sarcastic rage; he used to say that eighty percent of being a good sheriff was acting. Anyway, he starts: "Who do you think you are, endangering the lives of the citizens of Cooper by whipping through here at eighty-two miles an hour?" And the guy goes: "I'm Dan Blum, and I'm late. Who do you think you are?" Whitney loves that, an opening. "I'm Whitney Shepard and I'm the law around here." Well, Dan Blum, as his name actually turned out to be, thought that was the funniest thing he'd ever heard, and after a little chuckle, he said, "Say, that's great. So, it's your wife that sleeps with the law." That comment seemed to confuse Whitney, even though he slapped the guy for seventy-five big ones, and he never said that about being the law again.

That was, like I said, four years ago, and since then Whitney's in-laws have had troubles outside Chicago, and he and Dorothy, who was also a Cougar with us, and whom I had also known for forty-one years, moved over there, and they might as well be on another world for all I hear from them. This is all to say, I'm not the law. I'm fifty-five years old and I've lived in this county all my life, except for fourteen months when I lived in Korea employed by Uncle Sam. My name is Derec Ferris and that's who sleeps with my wife.

The fact is, I'm still surprised that Whitney left. I mean, where is he? I still expect to see him squashing his stool at the counter at The World every time I walk in there. Hell, he grew up here along the river just like I did; he and I and Harold were the three musketeers. We worked for Nemo at Earth Adventure two summers in high school, and we gained four hundred and forty-four yards passing as Cooper Cougars in 1949, setting a record that stood until 1957. Then, poof! he's gone, and I'm sheriff. I've got his car and everything. It still smells like him.

And then as deputy, the council signs some guy, Leon, and he's not even from here. He's from Griggs, for Chrissakes. This guy drops in from Griggs and he takes over my car and my desk and starts acting like a deputy. I mean, he's a nice kid and he likes me, *but:* who is he? The hardest thing about dealing with young people who think they know anything is that you've got to sit there and listen to the same bullshit you tried out on somebody else thirty years ago. It makes me tired. It makes me want to go to bed. I don't want to talk about it. At all. What I want to talk about is the Unidentified Object that has come into my life, the whole unidentified flying object day, so that you can see I'm not a phenomena weirdo; I'm only Derec Ferris, the sheriff here in Cooper.

First of all, I'm not going to give you any theory, because I don't have any. And I don't want any. Where did it come from? I don't care. I've been here in Cooper all my life and it might have come from over in Mercy or even Griggs. It kind of looked like something from Griggs. I don't care. It was a U.F.O. It might have come from Korea; try to tell me that's on this earth. And why did it come? Ha ha. None of that. I'm going to give you the day, the whole day, and—really—nothing but the day.

When I arrived at the jail, Leon was finishing the papers on Chaney and Gibbs, who we had collared the night before in the dumpster behind Plenty-a-Chicken. They didn't give us any trouble, partly because they both had a good faceful of fiberglass insulation from forcing themselves through that little hole in the K-Mart roof, and Gibbs had sprained his ankle. They had jumped into a bin of purses or they'd both broken all their legs. Breaking into K-Mart, for Chrissakes. It was one of the few times a year when I wished we had two cells, but the two bad guys themselves looked pretty subdued—that's the way it always is the morning after—and I only had to hold them two days until District came by.

Right after I arrived, here comes Martin from the K-Mart for a look. He was confused. I mean two guys saw a hole in your roof and it hurts your feelings. Chaney came to the bars and smiled at him. "You dumb shit," he said. "It's K-Mart. Don't take it personally."

I took Martin outside and told him not to worry, just to clean up and go over and get a blue light special going on those purses. We all knew Chaney was no damn good ever since the Pontiac-a-Thon over in Mercy when he tried to get all the other contestants to let go of the car by threatening to murder them later.

"This is never going to happen again," I told Martin, and he seemed to believe me. I remember Whitney saying that thing about sheriffs having to act and I wondered if I was just acting with Martin. Somebody might saw into K-Mart again; I don't know. I'm not God.

Back inside, Chaney's still smiling, and Sarah calls. She says we received a card from Derec; that's our son, same name. He works for a textbook publisher in Palo Alto, California, and he's a painter. Paints pictures. Well, it's a little news, because we haven't seen him in five years, and we don't get that much mail. Every time I drive by Cooper Regional I think about him, though. Even then when he was in high school refusing to play football, he said he couldn't wait to get out of here, Cooper, and go to California. Which he did. I feel bad about it, and I miss him, but I figure it this way: at least somebody got what he wanted.

Sarah says the card says that Derec is going to have a show. Well. I don't know what that is, and she explained that it is a show of his paintings and it is good news. She wants to go. I'm looking at Chaney and his wrong-ass smile, and Sarah is excited on the telephone. I tell her great, that I'll talk to her later and I hang up. I thought: I want to go, too. But the thought came to me as something else. Here it was, just a Monday. Leon was taking off at noon; I've got two idiots in the cell; we've got a card from Derec; and there's a radio call coming in. It's not ten o'clock in the morning of the day I'll see a U.F.O.; I should have seen it coming.

What I want to do is go and hold down my stool at The World and drink my gallon of coffee, but Arvella at District says it's something from Nemo out at Earth Adventure, a bear attack or something. So I tell Leon, no problem, to lock up and enjoy his folks over in Griggs, that hellhole, though I don't say that, and I drive out to Earth Adventure.

On the way out I'm thinking about Derec and his show, and I'm kind of blue thinking about what he ever thinks of his old man. Did you ever do that, wonder what your grown kids think of you? The times you tried, the times you didn't try. No matter who you are, I think, you still want your boy to be like you. Just as some kind of compliment. Derec *is* like me, with his ears, and he's got the build, but the rest . . . I don't know. He never liked Whitney and all his macho kidding, but he did work for Harold at the Passion Play for a while the summer before he left for California.

Old Earth Adventure is about on its last legs. If you didn't know where you were going, I doubt you could find the place. The two great signs Nemo put up the summers before Harold,

Whitney, and I worked for him are all peeled to hell, and a Chinese elm has taken the best one, the one with the dinosaur peeking over at the boatload of people. You can still see the profile of the dinosaur poking up above the sign, but you can't read a word through the bushes.

It turned out not to be a bear attack. I knew it wouldn't be. Nemo's bear, Alex, hasn't been awake for about two years. It turned out to be Monty, the old cougar, who must be forty now and who's lost most of his hair and teeth and whose skin sags off his bones like it was somebody else's suit; Monty had fallen out of a tree and broke his hind leg on the hood of some tourist's Ford. By the time I arrived, Monty had already dragged himself into the women's restroom and he was growling in the corner like an old man getting ready for his last spit. His poor old rheumy eyes were full of tears. Hell, I'd known him from a kitten when they found him west of Mercy at the Ringenburgs', crying in the barn being harassed by a dozen swallows. I'd fed that cat a lot of corndogs the summer I was seventeen and worked the boats.

So I kept guard by the women's room door, so nobody would get a surprise, while we waited for Werner to come out from his practice in town. The guy from the Ford was arguing, or trying to argue, with Nemo about the damage and the scare and the hazard, and all Nemo would do was point at me and say, "There's the sheriff." But the guy wasn't coming near me or the shack where Monty lay dying. Finally he left and the doctor pulled up in his black van. I knelt with him while he drugged the big old cat. Then he and Nemo had a little talk outside while I watched Monty's tongue loll farther and farther out of his mouth. Just above him in the stall, somebody had carved "Kill All Men" in a wicked, but precise printing.

When the two men returned they had decided that this was it for Monty, and Werner said he'd haul him off. But Nemo said no, said to put him to sleep right there in the women's room, so Werner did. Monty, who was already asleep, didn't even quiver.

Outside, he and Werner argued about money for a while, Nemo trying to give the doc a twenty and the doctor not even looking Nemo in the face, saying, "No way, Nemo, not this time. No charge." They pushed that twenty back and forth twenty times like two men in a restaurant, and finally the doctor climbed in his van and headed out.

Old Nemo was in pretty bad shape. He stood there with his twenty still in his hand in the middle of the dirt road and said he was pretty close to it this time. If he lost any more animals, Earth Adventure would have to close. You couldn't charge people four bucks a car to drive along a half mile dirt road to see one bear sleeping in a way that showed his worn out old ass, a plastic tiger Nemo had gotten from the old Exxon station in Clinton, six peacocks, and four hundred geese. "It was different with a mountain lion," he said. "Monty was *something.*" Old Nemo. He stood there, pretty long in the tooth himself, knowing that Alex, the brown bear from Sheridan, was in one of his last dozen naps, and shit, I know Nemo didn't care two sticks about any of them birds. I told him not to worry, he still had the underground canal trips, but that wasn't too good either, since the boats—the same boats I worked—are in pretty bad condition. One sank last summer out from under a family from Mercy. It was lucky for Nemo the boat went down just outside the tunnel, where the water is only a foot deep, or he'd have had genuine legal action.

So I stood there with old Nemo, looking around at Earth Adventure crumbling in the weeds. Poor old Nemo. I could see it clearly: the closed sign across his gate next summer. After a while, he thumbed his overall strap and disappeared.

I thought I should stay around to see that Nemo was going to be all right, and I'm kind of sorry I did. He came back with an old canvas mail bag and started filling it with the round white rocks that he uses to line the paths.

"Can I help you, Nemo?" I said, and he opened the bag.

"Right here," is all he said.

So I lifted Monty, who must have weighed ninety pounds, and Nemo helped guide him into the bag. He cinched the tie and started dragging it toward the canal. But when we got there it was different than I supposed. He wanted to put it in one of the boats. By the time I'd helped him do that, I was committed. He climbed in the bow of the old peeling boat and there was that seat in the stern. I found one paddle in the weeds and took my place. The boat was so weathered and shot I couldn't tell which one it had been; it could have once been mine.

When I was seventeen, we came out here, Whitney, Harold, and I, and Nemo hired us piecework. We each had a boat and we got seventy-five cents a tour. In those days Nemo had a little dock strung with Christmas lights, and summer nights it was kind of lovely. There was a popcorn stand right there too, so people could buy some of that and feed the ducks, all those mallards tame as barnducks in the bright water. We'd tear the tickets and Whitney would feed those to the ducks whenever he ran out of other bad jokes. I'd get five people in my boat, the park was full of people then, and I'd pole off. "These are the natural wonders of Cooper," I'd say as we entered the cave. "They were formed a million million years ago. They have found albino perch in these waters and there may still be creatures as yet undiscovered beneath us. The legend is that a trip through this wonder makes you five years younger or five years older depending on how you've been to your mother and father. Please keep your hands inside the boat."

Nemo perched on his seat rigidly, his knees together, his arms folded. It could have been his funeral. I steered us out into the soft current and we entered the cool dark of the cavern. I hadn't been in here for years. I used to have to come down and chase teenagers out and break up their beer parties, but it wasn't too hard, because I knew my way around. There in the quiet dark with Nemo, I could almost hear Harold in the old days doing his romantic version of the tour for his boat. It was like singing. Behind me, in his boat, sometimes I could hear Whitney kidding with the passengers, laughing and telling off-color jokes, "Keep your hands inside the boat, not there, buddy. Lady, keep your hands to yourself; just because it is dark there is no need to turn into an aborigine." The passengers in his boats would laugh and call back and ahead and go "Wooo-woooo!" And at the other end, Whitney always got the tips.

For me it was a job. I was saving my money for a car that turned out to be a used 1939 Buick. For Harold, it was romantic, each little trip got him a little. He believed it; he even painted a name on his boat: *The Santa Maria.* For Whitney, it was fun.

Later that summer Whitney and I swam through once after hours. Harold wouldn't go. He wasn't fat then, no, thin as a baton, but he wouldn't go. He didn't think it was right to swim naked through the Underground River. And then later, after

I met Sarah, we all used to stay around almost every night, make a tour or two. Stop in the middle, bump around in the boats. It smelled nice then, like sand and willows, before the water treatment plant went in and raised the temperature. The five of us would take a boat in. Whitney and a date, Sarah and I, and Harold. Whitney would start on his spiel about how no virgin had ever emerged from these caverns, and he would let Sarah and me off midway on the limestone ledge, and then he'd take Harold to the far end where Harold would sit with his guitar and just play and play. Sometimes he'd sing "Stormy Weather" or "Pennies From Heaven." Sarah and I would eat the popcorn and talk about high school or the families who came to Earth Adventure. We could hear Whitney hauling around in the boat, saying, "Come on; come on," to some girl from Mercy, a waitress, or somebody he'd picked up that night. He and I were clearly different that way. I never touched a girl casually in my life, not to this day. Whitney never touched them any other way. And I guess, Harold never touched one at all. I don't know. Anyway, they were great nights.

When Nemo and I passed the ledge, he lifted his hand and looked ahead. There was one rock column and then we could see the end, the rough triangle of light that opened on the river.

"This is good right here," he said.

He started to stand, but I motioned him down, and I rose and took hold of the bag. The bright stripe of light from the cavern mouth ran roughly up the water to our boat. I remembered once being here with Harold and Sarah, late one night during a storm. We glided in the boat waiting for the next flash of lightning to explode in the jagged window down there. Harold had said, "Floating in a mountain during War of the Worlds." That was a long time ago.

I set the bag carefully on the gunnel and looked at Nemo. All I could see against the light on the water was his silhouette, and it didn't move. I waited. He didn't say anything, so I set the bag out and let the water take it.

Now, remember this is the day of the phenomenon. I went back to the jail and took the crooks a couple of tuna sandwiches from The World; I just kind of threw them in the cage. I knew that two guys with the sense of Chaney and Gibbs wouldn't try to drown themselves in their milk or suffocate in the little bits of cellophane that the sandwiches came in. Then I went back to The World and had the liver and onions for an hour. All that reminiscing had me hungry.

It was Monday, like I said, and so I knew they'd have a good hard workout at the high school. I parked across the tennis court with the radio on in case Arvella came up with something, and watched practice. I don't know the coaches now; they're two boys from State who have done a fair job so far. They like to split the hell out of the line, two ends way out there, one clear across the other side. Half the time you think the tackle is eligible.

In 1949, we never split anybody. I had to take a hard shot and still get out and get clear. But I don't care; football changes a little, just so they beat Griggs. I stayed all through the blocking, tackling and the scrimmage, to see what kind of work they'd do late. Old Coach Belcher used to yell, "You've not started, *boys,* until you're running in the dark and you're sure of yourselves!" And we'd run the cinder track until the profile of the technical building would fade right into the night sky. Whitney and I would circle the track together, our pads creaking, our cleats crunching step by step.

Well, here it was only the second week of school, still summer really, so I knew no one would be running in the dark today, but still, I was disappointed when one of the boy-coaches blew the whistle and the practice fell apart and the kids sauntered off toward the gym. I had been dreaming a little, but I still didn't see anything that was going to beat Griggs. For a minute I thought of the sheriff going over to the two coaches and giving them a word to the wise. But: nope.

It made me a little sad, sitting there in the car after the field had emptied. Football. As great as it was for Whitney and me, football was one of the first things Derec and I argued about. I couldn't understand why he didn't want to play, but after I saw that he really didn't want to, I let it go. I didn't care if he played or didn't; it wasn't worth fighting over. But I don't think he ever understood that. I think to the day he left Cooper he thought I was disappointed. As a man, sometimes, I find there are some things I can do nothing about. The words just won't line up in my mouth.

I went down to The World for my evening coffee until it was dark and then I took my two breaker-and-enterers a hot plate of kraut and dogs. I had to sit with them to get the silverware back, and then I got the call from Arvella, the only other call that day. It wasn't the U.F.O. Somebody was injured out to the Passion Play Center. I have a call or two out there every summer. Somebody gets a snakebite behind the stage or a flat settles on somebody's foot as they're shifting scenery in the dark. But this time I was a little worried because Arvella said, as she was signing off, that she thought it was Harold Kissel. And Harold is now pushing three hundred poundsand if he missed a step out of his trailer or fell off the apron, it would be serious.

I've been told that every community has a Harold Kissel, my old friend. I doubt it. He'd moved to Cooper with his mother when we were in tenth grade and for two years everybody thought he was from New York, and he didn't tip his hand about it either. His manners were amazing. I mean it was amazing that he had any, because I guess, none of the rest of us did. But he had a hat, a dark derby sort of hat and he'd tip it, and he'd hold doors for about everybody, and the things he'd do with his napkin even in The World were worth watching. It's funny, but he never took much shit for any of it, everybody just kind of knew him: eccentric. That's why I liked him and why he was the only friend I had who wasn't on the football team. Later he told me he was from Pierre, and that's when I knew it was *him,* not anyplace he was from.

He wasn't allowed to go to Korea either, which was a relief for just about everybody in town, because by that time, the year after we graduated, everybody liked Harold in their own way. While I was gone, he started and became director of the Cooper Players and was just known for that. He was the theatre. Sarah wrote me about the productions. She helped sew costumes, even the curtain for the stage at the old Episcopal Church. She wrote how the Buckley sisters had fought his using the church as a theatre even after it closed and the Episcopalians from Cooper had to go to the Lutheran or drive over to Mercy on Sunday mornings. Most went to the Lutheran.

When I came back from Korea, which is a cold place mostly, Sarah and I were married in the Lutheran Church, and Harold was one of the ushers along with Whitney who was also best man. The first year I was a deputy, Harold's mother died, and everybody thought he'd move away. Sarah was real worried. She and Whitney's wife, Dorothy, had been in two plays by then. They kind of starred in *Arsenic and Old Lace* as the aunts. You should have seen Sarah as an old lady. I told her right then that I'd love her my whole life, because even with white hair and big gray lines all over her faced, she was too pretty to stand. And when Harold's mother passed away, there was a lot of talk. The Playhouse, as they were calling the church, had added a lot to Cooper, especially in the winter, and people said it would be a shame to lose it. We had him to dinner and Sarah put it right to him, that was her way. "Are you staying?" she said. He said he was going to go away for a while and decide. The next day, he took the bus to Pierre.

Where he went for four years, nobody knows. I know that, because he never told me. Some say he finally went to New York and there was a rumor about his going to France or Africa. No clues. When he came back, he had the beginnings of the fat and he looked worn. Hell, we all do. He had a meeting of the old Cooper Players and announced that what this town needed was "a passion play." That set people off. The Buckley sisters had moved to Mercy or they'd have had a tingle or two about his plans for a *passion play.*

That was thirty years ago. The passion play has become the biggest thing about Cooper really. People say, "Have you been over to the Cooper Passion Play?" It's a real institution. Every summer thousands of people see Harold play the life of Christ, and I've seen it quite a few times myself. The local joke is that whenever anybody says Jesus H. Christ, the H. stands for Harold. He's real good in all the parts where he's among the children and disciples. He knows how to walk and he's got great hand movements, but the part which everyone remembers, the part which has been told across the counter in The World ten thousand times, is when the music starts and the lights go out. The last thing you see is Mary Magdalene and the others on their knees weeping and praying and then the darkness in the amphitheatre, just the sky with all our stars, sometimes the moon on a little cloud cruise, and the music real low and sad along with the sound effects of some hammering. Then, Harold climbs those stairs behind the cross and steps out and places his arms on the crossbars, his head hung down at the perfect angle, and pow! the spotlight puts everybody's eyes out with the white circle of Jesus on the cross: you can feel the chilly waves of goose bumps cross over the whole audience.

In these last few years, Harold is so big that he looks like Santa Claus or somebody in that loincloth, but the effect is still the same. Even his bald spot jumps at you in the scene like a halo. He's something. I remember listening to his voice in the Earth Adventure Caverns as he sang "Stormy Weather," and I know he's just a man with the God-given ability to give others the chills.

I cut the back way through Gilmer's abandoned farm to the Amphitheatre and when I get there: it's bad. The cross has come down while Harold was setting his arms up on the cross-bar. The old timber leaned over and ripped out of the stage like a tree in a storm. They said it sounded like a bomb. Harold had hit the stage hard and the full weight of that cross had killed him I was sure. There was blood and make-up blood everywhere. He wasn't moving. The cross had clobbered Bonnie Belcher who was playing Mary Magdalene and a high school girl from Mercy, but they were both okay, just lots of blood. They hadn't moved a thing. Feely told me they were afraid they would break his back. So, I had it all right there. I thought this is what happens: Whitney is gone, dead to me, and now Harold is killed. I felt the space right in here open up so I could be empty. Harold is crushed.

I knelt over him, but I couldn't feel a pulse and I couldn't tell if he was breathing. In that loincloth he looked like a great big dead kid, a two-year-old. By this time I was crying, or tears were just coming, I don't know. And I didn't care. I had to get Feely and Jerry—who plays Judas—to help me lift the cross off Harold and we dragged it back and dropped it off the rear of the stage. But it was odd. When Feely and Jerry and I lifted it up, I heard this noise. It was clapping. Out there in the dark, about half the audience still sat there waiting to see what was going to happen to Jesus now. It must have looked pretty strange to see the sheriff bending over him. And it was strange for me too; I couldn't see the people at all. It didn't—none of it—seem real.

Boyce brought the ambulance and when the four of us hoisted Harold on the stretcher, there was another raging applause. I was scared. We wrestled Harold in the van and he never made a noise, not a gurgle or a groan. It killed me. Then Jerry shut the doors and Boyce drove away. Jerry turned to me and said, "You better say something, Derec. The people aren't leaving." There I was out there in the dark talking to Judas in his nightgown, Jerry Beemer, who is going to be the assistant manager at the Dairy Creme in Griggs all his goddamned life, and he is instructing me as to what I had better do. And what really made me boil, on top of being sick and scared, was that I knew he was right. I didn't want to say anything. But I'm the sheriff. I went back up onto the stage in the lights and stood in front of the blood stain and said, "He's going to be all right, folks. You can go home now. And be careful driving. Those of you parked to the side can slip back to 21 through Gilmer's place, even though it is the entrance."

It was real quiet for a second, but then I heard the shuffling, and the families sorted themselves out and went off in the dark.

Back at the office, Chaney and Gibbs are gone. I'm still thinking about Harold, about how he could sing "Stormy Weather" and how I was a boy once, and about how he is going to die. I know he's going to die. Then I was thinking about Sarah in *Arsenic and Old Lace,* when I walk back to the cell and there's that goddamned mess all over the floor and a hole in the ceiling the shape of Ohio. I should have known. Once a couple of bums start sawing through ceilings there's no stopping them. Well, I went and got the broom, and then no: it's too much. I didn't even sweep up. I called Arvella and placed an A.P.B. on those two, locked the door, and started home.

I didn't want to see another thing. I didn't want to see the U.F.O. I'd seen enough for one day already. I just wanted to see Sarah. It was after one in the morning and I just wanted to see her. She'd be asleep, which was good because I didn't want to go over anything again. I try not to tell her any of what goes on with my work; it's all either ridiculous or hideous—who wants to hear that? If she asks me about something, I try to wait and let it pass. I can wait.

There's a lot inside a man that never gets out; I don't understand that or pretend to understand it, but if women ever knew that those waits, those times that I stir my coffee, twenty times right, twenty times left, were just full, full of the way a day crams my heart full, while I sit silently, almost humming like the biggest dummy that ever came to Cooper—if women knew how much was in a man, they'd never let up. But there's nothing I can do about it. The worse something it is, the deeper I keep it. That's the law.

If Sarah won't let it go, if she gets on me, I have a simple strategy: I turn it and ask when she's going to have that rummage sale and get rid of some of the junk in the garage and the basement. That'll start her. She's a woman who has saved everything she's ever had in her hand. I won't go into it, but she has a box of egg cartons once touched by her Uncle Elias and they remind her of him. Actually, they do me too.

Anyway, I don't tell her all the ugly details of being sheriff. And I especially didn't want to tell her about Harold and how he fell and killed himself. All I want to do is see her there sleeping and to crawl into the bed by her.

It was 1:20 A.M. I was driving home and I was a tired man. That cross was heavy.

Now get ready. At 13 and 30, where I turn for home, there at Chernewski's Tip-a-Mug, I saw the U.F.O. It set down in the road right in front of me. Actually, I heard it as I slowed for the four way. There was a clanking— awful—like a pocket knife in the dryer. I mean a real painful sound, some machine about to die, and then: *whomp!* The whole contraption dropped onto Route 30, hard as a wet bale.

At first I thought a combine had turned over; I didn't know what was going on. I couldn't see it too well; there wasn't a light on it, not a bulb. It just sat there clanking and hissing, and some low growl the way a still sounds before it commences to boil. I could also hear it spitting oil on the pavement; honest to God, this U.F.O. was a wreck. I stood out of the car and trained my spot on it, and it looked like a crashed helicopter. I could see all the terrible plumbing caging several gray oil drums and rusty boxes, like coke machines trapped in there, and lots of little ladders, some missing rungs. The wiring ran along the outside of the heavy ductwork, taped there by somebody in a hurry.

Then the smell hit me. Jesus, the smell. It had been burning oil and something else, something like rubber or plastic. The fumes were thick, billowing off one side just like the train wreck over at Mercy when the asphalt truck got creamed last winter.

I was going to go up to the thing to see if anybody was hurt, but the way it was settling, jumping around like a winged duck, and banging, I was afraid it would all give way and fall right on me.

Besides, about then I saw the alien. A door slammed open, falling out like the gate on the back of a pickup. And I stood there in the dark while the alien climbed down.

Now the alien, the alien. The alien looked a lot like my boy Derec. To me, the alien looked like my son. It was a kid about twenty-three years old wearing a sleeveless white T-shirt with the words JOHN LENNON on the front. He wore greasy green surgical pants and tennis shoes. No socks. He jumped onto Route 30 and walked past me this close and looked in the back seat of the car. Then he folded his hands like this, across his chest like he was confused. Then he looked in again and put his hands on top of the car like this, like he was waiting to be frisked or just thinking it all over. I don't know what he'd expected to be in the car, but it wasn't there. Then I found out. He looked at me, and this is going to make me sound like a weirdo, like some airbrain who likes these encounters, but he looked in that moment just like Derec. He said to me, "Where's Harold?"

Well, I was a little surprised by that. I didn't know what to say. And I didn't have to say anything. He skipped past me again, walking just like Derec, bouncing a little in those tennis shoes, and he climbed back up in that crazy rig. He had to slam that tailgate hatch or whatever it was four times to get it to stay closed, and the last time I heard glass break and sprinkle onto Route 30.

I stepped back, watching all the time. The U.F.O. cranked itself up into a frenzy, the hissing made me squint. He had it revved up and shaking, just a raw sound for three or four minutes, more than any engine I know could take. Then it jumped, and that's the right word: *jumped,* ten feet straight up, and it came down again hard, really shaking, and then it jumped and hovered up over Route 30 unsteadily. As it climbed up a little ways, I could see a small propeller on the under carriage and the oil was dripping onto that and it sprayed me a good one going by. After I couldn't see the U.F.O. anymore or hear it, thank God, or smell it, and all I could hear were the crickets and the buzzing of Chernewski's Tip-a-Mug neon sign with that silly cocktail glass tipped and fizzing the three green bubbles, and all there was left on the road was the worst oil spill you'd want to see. I went over to it and it was oil all right, dirty oil that hadn't been changed in five or six thousand miles of hard driving, and I found all these pieces of glass. Looks like some kind of mason jar. And I found this one bolt. It's left handed. The oil stain is still out there—over both lanes, for you to see for yourselves. You can't miss it: four or five gallons—at least.

That was the U.F.O.

I slumped back in the car and lifted the mic to call Arvella, but then I put it back. It had been a day. I was making no more calls.

I was a boy in this town. And now I am a man in this town. A lot of things happen some days. Somebody'll die and there'll be a mattress in the backyard. Some kid driving a hard hang-over and an asphalt truck won't see a train and there'll be smoke, clear to Griggs. And some days nothing happens. The flies won't move five inches down the counter in The World. Some days things happen, and some days nothing does, but at the end of each I have to lie down. I lie by Sarah, the collector of treasures, in our bed which is surrounded by rooms full of the little things of our lives. She still has the ticket stubs from the game with Mercy, our first date, and they too sleep in some little box in some drawer in our house. I lie by Sarah in my place on earth, and slowly—it takes hours—I empty for the earth to turn and prepare me for the next thing, another day.

Sarah is in the bed under the covers in the shape I will always identify. Her form is identifiable. "The hospital called," she says. She's awake. I button my pajamas and don't answer. I don't want to get started. I don't want to get started on Harold and go over the whole thing. I climb heavily into bed. "Delores called from the hospital." I weigh nine hundred pounds; sleep is coming up around my eyes like warm water. "Delores called from the hospital. She said Harold is going to be all right."

I float in the bed by my wife Sarah's side. I know she is going to go on. "I made reservations for Palo Alto, for Derec's show. We're going next Thursday, so get the time off. You want to go, don't you?"

"Yeah," I say. "Yeah." Sleep rises in me like sweet smoke. It is late here in Cooper. It kind of feels late everywhere. Maybe it is just late for me. My son Derec. We're going to Palo Alto, California. We're going to fly out there.

BILL RIPLEY

DESERT OWLS

I'm sitting in an air-conditioned espresso shop, hung over, trying to write a poem about guilt. Boy, do I feel guilty. People working everywhere. People starving everywhere. Minorities everywhere. Poor minorities. And me writing poetry. It's just not fair.

It all started when we went over to see my friend Houdini and tried to explain to him that he shouldn't work. We think work causes you to miss the magic in life and conceivably causes wars. We told him that he should become a poet like us, because all we have to do is drink. But Houdini got quite sad. His wife hates both poets and bums and he said that he couldn't become one, but that he would have another drink. Then we got sad and had to have another drink. Things got so morose over at Houdini's that we had to leave.

When we got in my car I noticed all the trash and beer cans and then I almost cried. But Dagoberto told me that all true poets lived in filth, and then I didn't feel so bad, and we started to worry about where we were going to get our next drink.

We got our next drink at the Tiddy Bar, the first bar we came to. This is not one of our favorite bars because we don't have enough money for the girls and they don't make pokey for poetry like they did in the sixties. This is a source of depression for Dagoberto and me since we both teach a little English and write a little poetry, but would rather be with the girls from the Tiddy Bar. Sleeping with a girl from the English department is like working on a crumbling Stutz Bear Cat when you are the last mechanic on earth—it becomes too much responsibility and thus interferes with your poetry.

Inside the Tiddy Bar a girl danced naked on the stage to "I See a Bad Moon a Rising." We sat down away from the stage because we wanted to seem like we came there to drink and not to chase girls because, somewhere in the back of our minds, we're still convinced that one day, one of these girls, the barmaid maybe, will fall for a poem. Being nearly broke, we try to seem special. Dagoberto is half Mexican and better at seeming special than I am.

After a couple more drinks a new, skinnier girl came on stage and took off her clothes to Bob Dylan's "Knocking on Heaven's Door." But the drinks didn't cheer us up and I told Dagoberto that it was Houdini's fault for marrying a woman who made him sell Amway.

After another drink, we decided to go see Fishback and Norton who are fun to be around because they are drunk all the time and happy even when they don't get girls. Sometimes the happiness rubs off and makes me feel guilty for being so depressed. So I thought I might be able to combine business with pleasure and get guilty enough to write the poem about guilt.

Norton lives in a cave beneath the owl holes on the side of Red Mesa, in the desert outside of town. He is a Vietnam veteran and the reason he moved into the cave was to prove a point to his wife. He said:

"I'd rather live in a cave beneath the owl holes than spend one more night in this house."

So she took his house, and though a lot of people invited him to live with them, Norton insisted on moving to the owl holes where he hooks his stereo up to a series of car batteries and listens to Jr. Walker and the All Stars. The view from the mouth of the cave, across the desert into the sand hills, is serene.

We caught up with Fishback's battered pickup about six miles out of town, on the gravel road to the owl holes, barreling through the dust until Fishback and Norton ran us off the road into the desert, where we ground to a stop over a dried dog.

The path to the cave runs up the steep slope of the mesa diagonally. The sandy cliff is full of holes made by burrowing desert owls. Scattered beneath each hole like a ghoul's waterfall are the skulls and bones of kangaroo rats, baby chicks, small snakes, etc. Close up, it looks like someone has disinterred a small animal cemetery.

Norton, Fishback, and Dagoberto each carried three six-packs up the path, and I followed with sacks of ice over my shoulders. Except for the rocks tumbling down the path, it was pretty good duty, cool at least. Once Norton stopped and stuck his big head into a hole and I imagined the owl crouched at the back of the cave, beak open, claws spread.

The cave is three quarters of the way up the mesa, behind an outcropping of sandstone, which hides the entrance from the road. The skulls and bones of all the creatures which litter the slope hang from a curtain made of fishing line in the entrance to the cave. When the wind rattles the bones, weird shadows roll around the dirt walls.

We were almost there when I stopped to rest. They went on. Sitting on a bag of ice, I wished my son was there to watch the hills change color. He would love the cave, of course, as do Norton's kids, when they get to visit, but something about cave dwelling alienates Norton's ex-wife. I was thinking about my kid when a rattlesnake flew by my face and bounced and writhed down the hill, and I remembered staring down into a pit of albino rattlesnakes as a child, my grandmother holding my hand and warning me that where there was one rattlesnake, there would always be another. The next snake that Norton tossed out of the cave wrapped itself around my neck. Though Dagoberto had crushed its head with a six-pack, it still curled and twisted on my shoulders and it wasn't until after we'd had a few more beers that I was able to calm down. Then I tried to think about this poem about guilt. I am enrolled in a poetry class, and the teacher, a poet who drives a Mercedes, wants us to write a poem about guilt.

Norton leaned back against the cave wall with his eyes rolled back in his head. In Vietnam they'd drop him from a chopper, his dog first, in the middle of a mine field to lead trapped soldiers out. He lost eighteen dogs as they put their faithful noses to the ground. They nicknamed him "Doggy Brains" because of the splattered way he'd come out of the mine fields. In the shadows of the skulls, in the back of the cave, Doggy Brains looked like a lobotomized Buddha, whispering to himself.

"It's almost time," he mumbled. "Almost time." Then, as the valley filled up with red light, he crawled over between the stereo and the car batteries and made the connection. Jr. Walker and the All Stars came on full tilt, shaking the mesa and blasting thirty or forty great startled desert owls into the evening sky like *Apocalypse Now*— Wagner blaring and the big choppers lumbering in to waste the village, machine-gun fire chopping chunks out of kids—only this time it was just desert owls out for baby chicks and mice and there was no smell of napalm or gasoline, for the owl holes are pretty uncivilized.

I couldn't think with the music that loud so I slipped outside with a couple of beers and walked up to the top of the mesa, feeling the music through the earth. On top the air was clear, you couldn't even hear a car. I wondered why I didn't live out here. It happens every time. My heart unwinds and I realize I'm wasting my life. I tried to think about this poem about guilt. But as I looked out over the mesa, all I could think about was how happy I was the snake hadn't bitten me. I almost felt guilty because I was so happy. Why should I be happy? People were starving to death across the river and somebody had run over that dried dog more than once.

Fishy had put the dog in the back of the truck and it looked like a flounder in the moonlight. A "sail dog," actually. Fishback had collected sail cats for a year or two, and even had a couple of sail squirrels, and one sail fox, but he lost interest in the project when Norton discovered that there was actually a national "sail cat" club that exchanged pictures, and even mailed flattened, dried cats back and forth, swapping collections. Norton got some pictures of families of sail cat swappers, gap-toothed folks standing in garages with collections of sail cats hung like stringers of strange fish which humbled Fishback forever and caused him to give up the nasty habit.

But there was something about this flattened out flounder dog that interested me. We'd found him on a dirt road, and he was a pretty big dog—too big to have been flattened out like that by a mere pickup. It looked like a semi had backed back and forth across him eleven times at least. There was no way you could get a truck that big on a dirt road that small.

But then all the lights of El Paso and Juarez came on, using up all that electricity, using up all that water in all those dams that are turning all those reservoirs that used to be pretty rivers into ugly mudholes, and I didn't feel so guilty. You didn't see me out there working away, building dams. I taught one little class of English, and tried to use that class to brainwash the kids out of work. Did they want to trudge the same treadmill their parents trudged? Did they want more automobiles, more aluminum siding, more carbon monoxide, more dams, more work?

Yep.

And they loved to comb their hair and drive cars and spout platitudes about success. Oh well. At least we were in America. Across the river an evil orange glowed above Juarez, where they didn't pretend to care about carbon monoxide. It was hard to eat lunch over there anymore what with hungry mothers impolitely holding emaciated infants up in front of the cafe window. Other innovative beggars mutilated children, then sent them out to hustle chubby white folks, taking unfair advantage of our underexposure to starvation.

So I began to wonder if it was a redneck or greaser who ran over the dog at least eleven times to make a buck selling the prize carcass to some top collector of sail animals in Duluth or Atlanta. You just couldn't be sure. But one thing you could be sure of—Detroit and Japan made it all possible. Without cars there could be no sail dogs.

Another confusing thing was this: the flattening had to be done on pavement. You don't get work of this quality on a dirt road. Norton had discovered that sail cat swappers don't just sit around and wait for God to bless them with an unexpected sail cat. The more discerning swappers saw that the thing to do was to custom make new ones—flatten, dry, and sell them. There are virtual mail order houses for Blue Point Siamese, Chinese Conga Cats, Australian Weegees—the works. But the most mysterious thing was: what was this dog doing out here on a dirt road in the desert? It was an unusual piece of work, possibly a Golden Retriever. I wondered if Norton had done it, and brought it out here as a trick on Fishback. But that didn't hold up. Losing all those dogs in Vietnam hadn't hardened Norton to quadrupeds.

Maybe somebody hadn't recognized its value, just sort of picked it up out of curiosity on their way to the owl holes, and then got bored and thrown it away. Some folks are that insensitive. Some folks feel guilty if they don't work like mad and breed like rats. But not me. I hang out at the owl holes. It's the tattered edge of civilization, what's left of the planet. I felt guilty looking at that dog mashed so flat and dry that you could've sailed it across the Rio Grande like a big Frisbee and some kid would've eaten it. I could see the kid munching away, sort of superimposed beneath a vision of Norton's wife's high heels, click click clicking down the tidy sidewalk on the way to the bank. I should have sailed old Fido across the Rio Grande in the hammering moonlight like the flat flying squirrel of charity—maybe even tossed across a beer. That would have been the utilitarian thing to do, the kind thing. But I wasn't going to do anything about starvation in Mexico. I was a poet.

ALLEN WIER

BOB AND THE OTHER MAN

Blanco, Texas, 1903, in the heat. In beards and board houses and long heavy dresses. In brown. In the dust of Texas.

In their wagon, in the hot shade of scrub cedar, Boon waited for his father, Brown Smith Speer, who stood in the circle around the grave. Juno Durham Speer wobbled down two ropes into the warm grave. Boon was five. He would miss stories about Juno fleeing Mississippi in the wake of cotton planters. Boon pictured an endless black line of slaves chasing his grandfather into Texas, and his grandfather fighting the land and the drouth and Santa Anna. Beard and flop-brim hat. Soft brown and off- white. Boon rocked on the wagon seat.

The wagon rocked to one side. A man not much taller than the wagon wheel was boosting a boy up beside Boon. The boy, dressed like Boon in overalls and a stiff clean shirt, grinned and settled on the wagon bed, legs folded Indian style. The man beside the wagon hoisted himself up, dabbing his face with a big white handkerchief. He was dressed like a man in Boon's picture book, in a tight-fitting black coat with long pointed tails like a snake's tongue. His pants were black with thin white stripes, and diagonally across his white ruffled shirt was a red shiny sash. Boon had asked about the sash in the picture book, wondering if it held an arrow quiver across the back, beneath the coat.

He handed Boon a small engraved gold plate: BOB AND THE OTHER MAN. He bowed shortly, wrinkling his red sash against his tight stomach. His long pink nose slowly rose and fell as he breathed. "I am Bob; this is The Other Man," he said, straightening from his bow and opening his palms to The Other Man.

The Other Man grinned, his round child's eyes widening, and pulled a bright orange yo-yo out of his overalls. "I can do around-the-world," he said, working the yo-yo off the side of the wagon.

Boon thought of his yo-yo, made by his grandfather, left at home for the funeral.

Bob crooked a finger and nodded to Boon. The sun reflected off his plastered-down black hair, his head moving up and down to the rhythm of his speech, "This here, this here's your first funeral, sonny boy?"

Boon nodded, looking at the soft gray fuzz on Bob's neck. He figured The Other Man was about his age, but Bob seemed ageless.

Bob smiled quickly and stroked the lapel of his coat, "Well, sonny boy, we'll go to more. There'll be more."

The Other Man was spinning the yo-yo around and around the world.

Bob laughed shrilly and pulled a great gold watch from beneath the silk sash. "Plenty of time. Time enough," he said.

The Other Man kept spinning the orange yo-yo.

Boon asked The Other Man if he had a knife, remembering he hadn't left his knife behind. The Other Man sucked the yo-yo into his hand with a soft slap and pulled a yellow-handled barlow from his overalls. They played splits in the back of the wagon while Bob dealt cards on the wagon seat. He quickly scooped the cards up when the people around the grave began singing "Nearer MyGod to Thee," tapped The Other Man on the shoulder, and said it was time to go.

"Where?" asked Boon.

"Got to get out of the heat, sonny boy. Get out of this dry heat. Your grandfather had the best ride out here. That hearse was the best ride."

Boon's mother was crying and his father frowned when he saw the jackknife. They got silently in the wagon and started back to town. Boon sat in back, looking backwards. The man from the funeral home turned the hearse around and followed. Bob and The Other Man rode in the hearse, behind the isinglass, out of the sun and the dust of Texas.

• • •

Brick Front Store, 1906. Only one in town. Boon's father inherited the store. The sign was new, not the name: JUNO D. SPEER & CO. GENERAL MERCHANDISE. Boon's father thought he was unselfish and smart not to change it. But, now that Juno was dead, there would be some improvements. Like the brick front. And another new sign: UNDER BUY, UNDER SELL.

Boon was in third grade, now, and hated it. The Other Man went with him, and he hated it too. Bob said it was a necessary waste of time. He said to learn enough to figure train fare and time schedules.

"We'll catch a fast express," he'd say. "Yes, sir," fingering his watch chain beneath the silk sash, "a mighty fast train one of these days."

Saturdays Boon helped in the store. He got a nickel an hour, his mother saved for him in a coffee tin. One or two nickels a week he could spend on what he wanted. His mother said working in the store was good practice for when he was older.

A Saturday, warm afternoon in April, they met Spider. Bob was sleeping in a pile of feed sacks and The Other Man was helping Boon sweep the storeroom. Boon and The Other Man had never seen anything to top it. Bob had, but it was in some foreign land. Spider was wrapped around the filament in a broken light globe Boon reached to throw away. He was afraid it might bite, but Bob stuck his pudgy finger into the broken light and Spider climbed aboard his finger like a parrot getting on a pirate's arm. He found an empty kitchen match box and slipped Spider inside.

"What we gonna do with it?" Boon asked Bob.

"We could pin it in the cigar box with the butterfly collection, but it'd be better to make friends with it and have it for a pet."

"Can't make a spider a pet."

"Sure. What happens when you give a cat milk? It settles."

"Can't give milk to a spider."

In the storeroom Bob found a busted box of oatmeal and a jug of syrup that had sugared.

While Spider rested in the match box, they made plans. A picnic. Out back, under the big mesquite.

"Need Mother's china plates, the silver forks and bone handle steak knives."

The Other Man shook his head, "She'll never let you have them."

"Four plates we need," said Bob, "and four cups for coffee."

Boon sucked in air; he wasn't allowed coffee. For an excuse to go home in the wagon Boon hooked the seat of his overalls on a jutting-out nail in the storeroom and slid down the wall into a sitting position. Bob and The Other Man could get things started while he was gone. "After the meal," Bob whispered, "we'll each have a cigar." Boon sucked in air again, but Bob said cigars were an absolute necessity.

Getting the plates, cups, and silverware was easy. His mother was washing clothes behind the house. He stashed the plates under the wagon seat, changed overalls, and hurried back.

The oatmeal and syrup made a paste they spread between crackers. The coffee Bob wanted wouldn't mix with the lukewarm water so they went thirsty. Boon broke one of the cigars, stuffing it in his overalls when he thought his father was looking. Bob said it would still smoke. Boon carried Spider in the Red Dot match box to the bare spot beneath the mesquite tree where Bob spread four feed sacks. Boon couldn't tell which end of Spider was his mouth, so he sat him on top of the stack of oatmeal-paste and cracker sandwiches. Boon ate two sandwiches, then lit the cigars.

His father was angry at first, but on the way home, when Boon was feeling better, he laughed and kidded Boon about the cigars. Three cigars. He said Boon was a hellion. Boon's mother was not too mad about the bent knife, Boon said he'd replace it with extra work at the store, and they didn't tell her about the cigars.

That night, after supper, Bob and The Other Man came around the house to Boon's room to see what had happened. Bob had Spider's unsmoked cigar. Spider was dead. They decided to have a cremation. Bob spoke the sermon. The cardboard coffin was raised up on an altar of flat stones from the river, and with the window up and Boon fanning smoke away from his parents' room, they hummed "Nearer My God to Thee." When it was over Boon brushed the ashes into his boots and went to bed with the bitter aftertaste of cigar in his mouth. Tomorrow was Sunday, up early for church. He would pray for the spider and his grandfather, the only people he knew in heaven.

Fourth of July picnic. New Blanco River Dam, 1913. Celebration at the river. Boon played ball until the game got crowded and he got bored. He thought of talking to Ella Burnett, maybe get her to go in the woods. But she wouldn't.

He walked along the dirt road parallel to the river. He went above the dam to the oak grove where a vine swung over a cold catfish pool. Someone had cut the vine, but he stripped to his shorts and swung on a limb, hand over hand, to the edge of the bank. Swung for momentum to make deep water. Pushing off, arms up, he hit. His feet got colder and colder. He thought he was dying feet first. Still in his black suit and red sash, sinking deeply beside him, he saw Bob. He heard The Other Man laugh out loud and felt bubbles against his toes.

His lungs ached. He looked up and saw a dull yellow light. Kicking, he brought his arms down and popped through the surface into the hot air. He spat water, gulped air. Nose burned. Bob and The Other Man were gone. He caught the limb again, swung hard, sank. He heard Bob beneath him. The Other Man floated up, waved.

Certain he must be near bottom, he had to breathe. He kicked and stroked, thinking he would never make it, but when he came gulping into the bright heat, he had air left.

The third time, his foot touched something and he came up too soon, scared. He heard Bob and The Other Man deep in the pool and wanted to reach bottom, but his father was whistling for him. He hurried back to the park, buttoning his shirt as he ran, trying to think of an excuse for his wet hair.

They were waiting, the motor of the new automobile sending heat rays up from the hood. His father frowned at him but didn't ask about the wet hair. He climbed in back and saw his mother's face reflected in the windshield. He saw Bob's face there too, before glare off the hood made him disappear.

Working at the store he got the idea of the letters. Waiting for Easter to pick out some penny candy—Easter worked for different people in town and was a credit customer so Boon had to write down everything he bought—waiting for Easter one August morning, Boon began writing notes to himself on the credit pad. When Easter had made up his mind Boon had filled the page. That night he added to what he had written: *This is like a shipwreck note. My name is Boon Speer. I live in Texas. It is hot and the mountains are dark brown with rounded tops. There is Austin and San Antonio to go to where you can see a movie, but I like the Alamo better. I went to the Alamo four times. My friends live with me and we are going away to the ocean in a Ford car when I am older.* Boon kept the letters in a shoe box under his bed. Sometimes he got them all out and read them, changing some of the words.

In the store again, he got the idea of mailing the letters. He was unpacking crates with The Other Man. Bob was sitting on a crate telling them stories about India. Boon read the shipping labels: *Chicago, Ill., Cleveland, Ohio, San Francisco, Calif.* He took a long brown envelope home from the store and, that night, sealed his first letter inside. On the front of the envelope he printed *Chicago, Ill.,* leaving space above, where he filled in, *Mr. Boon Speer, 111 Main Street.* His name looked good with *Mr.* in front.

The letter came back stamped ADDRESS UNKNOWN. He looked over the envelope for signs of the long distance to Chicago. He sent other letters. Made-up names and addresses. He wrote to *Mr. Ivy Hobbs* in *Trenton, New Jersey,* and to *Mrs. Trenton Ivy* in *Hobbs, New Mex.* The Other Man always went with him to the post office, and once he addressed a letter to *Mr. T. O. Man, in Omaha, Neb.* He went to the store early every morning to get the mail before anyone arrived. He thought of sending a letter to England or France, but he didn't know how many stamps to use, and didn't want to ask; he wanted to keep the letters secret.

Mr. Kitter, at the post office, asked Boon's father about the letters. Then it was no good. His father teased him, said it was girls who always wanted pen pals. Boon continued to write the letters and keep them in the shoebox, but he never mailed them unless he got a chance to go to Austin or San Antonio. He was not known in Austin or San Antonio, and he no longer wrote a return address. Now the letters never came back, and he made up stories about the people reading them.

Summer, 1915, Boon finished high school. Mike Burnett went to San Antonio and joined the army. Boon wanted to join; his mother wanted him to wait. He was needed at the store. Mike Burnett left three brothers and a sister to help his folks.

One of those brothers, David, hopped a freight train and went to California. After he got back and told Boon the things he'd seen, Boon liked to walk through the train yard on his way home from the store.

Sprawled out in rows like lazy centipedes the iron rails shimmered, oily in the heat. Piles of grain, sulphur, salt between the rails, spilled from cars. Boon breathed rust and creosote and diesel. Flies buzzed ahead of him. He squatted on the gravel and looked up under the belly of a boxcar, a cool draft between the iron wheels. When a freight slid past he wanted to throw himself beneath a car, see if he could make the other side before the rear wheels got him.

David Burnett had ridden across New Mexico and Arizona. He had raced speedboats in California. He told Boon they chose a different winner each week and bunched behind him so no boat could pass. David said he had held a world's record for a week, until the next race when the team picked someone else.

When Santa Fe 11687 rolled by Boon heard The Other Man yell and saw Bob's long coattails flapping in the open doors. He almost jumped on, but he thought of the store and went home.

He worked full time now. Some nights he went to San Antonio, saw a movie, or got drunk, but he never came home drunk. Mike Burnett was in the Army, in San Antonio. Mike got Boon a girl, and a crowd of them went to Gray Moss Inn, drank beer and ate fried chicken. They went to the Kitty Kat Klub and danced to music by the Melody Men. Then the entire platoon was transferred to Liberal, Kansas. At the going away party Boon had a date with a girl named Dorothy Gomez. He liked her, and a few weeks later he called her and the two of them went out, but it was no fun.

He tried to enlist, secretly, but didn't weigh enough. A guy he met at the recruiting station said he should try again at a different station—Houston, he said. He told Boon to eat bananas and drink plenty of water and he would weigh enough to get in at Houston. Boon never tried it. He worked in the store until the war was over and Mike Burnett came home saying that Boon didn't miss nothing.

• • •

Died 1930 on the stone. Sweat trickling down his spine, Boon rocked on the balls of his feet in stiff shoes and watched the sun on the glossy coffin. His mind wandered during the prayer and he wanted to get away from the smell of flowers and Mr. Wilkinson's cologne. A gust of breeze hit his sweat-soaked shirt, his nipples tightened against the sting. Through the long prayer his mother leaned grayly against him. Mr. Wilkinson helped her to the limousine. Two men shoveled the hole full.

Boon thought of Dorothy Gomez and wondered if she was still available. A shovel stood in the dirt throwing a shadow like a sundial.

He climbed in the car beside his mother and listened to Mr. Wilkinson talk about the cooling system in the engine of the new limousine. Bob and The Other Man, nodding silently, rode in front with Mr. Wilkinson.

1934. A century of Progress. Chicago World's Fair. Boon got a boy from the high school to help with the store. Boon's mother told him not to worry. To have a good time. He said he'd be back in a week.

The silver and blue bus whooped and wheezed past JUNO D. SPEER & CO. rattling the front doors. Passed the Spicer Lumber Company and turned sharply toward Oklahoma. Boon stared out the window. The gray, moonless sky pressed down, keeping the heat heavy on the land.

The man in the seat next to Boon was thick and bulky, like his suit. His double chin bumped along on his chest, and he slumped against Boon. Boon wanted to get out for coffee when the bus stopped in Oklahoma City, but he hated to wake the man, so he tried to sleep.

When the bus finally bounced up the ramp of the Chicago depot, Boon was cob-webbed with wrinkles and sweat, the stubble under his chin itching to be shaved. The porter in the men's room recommended the Majestic Hotel where he said Boon could get a package deal, room and three-day tour of the fair.

Boon was up early the next morning, padding down the hall of the Majestic to the toilet.

"Yes sir, nothing quite like pissing," Bob said, standing beside Boon, his striped pants down around his knees as he leaned into the urinal. Boon laughed and wrung the silver handle with a flourish.

At the fair he went to the Firestone Building and watched tires made from African rubber. He imagined black African natives twined into a hoop, ankles grasped by long fingers, feet locked over rubbery hair. He saw a mural of jungle forest where giant rubber trees were cut.

A big dog peed on the tires of the Gray Line tour bus. Black tires that grew as great trees in dark land, in rain and shadows of the hot sun of Africa. The dog peed on the rubber tree, stretched, ran in place, and traveled across continents.

A new DeSoto raced around the outdoor track at the Chrysler Building. On the beach midway he had his photograph made. A cardboard woman in her slip with a huge airplane over her head, "Hell's Angels" painted across the sky. The photograph came in a folder that said, "Look Who's Here!"

In the photography exhibit he saw a display about a man in 1901 who got excited about widths and heights and built a camera weighing fourteen hundred pounds so he could photograph the Chicago and Alton Railroad Company's new luxury express with one shot. The huge camera was called Mammoth and had to be transported by a specially built car. It took fifteen men to take that one picture. Today, the exhibit explained, we have small precision cameras, wide-angle lenses. Today anyone can buy a camera that will do the job.

Sixty miles across Lake Michigan on the Chicago Roosevelt Steamship. On the other side he waited for the night cruise. A dollar for two more hours on the great lake—the Mississippi, the Gulf of Mexico, the Pacific. Steamed through the floating lights of the Firestone Building.

The last day of his visit he went into the Adler Planetarium and looked at stars at high noon in Chicago and the announcer took him backward and forward in time.

He had been to most of the state exhibits. States where made-up people lived. People he had mailed letters years before. But he had avoided the Texas Pavilion, the sun and the dust of Texas.

Hour early. Slow stillness of afternoon. Sun leaves splattered across the hood of the Ford, the sky cloudless. Dry colors, grass blades in bas relief, texture of asphalt sparkling silica flakes. Asphalt clouds into dirt where one man refused to pay for blacktopping. Boon rolls the window tight against the dust, wipers making two humps on the windshield. Pockmarked, the sign points the way to town.

Yellow flashing light hangs over the highway, lone lantern, amulet to ward off evil spirits. Town is empty. Nearly two years since Boon's mother got sick and he closed the store. He moved her to a hospital in San Antonio and got work in a lumberyard. He came back to Blanco to sell the store, but no one was interested. The Railroad had left and taken most of the town. He got a room near the hospital and spent his time off with his mother. Now she is back in Blanco to be buried, and he is out of the boarding house.

The sign, JUNO D. SPEER & CO. GENERAL MERCHANDISE, is down, leaning against the brick front. A rusty BEECHNUT CHEWS BEST sign is nailed over broken windows.

Boon pulls up in front of Blackwell's Garage. Two pumps, lighthouse tops, digital eyes, rubber arms, silver fingers in silver ears. Gasoline dripped and dried to earwax. The garage where Mr. Blackwell pulled guts out and wheels off, tapped and screwed. Dappled grease and sunburned arms. Redhead stared at you from above the coke machine. Always August above the Coke machine. A tractor's width behind the gas pumps, screened door, opens soft—slaps shut. Boon has not seen Taylor since Boon moved his mother to the hospital. Taylor Blackwell, who went to high school with Boon, who took over the garage from his father.

"Boon."

"Hello, Taylor."

"I was closing for the funeral when I saw you pull up."

Boon thanks Taylor Blackwell for the gas; he won't take Boon's money. Boon gives him a ride to the funeral home.

Mr. Wilkinson's cologne is the same. There are fewer hands to shake. Marker already in place, the double stone Boon's mother selected—*Brown Smith Speer, Died 1930,* on his side, *Cora Yeats Speer, Died 19* , on her side. Have the *39* cut before leaving. 1939, in the heat. Boon thinks back to the heart.

His grandfather lies above the double grave. Boon remembers the orange yo-yo. His grandfather must have showed him a hundred times how to do around-the- world, but he never got the hang of it.

The Ford bumps over the empty tracks. Rows of theater seats on the station house platform, watched over by baggage cart, tongue up like a skunk's tail. Foot of the low hill, the church. Sunday's sermon: God's Commandment to Stewardship. Beyond the church, the cemetery. Scrub cedar and tumbleweed. Black iron fence, arrowhead points. Ashtray of chalky monuments stuck at random heights and angles.

More hills. Miles of road.

In the rearview, the buildings tiny. On the back seat Bob smokes a big cigar, peering over a road map unfurled across his lap, his legs too short to reach the floor.

"Plenty of time now, boy. All the time we need." He snaps his big gold watch up under the red silk sash and blows several perfect smoke rings.

Boon unfastens his collar and pulls his tie loose. He reaches to hang it over the rearview mirror, and his hand hits The Other Man's, who has also undone his tie. They look at each other and there is a spark of recognition. Both grin and begin to hum a made-up tune.

RON HANSEN

TRUE ROMANCE

It was still night out and my husband was shaving at the kitchen sink so he could hear the morning farm report and I was peeling bacon into the skillet. I hardly slept a wink with Gina acting up, and that croupy cough of hers. I must've walked five miles. Half of Ivan's face was hanging in the circle mirror, the razor was scraping the soap from his cheek, and pigs weren't dollaring like they ought to. And that was when the phone rang and it was Annette, my very best friend, giving me the woeful news.

Ivan squeaked his thumb on the glass to spy the temperature—still cold—then wiped his face with a paper towel, staring at me with puzzlement as I made known my shock and surprise. I took the phone away from my ear and said, "Honey? Something's killed one of the cows!"

He rushed over to the phone and got to talking to Annette's husband, Slick. Slick saw it coming from work—Slick's mainly on night shift; the Caterpillar plant. Our section of the county is on a party line: the snoops were getting their usual earful. I turned out the fire under the skillet. His appetite would be spoiled. Ivan and Slick went over the same ground again; I poured coffee and sugar and stirred a spoon around in a cup, just as blue as I could be, and when Ivan hung up I handed the cup to him.

He said, "I could almost understand it if they took the meat, but Slick says it looked like it was just plain ripped apart."

I walked the telephone back to the living room and switched on every single light. Ivan wasn't saying anything.

I opened my robe and gave Gina the left nipple, which wasn't so standing-out and sore; and I sat in the big chair under a shawl. I got the feeling that eyes were on me.

Ivan stood in the doorway in his underpants and Nebraska sweatshirt, looking just like he did in high school. I said, "I'm just sick about the cow."

He said, "You pay your bills, you try and live simple, you pray to the Lord for guidance, but Satan can still find a loophole, can't he? He'll trip you up every time."

"Just the idea of it is giving me the willies," I said.

Ivan put his coffee cup on the floor and snapped on his gray coveralls. He sat against the high chair. "I guess I'll give the sheriff a call and then go look at the damage."

"I want to go with you, okay?"

The man from the rendering plant swerved a winch truck up the pasture until the swinging chain cradle was over the cow. His tires skidded green swipes on grass that was otherwise white with frost. I scrunched up in the pickup with the heater going to beat the band and Gina asleep on the seat. Ivan slumped in the sheriff's car and swore out a complaint. The man from the rendering plant threw some hydraulic levers and the engine revved to unspool some cable, making the cradle clang against the bumper.

I'd never seen the fields so pretty in March. Every acre was green winter wheat or plowed earth or sandhills the color of camels. The lagoon was as black and sleek as a grand piano.

Gina squinched her face up and then discovered a knuckle to chew as the truck engine raced again; and when the renderer hoisted the cow up, a whole stream of stuff poured out of her and dumped on the ground like boots. I slaughtered one or two in my time. I could tell which organs were missing.

Ivan made his weary way up the hill on grass that was greasy with blood, then squatted to look at footprints that were all walked over by cattle. The man from the plant said something and Ivan said something back, calling him Dale, and then Ivan slammed the pickup door behind him. He wiped the fog from inside the windshield with his softball cap. "You didn't bring coffee, did you?"

I shook my head as he blew on his fingers. He asked, "What good are ya then?" but he was smiling. He said, "I'm glad our insurance is paid up."

"I'm just sick about it," I said.

Ivan put the truck in gear and drove it past the feeding cattle, giving them a look-over. "I gotta get my sugar beets in."

I thought: the cow's heart, and the female things.

Around noon Annette came over in Slick's Trans Am and we ate pecan rolls hot from the oven as she got the romance magazines out of her grocery bag and began reading me the really good stories. Gina played on the carpet next to my chair. You have to watch the little booger every second because she'll put in her mouth what most people wouldn't step on. Annette was four months pregnant but it hardly showed—just the top snap of her jeans was undone—and I was full of uncertainty about the outcome. Our daytime visits give us the opportunity to speak candidly about things like miscarriages or the ways in which we are ironing out our problems with our husbands, but on this occasion Annette was giggling about some goofy woman who couldn't figure out why marriage turned good men into monsters, and I got the ugly feeling that I was being looked at by a peeping tom.

Annette put the magazine in her lap and rapidly flipped the pages to get to the part where the story was continued and I gingerly picked up Gina and, without saying a peep to Annette, walked across the carpet and spun around. Annette giggled again and said, "Do you suppose this actually happened?" and I said yes, pulling my little girl tight against me. Annette said, "Doesn't she just crack you *up?*" and I simply kept peering out the window. I couldn't stop myself.

That night I took another stroll around the property and then poured diet cola into a glass at the kitchen sink, satisfying my thirst. I could see the light of the sixty-watt bulb in the barn and the cows standing up to the fence and rubbing their throats and chins. The wire gets shaggy with the stuff; looks just like orange doll hair. Ivan got on the intercom and his voice was puny, like it was trapped in a paper cup. "Come on out and help me, will you, Riva?"

"Right out," is what I said.

I tucked another blanket around Gina in the baby crib and clomped outside in Ivan's rubber boots. They jingled as I crossed the barnyard. The cattle stared at me. One of the steers got up on a lady and triumphed for a while but she walked away and he dropped. My flashlight speared whenever I bumped it.

Ivan was kneeling on straw, shoving his arm in a rubber glove. An alarm clock was on the sill. His softball cap was off and his long brown hair was flying wild as he squatted beside the side-lying cow. Her tail whisked a board so he tied it to her leg with twine. She was swollen wide with the calf. My husband reached up inside her and the cow lifted her head indignantly, then settled down and chewed her tongue. Ivan said, "P.U., cow! You stink!" He was in her up to his biceps, seemed like.

"You going to cut her?"

He shook his head as he snagged the glove off and plunked it down in a water bucket. "Dang calf's kaput!" He glared at his medicine box and said, "How many is that? Four out of eight? I might as well give it up."

I swayed the flashlight beam along the barn. Window. Apron. Pitchfork. Rope. Lug wrench. Sickle. Baling wire. And another four-paned window that was so streaked with pigeon goop it might as well've been slats. But it was there that the light caught a glint of an eye and my heart stopped. I stepped closer to persuade myself it wasn't just an apparition and what I saw abruptly disappeared.

Ivan grinded the tractor ignition and got the thing going, then raced it backwards into the barn, not shutting the engine down but slapping it out of gear and hopping down to the ground. He said, "Swing that flashlight down on this cow's contraption, will ya, Riva?" and there was some messy tugging and wrestling as he yanked the calf's legs out and attached them to the tractor hitch with wire. He jumped up to the spring seat and jerked into granny, creeping forward with his gaze on the cow. She groaned with agony and more leg appeared and then the shut-eyed calf head. My husband crawled the tractor forward more and the calf came out in a surge. I suctioned gunk out of its throat with a bulb syringe and squirted it into the straw but the calf didn't quiver or pant; she was patient as meat and her tongue spilled onto the paint tarp.

Ivan scowled and sank to his knees by the calf. The mother cow struggled up and sniffed the calf and began licking off its nose in the way she'd been taught, but even she gave up in a second or two and hung her head low with grief.

"Do you know what killed it?"

Ivan just gaped and said, "You explain it." He got up and plunged his arms into the bucket. He smeared water on his face.

I crouched down and saw that the calf was somehow split open and all her insides were pulled out.

After the sheriff and the man from the rendering plant paid their visits, the night was just about shot. Ivan completed his cold weather chores, upsetting the cattle with his earliness, and I pored over Annette's romance magazines, gaining support from each disappointment.

Ivan and I got some sleep and even Gina cooperated by being good as can be. Ivan arose at noon but he was cranky and understandably depressed about our calamities, so I switched off "All My Children" and suggested we go over to Slick's place and wake him up and party.

Annette saw I was out of sorts right away and she generously agreed to make our supper. She could see through me like glass. At two we watched "General Hospital," which was getting crazier by the week according to Annette—she thought they'd be off in outer space next, but I said they were just keeping up with this wild and woolly world we live in. Once our story was over we made a pork roast and boiled potatoes with chives and garlic butter, which proved to be a big hit. Our husbands worked through the remaining light of day, crawling over Slick's farm machinery, each with wrenches in his pockets and grease on his skin like warpaint.

Annette said, "You're doing all right for yourself, aren't you, Riva."

"I could say the same for you, you know."

Here I ought to explain that Annette went steady with Ivan in our sophomore year, and I suspect she's always regretted giving him to me. If I'm any judge of character, her thoughts were on that subject as we stood at the counter and Slick and Ivan came in for supper and cleaned up in the washroom that's off the kitchen. Annette then had to gall to say, "Slick and me are going through what you and Ivan were a couple of months ago."

Oh, no you're not! I wanted to say, but I didn't even give her the courtesy of a reply.

"You got everything straightened out, though, didn't you."

I said, "Our problems were a blessing in disguise."

"I know exactly what you mean," she said.

"Our marriage is as full of love and vitality as any girl could wish for."

Her eyes were even a little misty. "I'm so happy for you, Riva!"

And she was; you could tell she wasn't pretending like she was during some of our rocky spots in the past.

Slick dipped his tongue in a spoon that he lifted from a saucepan and went out of his way to compliment Annette—unlike at least one husband I could mention. Ivan pushed down the spring gizmo on the toaster and got the feeling back in his fingers by working them over the toaster slots. My husband said in that put-down way of his, "Slick was saying it could be UFOs."

"I got an open mind on the subject," said Slick, and Ivan did his snickering thing.

I asked if we could please change the topic of conversation to something a little more pleasant.

Ivan gave me his angry smile. "Such as what? Relationships?"

Slick and Annette were in rare form that night but Ivan was pretty much of a poop until Slick gave him a number. Ivan bogarted the joint and Slick rolled up another and by the time Annette and I got the dishes into the sink, the men were swapping a roach on the living room floor and tooling Gina's playthings around. Annette opened the newspaper to the place that showed which dopey program was on the TV that evening. Slick asked if Ivan planted the marijuana seeds he gave us and Ivan shrugged. Which meant no. Slick commenced tickling Annette. She scooched back against the sofa and fought him off, slapping at his paws and pleading for help. She screamed, "Slick! You're gonna make me pee on myself!"

Ivan clicked through the channels but he was so stoned all he could say was, "What *is* that?"

Annette giggled but got out, "*Creature from the Black Lagoon!*"

I plopped Gina on top of her daddy's stomach and passed around a roach that was pinched with a hairpin. I asked Ivan, "Are you really ripped?" and Ivan shrugged. Which meant yes.

The movie was a real shot in the arm for our crew. My husband rested his pestered head in my lap and I rearranged his long hair. There was a close-up of the creature and I got such a case of the stares from looking at it you'd think I was making a photograph.

Ivan shifted to frown at me. "How come you're not saying anything?"

And I could only reply, "I'm just really ripped."

Days passed without event and I could persuade myself that the creature had gone off to greener pastures. However, one evening when Ivan was attending a meeting of the parish council, my consternation only grew stronger. Gina and I got home from the grocery store and I parked the pickup close by the feed lot so I could hear if she squalled as I was forking out silage. Hunger was making the cattle ornery. They straggled over and jostled each other, resting their long jaws on each other's shoulders, bawling *mom* in the night. The calves lurched and stared as I closed the gate behind me. I collared my face from the cold and, as I was getting into the truck, a cry like you hear at a slaughterhouse flew up from the lagoon.

I thought, I ought to ignore it; or I ought to go to the phone; but I figured what I really ought to do is make certain that I was seeing everything right, that I wasn't making things up.

Famous last words!

I snuggled Gina in the baby crib and went out along the pasture road, looking at the eight o'clock night that was closing in all around me. I glided down over a hill and a stray calf flung its tail in my headlights as its tiny mind chugged through its options. A yard away its mother was on her side and swollen up big as two hay bales. I got out into the spring cold and inspected the cow even though I knew she was a goner, and then I looked at the woods and the moonlighted lagoon and I could make out just enough of a blacker image to put two and two together and see that it was the creature dragging cow guts through the grass.

The gun rack only carried fishing rods on it, but there was an angel food cake knife wedged behind the pickup's tool box and that was what I took with me on my quest, my scalp prickling with fright and goosebumps on every inch of me. The chill was mean, like you'd slapped your hand against gravel. The wind seemed to gnaw at the trees. You're making it up, I kept praying, and when I approached the lagoon and saw nothing I was pleased and full of hope.

The phone rang many times the next day, but I wouldn't get up to answer it. I stayed in the room upstairs, hugging a pillow like a body, aching for the beginning of some other life like a girl in a Rosemary Rogers book. Once again Annette provided an escape from my doldrums by speeding over in the orange Trans Am—her concern for me and her eternal spunk are always a great boost for my spirits.

I washed up and went outside with Gina, and Annette said, "What on earth is wrong with your phone?"

I only said, "I was hoping you'd come over," and Annette slammed the car door. She hugged me like a girlfriend and the plastic over the porch screens popped. The wind was making mincemeat of the open garbage can. And yet we sat outside on the porch steps with some of Slick's dope rolled in Zig-Zag papers. I zipped Gina into a parka with the wind so blustery. She was trying to walk. She'd throw her arms out and buck ahead a step or two and then plump down hard on her butt. The marijuana wasn't rolled tight enough and the paper was sticking all the time to my lip. I looked at the barn, the silo, the road, seeing nothing of the creature, seeing only my husband urging the tractor up out of a ditch with Slick straddling the gang plow's hook-ups and hoses. Slick's a master at hydraulics. The plow swung wide and banged as Ivan established his right to the road, then Ivan shifted the throttle up and mud flew from the tires. One gloved hand rested on a fender lamp and he looked past me to our daughter, scowling and acting put-out, then they turned into the yard and Annette waved. Ivan lifted his right index finger just a tad, his greeting, then turned the steering wheel hand-over-hand, bouncing high in the spring seat as Slick clung on for dear life.

Annette said, "My baby isn't Ivan's, you know."

I guess I sighed with the remembering of those painful times.

Annette said, "I'm glad we were able to stay friends."

"Me too," I said, and I scooched out to see my little girl with an angel food cake knife in her hands, waddling over to me. I yelled, "Gina! You little snot! Where'd you get that?"

She gave it to me and wiped her hands on her coat. "Dut," Gina said, and though my husband would probably have reprimanded her, I knelt down and told her how she mustn't play with knives and what a good girl she was to bring it right to me. She didn't listen for very long and I put the knife in my sweater pocket for the time being.

Annette was looking peculiar and I could tell she wanted an explanation, but then there was a commotion in the cattle pen and we looked to where Ivan and Slick were pushing cow rumps aside in order to get close to the trough. They glared at something on the ground out there, and I glanced at the cake knife again, seeing the unmistakable signs of blood.

"I'm going out to the cattle pen," I imparted. "You keep Gina with you."

Annette said, "I hope your stock is okay."

The day was on the wane as I proceeded across the yard and onto the cowpath inside the pen, the cake knife gripped in my right hand in my sweater pocket. The cattle were rubbing against the fence and ignorantly surging toward the silage in the feed trough. Slick was saying, "You oughta get a photograph, Ivan." My husband kept his eyes on one spot, his gloved hands on his hips, his left boot experimenting by moving something I couldn't see.

I got the cattle to part by tilting against them with all my weight. They were heavy as Cadillacs. And I made my toilsome way to my husband's side only to be greeted with a look of ill tidings and with an inquiry that was to justify all my grim forebodings. He asked, "Do you know how it happened, Riva?"

I regarded ground that was soggy with blood and saw the green creature that I'd so fervently prayed was long gone. He was lying on his scaly back and his yellow eyes were glowering as if the being were still enraged over the many stabbings into his heart. Death had been good for his general attractiveness, glossing over his many physical flaws and giving him a childlike quality that tugged at my sympathy.

Again Ivan nudged the being with his boot, acting like it was no more than a cow, and asking me with great dismay, "How'd the dang thing get killed, do ya think?"

And I said, "Love. Love killed it. Love as sharp as a knife."

Slick gazed upon me strangely and my husband looked at me with grief as I sank to the earth among the cattle, feeling the warmth of their breathing. I knew then that the anguish I'd experienced over those past many months was going to disappear, and that my life, over which I'd despaired for so long, was going to keep changing and improving with each minute of the day.

RICHARD FORD

GREAT FALLS

This is not a happy story. I warn you.

My father was a man named Jack Russell, and when I was a young boy in my early teens, we lived with my mother in a house to the east of Great Falls, Montana, near the small town of Highwood and the Highwood Mountains and the Missouri River. It is a flat, treeless benchland there, all of it used for wheat farming, though my father was never a farmer, but was brought up near Tacoma, Washington, in a family that worked for Boeing.

He—my father—had been an Air Force sergeant and had taken his discharge in Great Falls. And instead of going home to Tacoma, where my mother wanted to go, he had taken a civilian's job with the Air Force, working on planes, which was what he liked to do. And he had rented the house out of town from a farmer who did not want it left standing empty.

The house itself is gone now—I have been to the spot. But the double row of Russian olive trees and two of the outbuildings are still standing in the milkweeds. It was a plain, two-story house with a porch on the front and no place for the cars. At the time, I rode the school bus to Great Falls every morning, and my father drove in while my mother stayed home.

My mother was a tall pretty woman, thin, with black hair and slightly sharp features that made her seem to smile when she wasn't smiling. She had grown up in Wallace, Idaho, and gone to college a year in Spokane, then moved out to the coast, which is where she met Jack Russell. She was two years older than he was, and married him, she said to me, because he was young and wonderful looking, and because she thought they could leave the sticks and see the world together—which I suppose they did for a while. That was the life she wanted, even before she knew much about wanting anything else or about the future.

When my father wasn't working on airplanes, he was going hunting or fishing, two things he could do as well as anyone. He had learned to fish, he said, in Iceland, and to hunt ducks up on the DEW line—stations he had visited in the Air Force. And during the time of this—it was 1960—he began to take me with him on what he called his "expeditions." I thought even then, with as little as I knew, that these were opportunities other boys would dream of having but probably never would. And I don't think that I was wrong in that.

It is a true thing that my father did not know limits. In the spring, when we would go east to the Judith River Basin and camp up on the banks, he would catch a hundred fish in a weekend, and sometimes more than that. It was all he did from morning until night, and it was never hard for him. He used yellow corn kernels stacked onto a #4 snelled hook, and he would rattle this rig-up along the bottom of a deep pool below a split-shot sinker, and catch fish. And most of the time, because he knew the Judith River and knew how to feel his bait down deep, he could catch fish of good size.

It was the same with ducks, the other thing he liked. When the northern birds were down, usually by mid-October, he would take me and we would build a cattail and wheat-straw blind on one of the tule ponds or sloughs he knew about down the Missouri, where the water was shallow enough to wade. We would set out his decoys to the leeward side of our blind, and he would sprinkle corn on a hunger-line from the decoys to where we were. In the evenings when he came home from the base, we would go and sit out in the blind until the roosting flights came and put down among the decoys—there was never calling involved. And after a while, sometimes it would be an hour and full dark, the ducks would find the corn, and the whole raft of them—sixty, sometimes—would swim in to us. At the moment he judged they were close enough, my father would say to me, "Shine, Jackie," and I would stand and shine a seal-beam car light out onto the pond, and he would stand up beside me and shoot all the ducks that were there, on the water if he could, but flying and getting up as well. He owned a Model 11 Remington with a long-tube magazine that would hold ten shells, and with that many, and shooting straight over the surface rather than down onto it, he could kill or wound thirty ducks in twenty seconds' time. I remember distinctly the report of that gun and the flash of it over the water into the dark air, one shot after another, not even so fast, but measured in a way to hit as many as he could.

What my father did with the ducks he killed, and the fish, too, was sell them. It was against the law then to sell wild game, and it is against the law now. And though he kept some for us, most he would take—his fish laid on ice, or his ducks still wet and bagged in the burlap corn sacks—down to the Great Northern Hotel, which was still open then on Second Street in Great Falls, and sell them to the Negro caterer who bought them for his wealthy customers and for the dining car passengers who came through. We would drive in my father's Plymouth to the back of the hotel—always this was after dark—to a concrete loading ramp and lighted door that were close enough to the yards that I could sometimes see passenger trains waiting at the station, their car lights yellow and warm inside, the passengers dressed in suits, all bound for someplace far away from Montana—Milwaukee or Chicago or New York City, unimaginable places to me, a boy fourteen years old, with my father in the cold dark selling illegal game.

The caterer was a tall, stooped-back man in a white jacket, who my father called "Professor Ducks" or "Professor Fish," and the Professor referred to my father as "Sarge." He paid a quarter per pound for trout, a dime for whitefish, a dollar for a mallard duck, two for a speckle or a blue goose, and four dollars for a Canada. I have been with my father when he took away a hundred dollars for fish he'd caught and, in the fall, more than that for ducks and geese. When he had sold game in that way, we would drive out 10th Avenue and stop at a bar called The Mermaid which was by the air base, and he would drink with some friends he knew there, and they would laugh about hunting and fishing while I played pinball and wasted money in the jukebox.

It was on such a night as this that the unhappy things came about. It was in late October. I remember the time because

Halloween had not been yet, and in the windows of the houses that I passed every day on the bus to Great Falls, people had put pumpkin lanterns, and set scarecrows in their yards in chairs.

My father and I had been shooting ducks in a slough on the Smith River, upstream from where it enters on the Missouri. He had killed thirty ducks, and we'd driven them down to the Great Northern and sold them there, though my father had kept two back in his corn sack. And when we had driven away, he suddenly said, "Jackie, let's go back home tonight. Who cares about those hard-dicks at The Mermaid. I'll cook these ducks on the grill. We'll do something different tonight." He smiled at me in an odd way. This was not a thing he usually said, or the way he usually talked. He liked The Mermaid, and my mother—as far as I knew—didn't mind it if he went there.

"That sounds good," I said.

"We'll surprise your mother," he said. "We'll make her happy."

We drove out past the air base on Highway 87, past where there were planes taking off into the night. The darkness was dotted by the green and red beacons, and the tower light swept the sky and trapped planes as they disappeared over the flat landscape toward Canada or Alaska and the Pacific.

"Boy-oh-boy," my father said—just out of the dark. I looked at him and his eyes were narrow, and he seemed to be thinking about something. "You know, Jackie," he said, "your mother said something to me once I've never forgotten. She said, 'Nobody dies of a broken heart.' This was somewhat before you were born. We were living down in Texas and we'd had some big blow-up, and that was the idea she had. I don't know why." He shook his head.

He ran his hand under the seat, found a half-pint bottle of whiskey, and held it up to the lights of the car behind us to see what there was left of it. He unscrewed the cap and took a drink, then held the bottle out to me. "Have a drink, son," he said. "Something oughta be good in life." And I felt that something was wrong. Not because of the whiskey, which I had drunk before and he had reason to know about, but because of some sound in his voice, something I didn't recognize and did not know the importance of, though I was certain it was important.

I took a drink and gave the bottle back to him, holding the whiskey in my mouth until it stopped burning and I could swallow it a little at a time. When we turned out the road to Highwood, the lights of Great Falls sank below the horizon, and I could see the small white lights of farms, burning at wide distances in the dark.

"What do you worry about, Jackie?" my father said. "Do you worry about girls? Do you worry about your future sex life? Is that some of it?" He glanced at me, then back at the road.

"I don't worry about that," I said.

"Well, what then?" my father said. "What else is there?"

"I worry if you're going to die before I do," I said, though I hated saying that, "or if Mother is. That worries me."

"It'd be a miracle if we didn't," my father said, with the half-pint held in the same hand he held the steering wheel. I had seen him drive that way before. "Things pass too fast in your life, Jackie. Don't worry about that. If I were you, I'd worry we might not." He smiled at me, and it was not the worried, nervous smile from before, but a smile that meant he was pleased. And I don't remember him ever smiling at me that way again.

We drove on out behind the town of Highwood and onto the flat field roads toward our house. I could see, out on the prairie, a moving light where the farmer who rented our house to us was disking his field for winter wheat. "He's waited too late with that business," my father said and took a drink, then threw the bottle right out the window. "He'll lose that," he said, "the cold'll kill it." I did not answer him, but what I thought was that my father knew nothing about farming, and if he was right it would be an accident. He knew about planes and hunting game, and that seemed all to me.

"I want to respect your privacy," he said then, for no reason at all that I understood. I am not even certain he said it, only that it is in my memory that way. I don't know what he was thinking of. Just words. But I said to him, I remember well, "It's all right. Thank you."

We did not go straight out the Geraldine Road to our house. Instead my father went down another mile and turned, went a mile and turned back again so that we came home from the other direction. "I want to stop and listen now," he said. "The geese should be in the stubble." We stopped and he cut the lights and engine, and we opened the car windows and listened. It was eight o'clock at night and it was getting colder, though it was dry. But I could hear nothing, just the sound of air moving lightly through the cut field, and not a goose sound. Though I could smell the whiskey on my father's breath and on mine, could hear the motor ticking, could hear him breathe, hear the sound we made sitting side by side on the car seat, our clothes, our feet, almost our hearts beating. And I could see out in the night the yellow lights of our house, shining through the olive trees south of us like a ship on the sea. "I hear them, by God," my father said, his head stuck out the window. "But they're high up. They won't stop here now, Jackie. They're high flyers, those boys. Long gone geese."

There was a car parked off the road, down the line of windbreak trees, beside a steel thresher the farmer had left there to rust. You could see moonlight off the taillight chrome. It was a Pontiac, a two-door hard-top. My father said nothing about it and I didn't either, though I think now for different reasons.

The floodlight was on over the side door of our house and lights were on inside, upstairs and down. My mother had a pumpkin on the front porch, and the wind chime she had hung by the door was tinkling. My dog, Major, came out of the quonset shed and stood in the car lights when we drove up.

"Let's see what's happening here," my father said, opening the door and stepping out quickly. He looked at me inside the car, and his eyes were wide and his mouth drawn tight.

We walked in the side door and up the basement steps into the kitchen, and a man was standing there—a man I had never seen before, a young man with blond hair, who might've been twenty or twenty-five. He was tall and was wearing a short-sleeved shirt and beige slacks with pleats. He was on the other side of the breakfast table, his fingertips just touching the wooden tabletop. His blue eyes were on my father, who was dressed in hunting clothes.

"Hello," my father said.

"Hello," the young man said, and nothing else. And for some reason I looked at his arms, which were long and pale. They looked like a young man's arms, like my arms. His short sleeves had each been neatly rolled up, and I could see the bottom of a small green tattoo edging out from underneath. There was a glass of whiskey on the table, but no bottle.

"What's your name?" my father said, standing in the kitchen under the bright ceiling light. He sounded like he might be going to laugh.

"Woody," the young man said and cleared his throat. He looked at me, then he touched the glass of whiskey, just the rim of the glass. He wasn't nervous, I could tell that. He did not seem to be afraid of anything.

"Woody," my father said and looked at the glass of whiskey. He looked at me, then sighed and shook his head. "Where's Mrs. Russell, Woody? I guess you aren't robbing my house, are you?"

Woody smiled. "No," he said. "Upstairs. I think she went upstairs."

"Good," my father said, "that's a good place." And he walked straight out of the room, but came back and stood in the doorway. "Jackie, you and Woody step outside and wait on me. Just stay there and I'll come out." He looked at Woody then in a way I would not have liked him to look at me, a look that meant he was studying Woody. "I guess that's your car," he said.

"That Pontiac?" Woody nodded.

"Okay. Right," my father said. Then he went out again and up the stairs. At that moment the phone started to ring in the living room, and I heard my mother say, "Who's that?" And my father say, "It's me. It's Jack." And I decided I wouldn't go answer the phone. Woody looked at me, and I understood he wasn't sure what to do. Run, maybe. But he didn't have run in him. Though I thought he would probably do what I said if I would say it.

"Let's just go outside," I said.

And he said, "All right."

Woody and I walked outside and stood in the light of the floodlamp above the side door. I had on my wool jacket, but Woody was cold and stood with his hands in his pockets, and his arms bare, moving from foot to foot. Inside, the phone was ringing again. Once I looked up and saw my mother come to the window and look down at Woody and me. Woody didn't look up or see her, but I did. I waved at her, and she waved back at me and smiled. She was wearing a powder-blue dress. In another minute the phone stopped ringing.

Woody took a cigarette out of his shirt pocket and lit it. Smoke shot through his nose into the cold air, and he sniffed, looked around the ground and threw his match on the gravel. His blond hair was combed backwards and neat on the sides, and I could smell his aftershave on him, a sweet, lemon smell. And for the first time I noticed his shoes. They were two-tones, black with white tops and black laces. They stuck out below his baggy pants and were long and polished and shiny, as if he had been planning on a big occasion. They looked like shoes some country singer would wear, or a salesman. He was handsome, but only like someone you would see beside you in a dime store and not notice again.

"I like it out here," Woody said, his head down, looking at his shoes. "Nothing to bother you. I bet you'd see Chicago if the world was flat. The Great Plains commence here."

"I don't know," I said.

Woody looked up at me, cupping his smoke with one hand. "Do you play football?"

"No," I said. I thought about asking him something about my mother. But I had no idea what it would be.

"I *have* been drinking," Woody said, "but I'm not drunk now."

The wind rose then, and from behind the house I could hear Major bark once from far away, and I could smell the irrigation ditch, hear it hiss in the field. It ran down from Highwood Creek to the Missouri, twenty miles away. It was nothing Woody knew about, nothing he could hear or smell. He knew nothing about anything that was here. I heard my father say the words, "That's a real joke," from inside the house, then the sound of a drawer being opened and shut, and a door closing. Then nothing else.

Woody turned and looked into the dark toward where the glow of Great Falls rose on the horizon, and we both could see the flashing lights of a plane lowering to land there. "I once passed my brother in the Los Angeles airport and didn't even recognize him," Woody said, staring into the night. "He recognized *me,* though. He said, 'Hey, bro, are you mad at me, or what?' I wasn't mad at him. We both had to laugh."

Woody turned and looked at the house. His hands were still in his pockets, his cigarette clenched between his teeth, his arms taut. They were, I saw, bigger, stronger arms than I had thought. A vein went down the front of each of them. I wondered what Woody knew that I didn't. Not about my mother—I didn't know anything about that and didn't want to— but about a lot of things, about the life out in the dark, about coming out here, about airports, even about me. He and I were not so far apart in age, I knew that. But Woody was one thing, and I was another. And I wondered how I would ever get to be like him, since it didn't necessarily seem so bad a thing to be.

"Did you know your mother was married before?" Woody said.

"Yes," I said. "I knew that."

"It happens to all of them, now," he said. "They can't wait to get divorced."

"I guess so," I said.

Woody dropped his cigarette into the gravel and toed it out with his black-and-white shoe. He looked up at me and smiled the way he had inside the house, a smile that said he knew something he wouldn't tell, a smile to make you feel bad because you weren't Woody and never could be.

It was then that my father came out of the house. He still had on his plaid hunting coat and his wool cap, but his face was as white as snow, as white as I have ever seen a human being's face to be. It was odd. I had the feeling that he might've fallen inside, because he looked roughed up, as though he had hurt himself somehow.

My mother came out the door behind him and stood in the floodlight at the top of the steps. She was wearing the powder-blue dress I'd seen through the window, a dress I had never seen her wear before, though she was also wearing a car coat and carrying a suitcase. She looked at me and shook her head in a way that only I was supposed to notice, as if it was not a good idea to talk now.

My father had his hands in his pockets, and he walked right up to Woody. He did not even look at me. "What do you do for a living?" he said, and he was very close to Woody. His coat was close enough to touch Woody's shirt.

"I'm in the air force," Woody said. He looked at me and then at my father. He could tell my father was excited.

"Is this your day off, then?" my father said. He moved even closer to Woody, his hands still in his pockets. He pushed Woody with his chest, and Woody seemed willing to let my father push him.

"No," he said, shaking his head.

I looked at my mother. She was just standing, watching. It was as if someone had given her an order, and she was obeying it. She did not smile at me, though I thought she was thinking about me, which made me feel strange.

"What's the matter with you?" my father said into Woody's face, right into his face—his voice tight, as if it had gotten hard for him to talk. "Whatever in the world is the matter with you? Don't you understand something?" My father took a revolver pistol out of his coat and put it up under Woody's chin, into the soft pocket behind the bone, so that Woody's whole face rose, but his arms stayed at his sides, his hands open. "I don't know what to do with you," my father said. "I don't have any idea what to do with you. I just don't." Though I thought that what he wanted to do was hold Woody there just like that until something important took place, or until he could simply forget about all this.

My father pulled the hammer back on the pistol and raised it tighter under Woody's chin, breathing into Woody's face—my mother in the light with her suitcase, watching them, and me watching them. A half a minute must've gone by.

And then my mother said, "Jack, let's stop now. Let's just stop."

My father stared into Woody's face as if he wanted Woody to consider doing something—moving or turning around or anything on his own to stop this—that my father would then put a stop to. My father's eyes grew narrowed, and his teeth were gritted together, his lips snarling up to resemble a smile. "You're crazy, aren't you?" he said. "You're a goddamned crazy man. Are you in love with her, too? Are you, crazy man? Are you? Do you say you love her? Say you love her! Say you love her so I can blow your fucking brains in the sky."

"All right," Woody said. "No. It's all right."

"He doesn't love me, Jack. For God's sake," my mother said. She seemed so calm. She shook her head at me again. I do not think she thought my father would shoot Woody. And I don't think Woody thought so. Nobody did, I think, except my father himself. But I think he did, and was trying to find out how to.

My father turned suddenly and glared at my mother, his eyes shiny and moving, but with the gun still on Woody's skin. I think he was afraid, afraid he was doing this wrong and could mess all of it up and make matters worse without accomplishing anything.

"You're leaving," he yelled at her. "That's why you're packed. Get out. Go on."

"Jackie has to be at school in the morning," my mother said in just her normal voice. And without another word to any one of us, she walked out of the floodlamp light carrying her bag, turned the corner at the front porch steps and disappeared toward the olive trees that ran in rows back into the wheat.

My father looked back at me where I was standing in the gravel, as if he expected to see me go with my mother toward Woody's car. But I hadn't thought about that—though later I would. Later I would think I should have gone with her, and that things between them might've been different. But that isn't how it happened.

"You're sure you're going to get away now, aren't you, mister?" my father said into Woody's face. He was crazy himself, then. Anyone would've been. Everything must have seemed out of hand to him.

"I'd like to," Woody said. "I'd like to get away from here."

"And I'd like to think of some way to hurt you," my father said and blinked his eyes. "I feel helpless about it." We all heard the door to Woody's car close in the dark. "Do you think that I'm a fool?" my father said.

"No," Woody said. "I don't think that."

"Do you think you're important?"

"No," Woody said. "I'm not."

My father blinked again. He seemed to be becoming someone else at that moment, someone I didn't know. "Where are you from?"

And Woody closed his eyes. He breathed in, then out, a long sigh. It was as if this was somehow the hardest part, something he hadn't expected to be asked to say.

"Chicago," Woody said. "A suburb of there."

"Are your parents alive?" my father said, all the time with his blue magnum pistol pushed under Woody's chin.

"Yes," Woody said. "Yessir."

"That's too bad," my father said. "Too bad they have to know what you are. I'm sure you stopped meaning anything to them a long time ago. I'm sure they both wish you were dead. You didn't know that. But I know it. I can't help them out, though. Somebody else'll have to kill you. I don't want to have to think about you anymore. I guess that's it."

My father brought the gun down to his side and stood looking at Woody. He did not back away, just stood, waiting for what I don't know to happen. Woody stood a moment, then he cut his eyes at me uncomfortably. And I know that I looked down. That's all I could do. Though I remember wondering if Woody's heart was broken and what any of this meant to him. Not to me, or my mother, or my father. But to him, since he seemed to be the one left out somehow, the one who would be lonely soon, the one who had done something he would someday wish he hadn't and would have no one to tell him that it was all right, that they forgave him, that these things happen in the world.

Woody took a step back, looked at my father and at me again as if he intended to speak, then stepped aside and walked away toward the front of our house, where the wind chime made a noise in the new cold air.

My father looked at me, his big pistol in his hand. "Does this seem stupid to you?" he said. "All this? Yelling and threatening and going nuts? I wouldn't blame you if it did. You shouldn't even see this. I'm sorry. I don't know what to do now."

"It'll be all right," I said. And I walked out to the road. Woody's car started up behind the olive trees. I stood and watched it back out, its red taillights clouded by exhaust. I could see their two heads inside, with the headlights shining behind them. When they got into the road, Woody touched his brakes, and for a moment I could see that they were talking, their heads turned toward each other, nodding. Woody's head and my mother's. They sat that way for a few seconds, then drove slowly off. And I wondered what they had to say to each other, something important enough that they had to stop right at that moment and say it. Did she say, *I love you?* Did she say, *This is not what I expected to happen?* Did she say, *This is what I've wanted all along?* And did he say, *I'm sorry for all this,* or *I'm glad,* or *None of this matters to me?* These are not the kinds of things you can know if you were not there. And I was not there and did not want to be. It did not seem like I should be there. I heard the door slam when my father went inside, and I turned back from the road where I could still see their taillights disappearing, and went back into the house where I was to be alone with my father.

Things seldom end in one event. In the morning I went to school on the bus as usual, and my father drove in to the air base in his car. We had not said very much about all that had happened. Harsh words, in a sense, are all alike. You can make them up yourself and be right. I think we both believed that we were in a fog we couldn't see through yet, though in a while, maybe not even a long while, we would see lights and know something.

In my third-period class that day a messenger brought a note for me that said I was excused from school at noon, and I should meet my mother at a motel down 10th Avenue South—a place not so far from my school—and we would eat lunch together.

It was a gray day in Great Falls. The leaves were off the trees and the mountains to the east of town were obscured by a low sky. The night before had been cold and clear, but today it seemed as if it would rain. It was the beginning of winter in earnest. In a few days there would be snow everywhere.

The motel where my mother was staying was called the Tropicana, and was beside the city golf course. There was a neon parrot on the sign out front, and the cabins made a U shape behind a little white office building. Only a couple of cars were parked in front of cabins, and no car was in front of my mother's cabin. I wondered if Woody would be here, or if he was at the air base. I wondered if my father would see him there, and what they would say.

I walked back to cabin 9. The door was open, though a DO NOT DISTURB sign was hung on the knob outside. I looked through the screen and saw my mother sitting on the bed alone. The television was on, but she was looking at me. She was wearing the powder-blue dress she had had on the night before.

She was smiling at me, and I liked the way she looked at that moment, through the screen, in shadows. Her features did not seem as sharp as they had before. She looked comfortable where she was, and I felt like we were going to get along, no matter what had happened, and that I wasn't mad at her—that I had never been mad at her.

She sat forward and turned the television off. "Come in, Jackie," she said, and I opened the screen door and came inside. "It's the height of grandeur in here, isn't it?" My mother looked around the room. Her suitcase was open on the floor by the bathroom door, which I could see through and out the window onto the golf course, where three men were playing under the milky sky. "Privacy can be a burden, sometimes," she said, and reached down and put on her high-heeled shoes. "I didn't sleep very well last night, did you?"

"No," I said, though I had slept all right. I wanted to ask her where Woody was, but it occurred to me at that moment that he was gone now and wouldn't be back, that she wasn't thinking in terms of him and didn't care where he was or ever would be.

"I'd like a nice compliment from you," she said. "Do you have one of those to spend?"

"Yes," I said. "I'm glad to see you."

"That's a nice one," she said and nodded. She had both her shoes on now. "Would you like to go have lunch? We can walk across the street to the cafeteria. You can get hot food."

"No," I said. "I'm not really hungry now."

"That's okay," she said and smiled at me again. And, as I said before, I liked the way she looked. She looked pretty in a way I didn't remember seeing her, as if something that had had a hold on her had let her go, and she could be different about things. Even about me.

"Sometimes, you know," she said, "I'll think about something I did. Just anything. Years ago in Idaho, or last week, even. And it's as if I'd read it. Like a story. Isn't that strange?"

"Yes," I said. And it did seem strange to me because I was certain then what the difference was between what had happened and what hadn't, and knew I always would be.

"Sometimes," she said, and she folded her hands in her lap and stared out the little side window of her cabin at the parking lot and the curving row of other cabins. "Sometimes I even have a moment when I completely forget what life's like. Just altogether." She smiled. "That's not so bad, finally. Maybe it's a disease I have. Do you think I'm just sick and I'll get well?"

"No. I don't know," I said. "Maybe. I hope so." I looked out the bathroom window and saw the three men walking down the golf course fairway carrying golf clubs.

"I'm not very good at sharing things right now," my mother said. "I'm sorry." She cleared her throat, and then she didn't say anything for almost a minute while I stood there. "I *will* answer anything you'd like me to answer, though. Just ask me anything, and I'll answer it the truth, whether I want to or not. Okay? I will. You don't even have to trust me. That's not a big issue with us. We're both grown-ups now."

And I said, "Were you ever married before?"

My mother looked at me strangely. Her eyes got small, and for a moment she looked the way I was used to seeing her—sharp-faced, her mouth set and taut. "No," she said. "Who told you that? That isn't true. I never was. Did Jack say that to you? Did your father say that? That's an awful thing to say. I haven't been that bad."

"He didn't say that," I said.

"Oh, of course he did," my mother said. "He doesn't know just to let things go when they're bad enough."

"I wanted to know that," I said. "I just thought about it. It doesn't matter."

"No, it doesn't," my mother said. "I could've been married eight times. I'm just sorry he said that to you. He's not generous sometimes."

"He didn't say that," I said. But I'd said it enough, and I didn't care if she believed me or didn't. It was true that trust was not a big issue between us then. And in any event, I know now that the whole truth of anything is an idea that stops existing finally.

"Is that all you want to know, then?" my mother said. She seemed mad, but not at me, I didn't think. Just at things in general. And I sympathized with her. "Your life's your own business, Jackie," she said. "Sometimes it scares you to death it's so much your own business. You just want to run."

"I guess so," I said.

"I'd like a less domestic life, is all." She looked at me, but I didn't say anything. I didn't see what she meant by that, though I knew there was nothing I could say to change the way her life would be from then on. And I kept quiet.

In a while we walked across 10th Avenue and ate lunch in the cafeteria. When she paid for the meal I saw that she had my father's silver-dollar money clip in her purse and that there was money in it. And I understood that he had been to see her already that day, and no one cared if I knew it. We were all of us on our own in this.

When we walked out onto the street, it was colder and the wind was blowing. Car exhausts were visible and some drivers had their lights on, though it was only two o'clock in the afternoon. My mother had called a taxi, and we stood and waited for it. I didn't know where she was going, but I wasn't going with her.

"Your father won't let me come back," she said, standing on the curb. It was just a fact to her, not that she hoped I would talk to him or stand up for her to take her part. But I did wish then that I had never let her go the night before. Things can be fixed by staying; but to go out into the night and not come back hazards life, and everything can get out of hand.

My mother's taxi came. She kissed me and hugged me very hard, then got inside the cab in her powder-blue dress and high heels and her car coat. I smelled her perfume on my cheeks as I stood watching her. "I used to be afraid of more things than I am now," she said, looking up at me, and smiled. "I've got a knot in my stomach, of all things." And she closed the cab door, waved at me, and rode away.

I walked back toward my school. I thought I could take the bus home if I got there by three. I walked a long way down 10th Avenue to Second Street, beside the Missouri River, then over to town. I walked by the Great Northern Hotel, where my father had sold ducks and geese and fish of all kinds. There were no passenger trains in the yard and the loading dock looked small. Garbage cans were lined along the edge of it, and the door was closed and locked.

As I walked toward school I thought to myself that my life had turned suddenly, and that I might not know exactly how or which way for possibly a long time. Maybe, in fact, I might never know. It was a thing that happened to you—I knew that—and it had happened to me in this way now. And as I walked on up the cold street that afternoon in Great Falls, the questions I asked myself were these: Why wouldn't my father let my mother come back? Why would Woody stand in the cold with me outside my house and risk being killed? Why would he say my mother had been married before, if she hadn't been? And my mother herself—why would she do what she did? In five years my father had gone off to Ely, Nevada, to ride out the oil strike there, and been killed by accident. And in the years since then I have seen my mother from time to time—in one place or another, with one man or other—and I can say, at least, that we know each other. But I have never known the answer to these questions, have never asked anyone their answers. Though possibly it—the answer—is simple: it is just low-life, some coldness in us all, some helplessness that causes us to misunderstand life when it is pure and plain, makes our existence seem like a border between two nothings, and makes us no more or less than animals who meet on the road—watchful, unforgiving, without patience or desire.

ELIZABETH TALLENT

NO ONE'S A MYSTERY

For my eighteenth birthday Jack gave me a five-year diary with a latch and a little key, light as a dime. I was sitting beside him scratching at the lock, which didn't seem to want to work, when he thought he saw his wife's Cadillac in the distance, coming toward us. He pushed me down onto the dirty floor of the pickup and kept one hand on my head while I inhaled the musk of his cigarettes in the dashboard ashtray and sang along with Rosanne Cash on the tape deck. We'd been drinking tequila and the bottle was between his legs, resting up against his crotch, where the seam of his Levi's was bleached linen-white, though the Levi's were nearly new. I don't know why his Levi's always bleached like that, along the seams and at the knees. In a curve of cloth his zipper glinted, gold.

"It's her," he said. "She keeps the lights on in the daytime. I can't think of a single habit in a woman that irritates me more than that." When he saw that I was going to stay still he took his hand from my head and ran it through his own dark hair.

"Why does she?" I said.

"She thinks it's safer. Why does she need to be safer? She's driving exactly fifty-five miles an hour. She believes in those signs: 'Speed Monitored by Aircraft.' It doesn't matter that you can look up and see that the sky is empty."

"She'll see your lips move, Jack. She'll know you're talking to someone."

"She'll think I'm singing along with the radio."

He didn't lift his hand, just raised the fingers in salute while the pressure of his palm steadied the wheel, and I heard the

Cadillac honk twice, musically; he was driving easily eighty miles an hour. I studied his boots. The elk heads stitched into the leather were bearded with frayed thread, the toes were scuffed, and there was a compact wedge of muddy manure between the heel and the sole—the same boots he'd been wearing for the two years I'd known him. On the tape deck Rosanne Cash sang, "Nobody's into me, no one's a mystery."

"Do you think she's getting famous because of who her daddy is or for herself?" Jack said.

"There are about a hundred pop tops on the floor, did you know that? Some little kid could cut a bare foot on one of these, Jack."

"No little kids get into this truck except for you."

"How come you let it get so dirty?"

" 'How come,' " he mocked. "You even sound like a kid. You can get back into the seat now, if you want. She's not going to look over her shoulder and see you."

"How do you know?"

"I just know," he said. "Like I know I'm going to get meat loaf for supper. It's in the air. Like I know what you'll be writing in that diary."

"What will I be writing?" I knelt on my side of the seat and craned around to look at the butterfly of dust printed on my jeans. Outside the window Wyoming was dazzling in the heat. The wheat was fawn and yellow and parted smoothly by the thin dirt road. I could smell the water in the irrigation ditches hidden in the wheat.

"Tonight you'll write, 'I love Jack. This is my birthday present from him. I can't imagine anybody loving anybody more than I love Jack.' "

"I can't."

"In a year you'll write, 'I wonder what I ever really saw in Jack. I wonder why I spent so many days just riding around in his pickup. It's true he taught me something about sex. It's true there wasn't ever much else to do in Cheyenne.' "

"I won't write that."

"In two years you'll write, 'I wonder what that old guy's name was, the one with the curly hair and the filthy dirty pickup truck and time on his hands.' "

"I won't write that."

"No?"

"Tonight I'll write, 'I love Jack. This is my birthday present from him. I can't imagine anybody loving anybody more than I love Jack.' "

"No, you can't," he said. "You can't imagine it."

"In a year I'll write, 'Jack should be home any minute now. The table's set—my grandmother's linen and her old silver and the yellow candles left over from the wedding—but I don't know if I can wait until after the trout à la Navarra to make love to him.' "

"It must have been a fast divorce."

"In two years I'll write, 'Jack should be home by now. Little Jack is hungry for his supper. He said his first word today besides "Mama" and "Papa." He said "kaka." ' "

Jack laughed. "He was probably trying to finger-paint with kaka on the bathroom wall when you heard him say it."

"In three years I'll write, 'My nipples are a little sore from nursing Eliza Rosamund.' "

"Rosamund. Every little girl should have a middle name she hates."

" 'Her breath smells like vanilla and her eyes are just Jack's color of blue.' "

"That's nice," Jack said.

"So, which one do you like?"

"I like yours," he said. "But I believe mine."

"It doesn't matter. I believe mine."

"Not in your heart of hearts, you don't."

"You're wrong."

"I'm not wrong," he said. "And her breath would smell like your milk, and it's kind of a bittersweet smell, if you want to know the truth."

DAVID LONG

HOME FIRES

Longer than anyone knows, fir and tamarack had clung to the sharp slopes of the canyon, ravaged by lightning fires and bark beetles and gravity, their tenacity witnessed only by the moody northwestern clouds, by birds of prey whose serrated wings bore them on the tricky thermals, by families of deer carefully following trails beside the fast gray water. In this century Jeep roads intruded until the entire eighty miles could be traversed by a strong rig, though it was never thought of as a way to get from one place to another. Then in the 1960s dynamite and giant earth-movers left a two-lane blacktop highway that matched the river's twists, ascending in places hundreds of feet above it through unguarded switchbacks.

It was an early morning in the dregs of a September that had frosted early. Scattered stands of aspen and weeping birch fluttered in the shadows. Down in the heart of the river, kokanee salmon were making their first run, a few now to be followed by great numbers, swimming upstream toward the waters of their spawning—surely it was a kind of miracle that they should find their way back, no longer feeding, their bodies already pulpy in preparation for death.

Traffic on the highway was sparse, relieved of the sluggish flow of motor homes and top-heavy camper outfits from other states. A few feet past mile marker 44, where the road climbs into a smooth northeasterly bank, a fresh pair of double tire tracks continued straight that morning, through the chunks of reddish clay, into the dry brush and the feathery upper branches of the firs.

The truck lay upside down, back end crushed like a soda can, cab folded into so dense a bolus of steel it would take Search & Rescue better than two hours working with welding torches and hydraulic jaws to discover it contained no body. Up slope, scattered among the outcrops of shale and limestone, in the trees and resting here and there on the flaps of freshly gashed topsoil, white packages of frozen fish were strewn, still rock-hard, though the exposed sides would feel mushy to the fingers of the first county deputy to huff down the slope, midafternoon. The truck had nearly made it to the river, stopped only by a slug of granite twice its size, where now the man named Pack squatted, head between his knees, glancing up every few seconds at the wreckage.

He could not understand why it did not include him. He should not have survived such a mistake, should not first have made it. He tried to picture the night just elapsed, the route that had led him to the lip of the road. He had no precise memory of it. Surely he had fallen asleep. Drivers fear the graveyard hours, though that fear is so close to the heart of what they do that it remains unsaid. They ride behind the wheel, pumping Dentyne or cigarettes or Maalox, half-thrilled by the power of the diesel and the reach of the headlamps, half-terrified by their limitations. They flick cassettes into the tape player and set the volume so high the treble jars them out of the dreamy hypnotic mood that comes just before the moment their heads drop. They sing, they banter with one another on the CB, they juggle weights and distances and velocity in their heads. Anything to keep them sharp until it is light again. In the end, though, the fear itself provides the energy.

But Pack was never like that. Driving those hours he found a kind of peace, a solitude that was its own reward. The darkness outside seemed to illuminate his loneliness, seemed to tell him it was only the natural way of the world. He aimed the passenger mirror inward at his own face so he could watch his eyes in the halo of dash lights. He never used the radio except sometimes to tune in an all-night talk show from the coast and listen to the paranoia and longing that gave the voices their peculiar timbre. He kept to himself at the truckstops, letting his cup be filled and refilled as he watched the other drivers kill their nights off under the acid lights. He would be privately pleased when the phone would ring and the waitress would wipe her hands and grab for it. It would never be for him.

He could not remember choosing to be a driver. He had fallen into the pattern of it a job at a time, found it suited his disposition. He had been to college but picked up nothing lasting there except the taste for reading, another solitary pastime. Sometimes on long nights he thought about his wife, but it was the same drowsy distant way he thought about what he had read. He did not doubt that he loved her, but he could not remember choosing her. She had been with him as long as he could recall—the adolescence she'd marked the end of only a blur now, dotted by occasional points of shame and excitement. When he came home to her, his desire quickened and he'd hold her and listen to her deep sure voice and be happy, but driving again, at night, he knew that the two were not one, after all, but two.

Pack sat on the crown of the boulder, surrounded by quiet and bird songs, trying to make sense of what had happened. He saw himself popping out the driver's door as the nose of the truck first hit, his body flipping backward through the branch tips, pitching like dead weight into the snarl of laurel where he'd come to.

He ran his fingers up and down his legs, over his ribs and back, finally touching around his skull, searching for the fatal exception to his good luck. Though he was dizzy and his forearms were devilled with long scratches, he could find nothing dreadful.

He climbed off his perch and bent over a sheltered pool. His face was thin and droopy-eyed, fringed with a beard the color of clay dirt. His eyes were the blue of an undeclared predawn sky. He smiled into the calm water, and it was then he saw that his front teeth were gone, ripped out by the roots. He touched the gums delicately, felt the clots forming over the holes, withdrew his hand, and saw the fingertips evenly stained, as if his body were nothing but a bucket of blood.

At that moment the sun first crossed the ridgeline and Pack squinted up the steep slope, bathed now in keen September sunlight. The dizziness gave way to a rush of clarity, as if he'd only now begun to wake up, not just from the accident and from the night, but from ten years of living in the dark. He looked at the crumpled truck, the torn earth. Clearly he was supposed to be a dead man.

He knows his loneliness better than he knows me, Elisabeth Pack, called Willie, wrote her sister who had moved east. *Maybe I am a jealous woman after all.*

She put her pen down, stared impatiently out the side window where the two pear trees had dropped their yield into long sweeps of grass. The leaves were brittle and gold. The road dead-ended here. If there had been children, it would have been a safe place for them to play, away from the hazards of through traffic. But there were none. In the distance, the parched foothills hung in a blue morning haze, curving out of sight toward the mouth of the valley where the river flowed wide and tame, accompanied by the tracks of the Burlington Northern and the placid interstate.

But I doubt it, Willie wrote.

She was a handsome woman, six feet even—slightly taller than Pack—with clear hazel eyes and soft lines around the mouth. At thirty she wasted no time mourning the woman she was or might have been. In uniform her presence was striking. Intensive care patients were guarded by her skills, comforted by her manner, perhaps mistaking her reserve for serenity or for a larger, more merciful view of things, one in which the sick always healed and the grieving were granted peace. It was good consuming work; with Pack gone so often she was happy for it.

His homecomings have become unbearable, she wrote, frowned at the words and stopped. It was not exactly what she meant to say. She preferred her letters to remain simple and full of news; even in the ones to her sister she was seldom confidential. She was embarrassed by the heaviness of her words. The fact was, though, his returns *had* become more difficult to cope with. She had long ago accepted that Pack—for all her love of him, for all her willingness not to judge him—was a man who came and went. In the ten years of their marriage he had gone off on the fire lines their first summers, after that had shuttled rental cars back to the Midwest, traveled with a bar band called *Loose Caboose,* and in recent years driven trucks on the long interstate routes.

He was always edgy just before he left, and she would have to turn away from him to avoid a fight. He always returned with a high-spirited exhaustion, coming to her bed for a spell of love-making, hard and wonderful for Willie, though lasting too long now, leaving her body sore and her spirit cut by resentment. She saw his passion soon spoiled by restlessness, as if she were not an object of love but of release. It had not always been like that, but she had to admit, privately, it was now. Still she forgave him that. What worried her more was that even between jobs he seemed to come and go, as though tracing an elliptical orbit around her and the part of his life that remained fixed. Sometimes she believed he might swing too far, snap loose, and keep sailing out into space.

"How do you put *up* with it?" her friends sometimes asked her over coffee.

"I don't see that it's really a problem," Willie said, willing to defend Pack from loose talk. She could handle the Pack whose nature it was to come and go, who hadn't settled into a life's work the way she'd imagined he might, who seemed an odd character put up against their husbands. But she knew they also meant: *How can you trust him to be faithful?* Faith was private, Willie thought. It irritated her the casual way her friends rated their husbands' performance, almost eager to see them fail and at the same time scared to death of losing them, especially to someone else. She was not afraid of losing Pack to another woman.

Once she told him: *I don't mind sleeping alone.*

"No?" Pack said, smiling at the darkness, rubbing her wide damp stomach. She had meant that it kept her from taking him for granted, that the emptiness of her bed, at night and again in the morning, stayed with her as a reminder even when he held her and warmed her. And she meant it as a kind of triumph, too, because it had not been easy for her at first; she'd needed to learn to be alone.

Unbearable, she'd written.

She craned her neck and squinted through the white sunlight at the clock on the kitchen wall, saw that it was already afternoon. She finished the letter quickly, dismissing her remarks as a morning's bad humor, sealed it, and laid it by her purse.

Though it was still early, she grabbed her uniform from the hook back of the bathroom door and slipped into it. She sat on the edge of the bed and double-knotted her white polished Clinics, rising then for a quiet inspection in the big mirror. She liked to see herself in the white uniform, her wheat-colored hair drawn smoothly over the ears and gathered in a silver slip at the neck. She liked not worrying about the quirks of fashion, but more than that, the whiteness itself pleased her.

She closed up the house and walked out to the car and idled it lightly in the driveway, a kind of nervousness overtaking her, the feeling that she'd left something undone. The afternoon light seemed suddenly frail, as if this were the exact moment the season turned. Her thoughts about Pack troubled her. She wished he were here, she wished he could walk down the hospital corridors beside her, feeling what she felt: the terrible precariousness of the lives and their links to one another. She wished he understood that.

Veins of worry began to dart through the halo of bright amazement surrounding Pack as he studied the ruined truck. The tires pointed absurdly in the air, splayed and flattened: the painted lettering emerged without meaning from the jammed aluminum. Unignited gasoline mixed with the freon from the fractured cooling unit and gave the air a gray stink. It was past time for precaution, but Pack was overwhelmed with being too close. All the sounds he had missed in his flight now swarmed into his ears. His stomach balled up like a fist.

He backed along the silt-caked stones, hands tucked into the tops of his jeans, staring at the wreckage as it diminished and began to blend with the other debris along the river. He walked upstream until the current bent sharply around a deposit of harder rock and he could no longer see the truck, kept walking a long time, the click of the small hard stones ringing in the narrow canyon. The roadway was high above him, out of sight. He wanted no part of it.

When he stopped, the sun was nearly overhead, its light broken into rich shadows by the low-hanging limbs of the cedars. As he knelt he felt the shakes coming on strong. He got up again quickly and caught the glint of orange rip-stop nylon, across the river and a short ways up a feeder creek. Above it rose a thin braid of smoke, the first sign of life Pack had seen. He waded into the shallows, the water rising over his boottops, then out where it was deeper, bending his knees against the current. Approaching, Pack saw two women crouched by the fire, for the moment unaware of him. The one facing him was slight—*wasted,* his wife would have said—even in a down vest. She pulled her blue stocking cap down over strands of pale hair as she leaned to flip a pair of fish skewered above the coals. The campsite looked small and orderly. The other woman, who had been sitting back smoking, head down, suddenly caught sight of Pack and grabbed up a shotgun he'd not seen resting beside her.

"*Hey!*" Pack said, freezing.

The woman aimed the gun at Pack's midsection and appeared willing to squeeze off a shot.

"There's been an accident," Pack said, hands lifted in a victim's posture.

"There could easily be another," the woman said. "You alone?"

"No trouble," Pack said. "OK?"

The woman in the vest got to her feet and squinted at Pack's face, turned, and shook her head at the gun. Her companion slowly lowered it until it pointed at the pine needles around Pack's feet.

"Tell us what happened," she said.

Pack moved in gingerly, squatted, and told them what he could remember. "I was headed home," he began. It sounded like somebody else's story, though the throbbing in his mouth reminded him it was neither made-up nor borrowed.

The women seemed to listen with special attention. Finally the one with the gun cracked a smile, but it was thin-lipped and made Pack more nervous. "It should be that easy," she said.

Pack looked at her, not understanding, not knowing what to do next.

"Here," the other said. "You want some food?"

Pack shook his head. He was beginning to feel truly bad. "You think it would be all right if I maybe laid down?" he said.

The women checked with each other. The one in the stocking cap nodded toward the tent. As Pack stood she caught his arm and said, "Let me . . ." dipping a corner of her towel in a pan of hot water, then dabbing at the blood dried around his mouth.

"Don't you get weird on us," the woman with the gun said. "You understand?"

Pack nodded. He crawled heavily into the tent, slid across the warm nylon and collapsed, watching the leaf shadows twitch above him.

While Pack slept the truck was spotted by a young man who had stopped above the ravine to photograph the eagles circling above the salmon run. He trained the long lens of his Nikon down the embankment, scanned the river bank for signs of life, and wondered what the little squares of white were. After a while he walked back to his van, dialed the CB to channel 9, and began calling for help. He was joined eventually by two county deputies, the highway patrol, Search & Rescue, and the coroner. The photographer followed the police down to the wreck and stayed until the light failed, snapping pictures of the truck and the broken slope and the faces of the workers, listening to their speculations, pleased to be so close to it all. The plates of the truck were checked through the Department of Motor Vehicles and identified. In Pack's darkened house the phone rang every hour, beginning at dinner time, continuing late into the evening.

Pack woke abruptly and saw that it was fully dark. It seemed as if a great flood of time had swept him away. He thought for a moment that he had dreamed but realized what he had seen and heard was the power of the fall itself, magnified and reiterated in the stillness of his mind. He ached everywhere; his lips and gums were swollen hard around the missing teeth. Peering from the tent flap, he saw the woman who had cleaned him sitting alone by the fire. Pack joined her. She smiled in an easy, sisterly way. It was as if they had gone in and studied him as he slept, reading into the man he was and deciding he was not a danger to them.

"Rita believes these are desperate times," she said. "She believes it's important to be armed and ready. Are you any better?"

"I don't know,"

"That was a miracle," she said.

"I don't know," Pack said again.

She laughed, her cheeks glowing round in the firelight. "Any fool could see that."

"*Kyle . . .*" Rita said, breaking the circle of light, armed now with a load of firewood, her voice reedy and careful. She knelt and dumped the wood, looked back at the two of them.

"Kyle," she said, "what have you told him?"

Kyle stared into the flames. "I just told him it was a miracle."

"Yes, that's true," Rita said. "But what will he do with it?"

"I don't think he knows yet," Kyle said gently.

Rita dusted the wood flakes from the front of her sweatshirt, then stooped and poured coffee into a tin cup and handed it to Pack, its steam puffing into the cold air. Pack nodded and took it, and it felt good between his hands.

"They'll be looking for you, of course," Rita said in a minute. "They'll figure your body fell into the river and was carried downstream. You could have gone several miles by now. It's not uncommon. For a while you'll be called missing, then presumed dead."

She stopped a moment to let that sink in. Kyle moved closer to Pack.

"I was missing once," Kyle said, quiet excitement in her voice. "My husband looked all over for me. No telling what he would have done if he'd found me. He'd done plenty already."

"Beaten her," Rita said.

"At first I was hiding upstairs at the hotel with a wig and a new name. I didn't know what I was going to do exactly. I couldn't sleep. Sometimes I could see his truck going down the main street and one night I saw it parked outside the Stockman's Bar, and he came out with someone else. I wasn't surprised. The next morning I took the bus to Pocatello."

"Yes," Rita said. "He was a bad man. A real prick."

Pack heard the tinkling of a brass windchime hung in the tree, drank his coffee in small careful sips.

"Still," Rita went on, "Kyle was smarter in the heart than I was. I waited until I was barely alive, barely able to help myself. But all that's changed now, as you can see."

"Can you eat yet?" Kyle asked Pack. "I saved a fish for you." She tugged a bundle of tinfoil from the edge of the coals.

"You'll need strength," Rita said. "Whatever you decide."

Pack took the fish into his lap and cracked it open and lifted out the long limp spine and tossed it into the fire. The meat crumbled in his mouth.

"But you're not a bad man, are you?" Rita said.

"What do you think?" Pack asked her.

"I think you're a lucky man," Kyle said. "But luck's only the start of it."

"Let me be blunt about this," Rita said. "They will be looking for you, but they don't have to find you."

As she spoke she stood behind Kyle, her fingers lightly stroking the shoulders of the down vest. The smoke twisted up before them, through the fringe of trees to a wedge of sky overcome with autumn constellations.

"Brother," Rita laughed, "have a new life."

Right then Pack stopped chewing and looked hard at the two women. "*New life* . . ." he said.

"Clean slate," Rita said. "Maybe you have the nerve, maybe not."

"I don't know," Pack said. "I can't tell you exactly how I feel."

"That's right," Kyle said. "That's how it is at first. You feel sick."

"You get this unmoored feeling," Rita said. "But then you start to see destinations and you go ahead." Her soft white face shone with patience. "Don't tell me you wouldn't like another chance."

Pack was silent.

Rita stood over him a moment, then said, "Now, we're going to bed. You can stay with the fire as long as you need, but it's going to be very cold here soon. Believe me."

Passing by, Kyle whispered to Pack, "Don't think it was an accident," and disappeared toward the tent.

"Thanks," Pack said.

He stayed watching the fire until the last cedar log burned through, showering the air with fine embers, stayed remembering the fires of his life, the blue-gray smoke of branding fires and the stink of burnt hide, the scattered fires of his childhood. He stayed listening to the steady clamoring of the creek, imagining the water's descent, how it wept from remote snowfields, came together, and followed high country drainages to the wide rivers that passed under the city's bridges disappearing west toward the sea. He thought of all the lighted places where he had stopped, the extravagance of his curiosities, and the careless ways he had broken faith with his wife. When he bent later to crawl into the tent, he heard the powerful contentment of the women sleeping. They had left one bag empty for him and were together in the other, holding each other like twins. Pack backed out and stood alone in the cold, measuring the foolish turns his life had taken.

The phone back in its cradle, Willie Pack let her uniform drop to the linoleum of the downstairs bathroom, wrapped herself in a terry-cloth bathrobe, took the Valium bottle from her purse and carried it to the kitchen, lit the gas under the tea kettle, stared at the clear blue flame until the water steamed, turned it off, and sat finally at the breakfast table, surrounded by the bright enamel, the saffron scalloped curtains, lacing her long fingers together in front of her, sure that this moment of control was a fast-fringing lifeline.

Save your tears, she could hear her mother saying. As a child she'd imagined great fetid reservoirs of unshed tears. *Save them why?* How lame and remote her mother's efforts were. Yet Willie knew, perched in the solitude of her own kitchen, that she had grown so much like that woman, believing life was best treated with caution and reserve, believing that loved ones could suddenly trade places with darkness.

Missing, the sheriff had stressed, his voice like fresh gauze.

All her life she'd wanted the exact names of things. Beneath his words she heard this: We haven't found a body yet—in country this wild we may never.

"What does *missing* mean?" Willie said.

"Anything's possible," the sheriff said. "I'm sorry."

"Thank you," Willie Pack said.

So in that time before the confusion and the shouting and crying took possession of her, she held her own hand and rested in an aura of clarity not unlike the one that had settled around Pack hours earlier, as he contemplated the boundaries of his good fortune. This is what tears were saved for.

She had long-ago accustomed herself to his absence, but though it looked the same as always it was not. She felt a flush of shame, to think she had ever enjoyed having him gone. Solitude meant nothing if it was infinite. She thought about death, the way it was taught to her in school, the predictable steps the minds of the living and the dying took in confronting it. Month by month she practiced its sacraments, sometimes finding in her discipline an antidote, mostly not. The farm wife died whispering: *Tell them.* . . . The twenty-year-old logger witnessed the bright splashing of his blood with a pure and wakeful knowledge. She heard the halting voices of old husbands turn suddenly eloquent in the white hallways, reciting an Old Testament catalogue of suffering and accommodation.

She thought then of Pack's missing body. She remembered the feel of her fingers sliding down over the arch of his ribs, she pictured his beautiful hip-swinging gait through the downstairs rooms, the angle of his fingers resting across this table from hers. The image of that body torn and broken rose in her like a searing wind, bringing a wave of sadness—for Pack's body having to die so far away and alone.

She drew a long, controlled breath. For the first time since the telephone call she forced herself to see Pack's face, straight on. It was then, in a burst, she understood what she'd hidden from herself: that she had not seen Pack as he actually was in a long time. What she saw now was not the face she had guarded in her imagination, the one she had married as a teenaged girl, the one she had always reckoned her own happiness by. What she saw now was a face with eyes crimped and glazed, a mouth constantly biting at something, a thumbnail or an emery board or the inside of his lip. It told her Pack had been missing long before this night.

She lurched to the sink and threw up and kept heaving though there was little in her stomach except the dark residue of cafeteria coffee. She ran the water and watched it swirl over the grate, gradually washing away her nausea. In a few minutes she straightened and snugged her bathrobe.

She spilled the blue pills on the table, spacing them evenly with her finger, imagining the sleep they would bring, each one clarifying it like sudden drops in the thermometer, until the muscles no longer flexed and the heart beat indifferently. The rooms were still dark around her: the front room where Pack's book was spread flat on the carpet beside his coffee mug, a book on snow leopards and survival; their bedroom where his workshirt had been carelessly thrown; the bathroom where Pack taped messages to the mirror—no longer the boyish love notes he'd once left, more like the one there now: . . . *and this is our life, when was it truly ours, and when are we truly whatever we are?* from something he had read.

Another chance, she thought, sitting again. She studied the pills lying before her, the tears beginning to burn her eyes. She scraped her hand across the tabletop, scattering the pills across the kitchen, spilling back the chair as she stood and ran out into the darkness of the house, turning on lights, screaming *Goddamn it* at the tears, screaming *No* at the treads of the stairs. *Goddamn it. Goddamn it,* throwing open doors, flipping switches, every one she could lay a hand on, until the whole house was burning and raging with life.

It was dawn again. Dawn of the husbands, Pack thought. He had been quiet all the way back, not letting on to the trucker who'd stopped for him who he was: the man presumed dead. It was still a private affair. The driver played a Willie Nelson tape, mostly ballads, and hummed along in fair harmony, blinking constantly at the road beyond his windshield. Pack hugged his arms inside the sweatshirt the driver had lent him. This was always a nervous and transitional hour, one kind of thought giving way to the next. Pack remembered how much of his life had disappeared working like the driver beside him, only with less sense of destination than this man surely had. He remembered the few times he had left a woman at that hour, the sadness of strange doorways and words that disappear like balloons into an endless sky, the whine of his engine as it carried him away. He thought of Kyle and Rita waking together in their tent, joined by affection and the belief that the only good road leads away from home.

Pack thanked the man and got down from the truck at the edge of town. He walked slapping his arms. The full white moon floated above the unawakened houses, above the familiar rise and fall of the mountains. In the next block somebody's husband had gone out and started a pickup in the semidark. Steam flared from the exhaust. Soon the heater would throw two rings of warm air at the frosted windshield. Pack broke into a run, loping through the empty intersections, cold air slamming into his lungs.

He stopped in the mouth of the short street that deadended at his house. Men on the road talk about coming home religiously, though they are not religious men or even, Pack thought, men who are at peace being there. What they want is to be welcomed each time, their return treated like the consummation of something noble, which is too much to ask. Unnecessary risks, Pack thought, too great and foolish to be rewarded with love. He had somehow thought he was immune.

Panting hard through the gap in his teeth but warm for the first time in many hours, Pack looked up to see the lights blazing from his house, even from the twin attic dormers and the well at the basement window. He could never know the fullness of his wife's grief, how it came with as many shades of diminishing light as a summer twilight, just as she would never know why his lonely disposition took him always away from her, or precisely what had happened to change him. Sometimes it is a comfort to believe that one day is like another, that things happen over and over and are the same. But accidents happen, and sometimes a man or a woman is lucky enough to see that all of it, from the first light kiss onward, could have gone another way. Pack ran to the front door of his house, alive, thinking *dawn of homecoming, dawn of immaculate good fortune.*

JOHN UPDIKE

NEVADA

Poor Culp. His wife, Sarah, wanted to marry her lover as soon as the divorce came through, she couldn't wait a day, the honeymoon suite in Honolulu had been booked six weeks in advance. So Culp, complaisant to the end, agreed to pick the girls up in Reno and drive them back to Denver. He arranged to be in San Francisco on business and rented a car. Over the phone, Sarah mocked his plan—why not fly? An expert in petroleum extraction, he hoped by driving to extract some scenic benefit from domestic ruin. Until they had moved to Denver and their marriage exploded in the thinner atmosphere, they had lived in New Jersey, and the girls had seen little of the West.

He arrived in Reno around five in the afternoon, having detoured south from Interstate 80. The city looked kinder than he had expected. He found the address Sarah had given him, a barn-red boardinghouse behind a motel distinguished by a giant flashing domino. He dreaded yet longed for the pain of seeing Sarah again—divorced, free of him, exultant, about to take wing into a new marriage. But she had taken wing before he arrived. His two daughters were sitting on a tired cowhide sofa, next to an empty desk, like patients in a dentist's anteroom.

Polly, who was eleven, leaped up to greet him. "Mommy's left," she said. "She thought you'd be here hours ago."

Laura, sixteen, rose with a self-conscious languor from the tired sofa, smoothing her skirt behind, and added, "Jim was with her. He got really mad when you didn't show."

Culp apologized. "I didn't know her schedule was so tight."

Laura perhaps misheard him, answering, "Yeah, she was really uptight."

"I took a little detour to see Lake Tahoe."

"Oh, Dad," Laura said. "You and your sight-seeing."

"Were you worried?" he asked.

"Naa."

A little woman with a square jaw hopped from a side room behind the empty desk. "They was good as good, Mr. Culp. Just sat there, wouldn't even take a sandwich I offered to make for no charge. Laura here kept telling the little one, 'Don't you be childish, Daddy wouldn't let us down.' I'm Betsy Morgan, we've heard of each other but never met officially." Sarah had mentioned her in her letters: Morgan the pirate, her landlady and residency witness. Fred Culp saw himself through Mrs. Morgan's eyes: cuckold, defendant, discardee. Though her eye was merry, the hand she offered him was dry as a bird's foot.

He could only think to ask, "How did the proceedings go?"

The question seemed foolish to him, but not to Mrs. Morgan. "Seven minutes, smooth as silk. Some of these judges, they give a girl a hard time just to keep themselves from being bored. But your Sary stood right up to him. She has that way about her."

"Yes, she did. Does. More and more. Girls, got your bags?"

"Right behind the sofy here. I would have kept their room one night more, but then this lady from Connecticut showed up yesterday could take it for the six weeks."

"That's fine. I'll take them someplace with a pool."

"They'll be missed, I tell you truly," the landlady said, and she bent down and kissed the two girls. This had been a family of sorts, there were real tears in her eyes; but Polly couldn't wait for the hug to pass before blurting to her father, "We had pool privileges at the Domino, and one time all these Mexicans came and used it for a *bath*room!"

They drove to a motel not the Domino. Laura and he watched Polly swim. "Laura, don't you want to put on a suit?"

"Naa. Mom made us swim so much I got diver's ear."

Culp pictured Sarah lying on a poolside chaise lounge, in the bikini with the orange and purple splashes. One smooth wet arm was flung up to shield her eyes. Other women noticeably had legs or breasts; Sarah's beauty had been most vivid in her arms, arms fit for a Greek statue, rounded and fine and firm, arms that never aged, without a trace of wobble above the elbow, though at her next birthday she would be forty. Indeed, that was how Sarah had put the need for divorce: She couldn't bear to turn forty with him. As if then you began a return journey that could not be broken.

Laura was continuing, "Also, Dad, if you *must* know, it's that time of the month."

With clumsy jubilance, Polly hurled her body from the rattling board and surfaced grinning through the kelp of her own hair. She climbed from the pool and slap-footed to his side, shivering. "Want to walk around and play the slots?" Goose bumps had erected the white hairs on her thighs into a ghostly halo. "Want to? It's fun."

Laura intervened maternally. "Don't *make* him, Polly. Daddy's tired and depressed."

"Who says? Let's go. I may never see Reno again." The city, as they walked, reminded him of New Jersey's little municipalities. The desert clarity at evening had the even steel glint of industrial haze. Above drab shop fronts, second-story windows proclaimed residence with curtains and a flowerpot. There were churches, which he hadn't expected. And a river, a trickling shadow of the Passaic, flowed through. The courthouse, Mecca to so many, seemed too modest; it wore the disheartened granite dignity of justice the country over. Only the Reno downtown, garish as a carnival midway, was different. Polly led him to doors she was forbidden to enter and gave him nickels to play for her inside. She loved the slot machines, loved them for their fruity colors and their sleepless glow and their sudden gush of release, jingling, lighting, as luck struck now here, now there, across the dark casino. Feeling the silky heave of their guts as he fed the slot and pulled the handle, rewarded a few times with the delicious spitting of coins into the troughs other hands had smoothed to his touch, Culp came to love them, too; he and Polly made a gleeful hopeful pair, working their way from casino to casino, her round face pressed to the window so she could see him play, and the plums jerk into being, and the bells and cherries do their waltz of chance, 1-2-3. One place was wide open to the sidewalk. A grotesquely large machine stood ready for silver dollars.

Polly said, "Mommy won twenty dollars on that one once."

Culp asked Laura, who had trailed after them in disdainful silence, "Was Jim with you the whole time?"

"No, he only came the last week." She searched her father's face for what he wanted to know. "He stayed at the Domino."

Polly drew close to listen. Culp asked her, "Did you like Jim?"

Her eyes with difficulty shifted from visions of mechanical delight. "He was too serious. He said the slots were a racket and they wouldn't get a penny of his."

Laura said, "I thought he was an utter *pill,* Dad."

"You didn't have to think that to please me."

"He *was.* I told her, too."

"You shouldn't have. Listen, it's her life, not yours." On the hospital-bright sidewalk, both his girls' faces looked unwell, stricken. Culp put a silver dollar into the great machine, imagining that something of Sarah had rubbed off here and that through this electric ardor she might speak to him. But the machine's size was unnatural; the guts felt sluggish, spinning. A plum, a bar, a star. No win. Turning, he resented that Polly and Laura, still staring, seemed stricken for *him.*

Laura said, "Better come eat, Dad. We'll show you a place where they have pastrami like back East."

As Route 40 poured east, Nevada opened into a strange no-color—a rusted gray, or the lavender that haunts the corners of overexposed color slides. The Humboldt River, which had sustained the pioneer caravans, shadowed the expressway shyly, tinting its valley with a dull green that fed dottings of cattle. But for the cattle, and the cars that brushed by him as if he were doing thirty and not eighty miles an hour, and an occasional gas station and cabin café promising SLOTS, there was little sign of life in Nevada. This pleased Culp; it enabled him to run off in peace the home movies of Sarah stored in his head. Sarah pushing the lawn mower in the South Orange back yard. Sarah pushing a blue baby carriage, English, with little white wheels, around the fountain in Washington Square. Sarah, not yet his wife, waiting for him in a brown-and-green peasant skirt under the marquee of a movie house on 57th Street. Sarah, a cool suburban hostess in chalk-pink sack dress, easing through their jammed living room with a platter of parsleyed egg halves. Sarah after a party, drunk in a black-lace bra, doing the Twist at the foot of their bed. Sarah in blue jeans crying out that it was nobody's *fault,* that there was nothing he could *do,* just let her *alone;* and hurling a quarter pound of butter across the kitchen, so the calendar fell off the wall. Sarah in miniskirt leaving their house in Denver for a date, just like a teen-ager, the sprinkler on their flat front lawn spinning in the evening cool. Sarah trim and sardonic at the marriage counsellor's, under the pressed-paper panelling where the man had hung not only his diplomas but his Aspen skiing medals. Sarah some Sunday long ago raising the shades to wake him, light flooding her translucent nightgown. Sarah lifting her sudden eyes to him at some table, some moment, somewhere, in conspiracy—he hadn't known he had taken so many reels, they just kept coming in his head. Nevada beautifully, emptily poured by. The map was full of ghost towns. Laura sat beside him, reading the map. "Dad, here's a town called Nixon."

"Let's go feel sorry for it."

"You passed it. It was off the road after Sparks. The next real town is Lovelock."

"What's real about it?"

"Should you be driving so fast?"

In the back seat, Polly struggled with her needs. "Can we stop in the next real town to eat?"

Culp said, "You should have eaten more breakfast."

"I hate hash browns."

"But you like bacon."

"The hash browns had touched it."

Laura said, "Polly, stop bugging Daddy, you're making him nervous."

Culp told her, "I am *not* nervous."

Polly told her, "I can't keep holding it."

"Baby. You just went less than an hour ago."

"I'm nervous."

Culp laughed. Laura said, "You're not funny. You're not a baby anymore."

Polly said, "Yeah and you're not a wife, either."

Silence.

"Nobody said I was."

Nevada spun by. Sarah stepped out of a car, their old Corvair convertible, wearing a one-piece bathing suit. Her hair was stiff and sun-bleached and wild. She was eating a hot dog loaded with relish. Culp looked closer and there was sand in her ear, as in a delicate discovered shell.

Polly announced, "Dad, that sign said a place in three miles. 'Soft Drinks, Sandwiches, Beer, Ice, and Slots.' "

"Slots, slots," Laura spit, furious for a reason that eluded her father. "Slots and sluts, that's all there is in this dumb state."

Culp asked, "Didn't you enjoy Reno?"

"I hated it. What I hated especially was Mom acting on the make all the time."

On the make, sluts—the language of women living together, it occurred to him, coarsens like that of men in the Army. He mildly corrected, "I'm sure she wasn't on the make, she was just happy to be rid of me."

"Don't kid yourself, Dad. She was on the make. Even with Jim about to show up she was."

"Yeah, well," Polly said, "you weren't that pure yourself, showing off for that Mexican boy."

"I wasn't showing off for any bunch of spics, I was practicing my diving and I suggest you do the same, you toad. You look like a sick frog, the way you go off the board. A sick *fat* frog."

"Yeah, well. Mommy said you weren't so thin at my age yourself."

Culp intervened: "It's *nice* to be plump at your age. Otherwise, you won't have anything to shape up when you're Laura's age."

Polly giggled, scandalized. Laura said, "Don't flirt, Dad," and crossed her thighs; she was going to be one of those women, Culp vaguely saw, who have legs. She smoothed back the hair from her brow in a gesture that tripped the home-movie camera again: Sarah before the mirror. He could have driven forever this way; if he had known Nevada was so easy, he could have planned to reach the Utah line, or detoured north to some ghost towns. But they had made reservations in Elko, and stopped there. The motel was more of a hotel, four stories high; on the ground floor, a cavernous dark casino glimmered with the faces of the slots and the shiny uniforms of the change girls. Though it was only three in the afternoon, Culp wanted to go in there, to get a drink at the bar, where the bottles glowed like a row of illumined stalagmites. But his daughters, after inspecting their rooms, dragged him out into the sunshine. Elko was a flat town full of space, as airy as an empty honeycomb. The broad street in front of the hotel held railroad tracks in its center. To Polly's amazed delight, a real train—nightmarish in scale but docile in manner—materialized on these tracks, halted, ruminated, and then ponderously, thoughtfully dragged westward its chuckling infinity of freight cars. They walked down broad sunstruck sidewalks, past a drunken Indian dressed in clothes black as his shadow, to a museum of mining. Polly coveted the glinting nuggets, Laura yawned before a case of old-fashioned barbed wire and sought her reflection in the glass. Culp came upon an exhibit, between Indian beads and pioneer hardware, incongruously devoted to Thomas Alva Edison. He and Sarah and the girls, driving home through the peppery stenches of carbon waste and butane from a Sunday on the beach at Point Pleasant, would pass a service island on the Jersey Turnpike named for Edison. They would stop for supper at another one, named for Joyce Kilmer. The tar on the parking lot would sting their bare feet. Sarah would go in for her hot dog wearing her *dashiki* beach wrapper—hip length, with slits for her naked arms. These graceful arms would be burned pink in the crooks. The sun would have ignited a conflagration of clouds beyond the great Esso tanks. Here, in Elko, the sun rested gently on the overexposed purple of the ridges around them. On the highest ridge a large letter E had been somehow cut, or inset, in what seemed limestone. Polly asked why.

He answered, "I suppose for airplanes."

Laura amplified, "If they don't put initials up, the pilots can't tell the towns apart, they're all so boring."

"I like Elko," Polly said. "I wish we lived here."

"Yeah, what would Daddy do for a living?"

This was hard. In real life, he was a chemical engineer for a conglomerate that was planning to exploit Colorado shale. Polly said, "He could fix slot machines and then at night come back in disguise and play them so they'd pay him lots of money."

Both girls, it seemed to Culp, had forgotten that he would not be living with them in their future, that this peaceful dusty nowhere was all the future they had. He took Polly's hand, crossing the railroad tracks, though the tracks were arrow-straight and no train was materializing between here and the horizon.

Laura flustered him by taking his arm as they walked into the dining room, which was beyond the dark grotto of slots. The waitress slid an expectant glance at the child, after he had ordered a drink for himself. "No. She's only sixteen."

When the waitress had gone, Laura told him, "Everybody says I look older than sixteen; in Reno with Mom, I used to wander around in the places and nobody ever said anything. Except one old fart who told me they'd put him in jail if I didn't go away."

Polly asked, "Daddy, when're you going to play the slots?"

"I thought I'd wait till after dinner."

"That's too long."

"O.K., I'll play now. Just until the salad comes." He took a mouthful of his drink, pushed up from the table, and fed ten quarters into a machine Polly could watch. Though he won nothing, being there, amid the machines' warm and impetuous colors, consoled him. Experimenting, he pressed the button marked CHANGE. A girl in a red uniform crinkling like embers came to his side inquisitively. Her face, though not old, had the Western dryness—eyes smothered in charcoal, mouth tightened as if about to say, *I thought so.* But something sturdy and hollow-backed in her stance touched Culp, gave him an intuition. Her uniform's devilish cut bared her white arms to the shoulder. He gave her a five-dollar bill to change into quarters. The waitress was bringing the salad. Heavy in one pocket, he returned to the table.

"Poor Dad," Laura volunteered. "That prostitute really turned him on."

"Laura, I'm not sure you know what a prostitute is."

"Mom said every woman is a prostitute, one way or another."

"You know your mother exaggerates."

"I know she's a bitch, you mean."

"Laura."

"She *is,* Dad. Look what she's done to you. Now she'll do it to Jim."

"You and I have different memories of your mother. You don't remember her when you were little."

"I don't want to live with her, either. When we all get back to Denver, I want to live with *you.* If she and I live together, it'll always be competing, that's how it was in Reno; who needs it? When *I* get to forty, I'm going to tell my lover to shoot me."

Polly cried out—an astonishing noise, like the crash of a jackpot. "*Stop* it," she told Laura. "Stop talking big. That's all you do, is talk big." The child, salad dressing gleaming on her chin, pushed her voice toward her sister through tears: "You want Mommy and Daddy to fight all the time instead of love each other even though they *are* divorced."

With an amused smile, Laura turned her back on Polly's outburst and patted Culp's arm. "Poor Dad," she said. "Poor old Dad."

Their steaks came, and Polly's tears dried. They walked out into Elko again and at the town's one movie theater saw a Western. Burt Lancaster, a downtrodden Mexican, after many insults, including crucifixion, turned implacable avenger and killed nine hirelings of a racist rancher. Polly seemed to be sleeping through the bloodiest parts. They walked back through the dry night to the hotel. Their two adjoining rooms each held twin beds. Laura's suitcase had appeared on the bed beside his.

Culp said, "You'd better sleep with your sister."

"Why? We'll have the door between open, in case she has nightmares."

"I want to read."

"So do I."

"You go to sleep now. We're going to make Salt Lake tomorrow."

"Big thrill. Dad, she mumbles and kicks her covers all the time."

"Do as I say, love. I'll stay here reading until you're asleep."

"And then what?"

"I may go down and have another drink."

Her expression reminded him of how, in the movie, the villain had looked when Burt Lancaster showed that he, too, had a gun. Culp lay on the bedspread reading a pamphlet they had bought at the museum, about ghost towns; champagne and opera sets had been transported up the valleys, where now not a mule survived. Train whistles at intervals scooped long pockets from the world beyond his room. The breathing from the other room had fallen level. He tiptoed in and saw them both asleep, his daughters. Laura had been reading a book about the persecution of the Indians and now it lay beside her hand. How short her fingernails seemed! Relaxed, her face revealed its freckles, its plumpness, the sorrowing stretched smoothness of the closed lids. Polly's face wore a film of night sweat on her brow; his kiss came away tasting salty. He did not kiss Laura, in case she was faking. He switched off the light and stood considering what he must do. A train howled on the other side of the wall. The beautiful emptiness of Nevada, where he might never be again, sucked at the room like a whirlpool.

Downstairs, his intuition was borne out. The change girl had noticed him, and said now, "How's it going?"

"Fair. You ever go off duty?"

"What's duty?"

He waited at the bar, waiting for the bourbon to fill him; it couldn't, the room inside him kept expanding, and when she joined him, after one o'clock, sidling up on the stool (a cowboy moved over) in a taut cotton dress that hid the tops of her arms, the blur on her face seemed a product of her inner chemistry, not his. "You've a room?" As she asked him that, her jaw went square: Mrs. Morgan in a younger version.

"I do," he said, "but it's full of little girls."

She reached for his bourbon and sipped and said, in a voice older than her figure, "This place is lousy with rooms."

Culp arrived back in his own room after five. He must have been noisier than he thought, for a person in a white nightgown appeared in the connecting doorway. Culp could not see her features, she was a good height, she reminded him of nobody. Good. From the frozen pose of her, she was scared—scared of him. Good.

"Dad?"

"Yep."

"You O.K.?"

"Sure." Though already he could feel the morning sun grinding on his temples. "You been awake, sweetie? Sorry."

"I was worried about you." But Laura did not cross the threshold into his room.

"Very worried?"

"Naa."

"Listen. It's not your job to take care of me. It's my job to take care of you."

TOM MCNEAL

TRUE

Loud men always made me edgy, except when I was a little girl, and then it was loud boys. So on this particular night, the new guys in the cabin next door were definitely making me edgy. They were whooping it up big, the two of them, yelling and throwing empties and generally carrying on in the way youth will.

The fracas had been going on a while, since before "People's Court," according to Letty, and that began at seven thirty. Letty was watching the set, holding Mr. Finny in her lap, doing her best to conduct business as usual. I was sitting in the kitchen watching the TV with one eye and the cabin next door with the other. A personality was doing the eleven o'clock news when one of them came out back of their cabin with a rifle bigger than I knew existed, pointed it carefully at the moon and let fly twice, *Ka-blam! Ka-blam!* Rattled our pans each time, was how big it was.

Letty without looking up from the set said, "Those two're dangerous."

All the one with the rifle was wearing were these black briefs and he was singing a song I didn't know. I'll say this. His voice was not bad, except for its loudness, and he himself was not ugly. Letty, on her way to visit the refrigerator, peered over my shoulder for a second, then, after she'd been back at the set for a while, said very casually, "Why you watching those goons anyhow?"

I didn't know, so I said, "What kinda gun is that, Letty?"

"Sharps, I think." Letty knows guns, I never knew from where.

The one on the porch had started in on "Blue Moon," a little softer, almost crooning it, then all of a sudden stopped, reloaded, and fired off another one over the pines. *Ka-blam!*

The phone rang. It was Earl in the cabin on the other side. He was talking loud about the new neighbors. Earl's not normally excitable but he was in a definite state. I held the receiver a couple of inches from my ear and listened to him calling them shiftless, malicious, and impolite. The impolite part made me laugh and Earl stopped short and said, "This Letty or Lois?"

"Lois," I said and was remarking on the niceness of the crooning goon's voice when another shot went off next door and Letty grabbed the phone from me. In one breath Letty said to Earl that she hadn't called the police but somebody ought to because besides everything else she'd heard a little rumor about there being a body in the goons's freezer though she wasn't at liberty to say anything more about it.

"What body would that be?" I inquired when she was done lighting a fire under Earl.

Letty, to compose herself, began feeding Hershey's Kisses to Mr. Finny one at a time. Mr. Finny was short, plump, and more her dog than mine. Finally Letty said, "There was a girl with them when they moved in. That was three days ago. You seen any live girls over there in the last three days?"

"There was a girl moved in?" I said. It was news to me.

"She looked maybe twenty," Letty said. "Hard to tell because it was dark, but she looked out cold. They had to carry her in. Took her straight toward the back bedroom."

Mr. Finny let a half-eaten Kiss roll out of his mouth and waddled off to his water bowl.

"Thirsty," Letty said for him, and picked up the moist Kiss and resealed it in its foil wrapper with a smoothness worth watching. "Course if I was sheriff," she went on almost to herself, "I'd check the freezer. They got a freezer over there big enough to stash three or four girls her size in."

Letty had a way of believing anything that knitted into her feelings about someone. She didn't care for the two goons so she had no problem believing there was a corpse in their cooler. Same with our neighbor Sally Ann Newville. At first we liked Sally Ann—she brought over a casserole the day we moved in—but then Sally Ann's viewpoint changed and she began leaning back from us as we talked to her in the street, like there was a smell to us or something, so one time, after reading a story in the newspaper called, "Is Your Neighbor a Space Alien?" Letty decided Sally Ann *was* one. She sent her a letter that went, *Your neighbors in Big Bear know you're a space alien and have notified the appropriate local, state, and federal authorities.* "All it did was make her meaner," I heard Letty telling Earl later, like this was a big surprise.

It was during Johnny Carson's monologue that the black-and-white pulled up next door. The goons's cabin didn't have any curtains so with all the lights blazing you could watch the goings-on on this side of the house like it was a play on a stage. I saw the ugly goon peek out the front window and yell something over his shoulder to the not-ugly one, who quick pulled on his pants and stashed his buffalo gun in the big freezer.

There was just the one deputy, knocking the first time and pounding the second. Eventually the crooning goon answered the door and they all stood in the front room. The deputy was doing all the talking for a while, then the goons looked funny at each other and led him toward the bedroom on the other side of the cabin. What they were doing in there was anybody's guess, but, after a bit, out they all came grinning and laughing, even the deputy. The three of them gathered again out on the front porch. I heard the deputy saying things about older neighbors and quiet neighborhoods, and the goons were nodding and agreeing and waiting for him to leave.

The minute the squad car crested the hill and disappeared from view the two goons began their sermon. They spoke to us one at a time. "You shrivelled old dick," one of them yelled toward Earl's place, "you go to bed right now and pull the pillow over your Dumbo-sized ears or this'll turn into a night you'll surely regret." Earl's ears don't lay back so well and one evening when he'd had a few he told us he'd taped them back at night all during high school. I probably would've enjoyed an element in the goon's speech—it was the kind of thing a man like Earl needed every now and then—if it hadn't've been for the fact that the two of them were now directing their attention to the cabin across the road, which is owned by the Feenstras, who are as nice as nice can be, and it didn't take Sherlock Holmes to figure out we were next. Letty switched off the TV and all the lights and opened the near window, which we huddled close to. It was like waiting in the basement for a tornado.

But with us the tactics changed. "And how about our two magnolias in their cozy little cottage?" one of them sang out in a sickening-sweet voice. And the other one in singsong said, "In their solitary cabin's solitary bed!" They didn't stop there either.

Letty wound shut the window. She looked at me through the dark and in a whispery voice said, "Don't you listen," and with her huge hands was softly covering my ears.

I don't dislike men. The problem is it's never simple. Take, for example, Arthur. I was thirty-five and living in Lincoln when Arthur moved in next door. I was with Cy at the time. My ex. Cy was an old story. High school football star, teacher's college dropout, beer distributor, borderline alcoholic. He was going slack in a hurry. Nights he spent sipping Scotch and watching the set. I did a little housework and got good at crosswords. Lots of days I never got out of the robe. So I was ripe for Arthur. At first it was just to see if I was alive anymore, but in a little time I began in my heart to take it seriously. I had it bad in fact.

Arthur was married, but his wife worked at Hovland-Swanson, so she wasn't home days, and neither was Cy. For a living Arthur was a steward for this charter airline that toted V.I.P.'s wherever in the world they wanted to go next. He'd served Don Ho, the Rolling Stones, and Tab Hunter, just to name a few. Anyhow, one day out of the blue he says he's been transferred to L.A. I went right home and packed. It didn't work out, of course, and there I was.

Hewlett-Packard is where I met Letty. We were the only ones in the whole lunchroom who ate alone every day, so we tended to pay attention to each other. She's a big woman but her lunches consisted of just candy bars and yogurt. One day I sat down nearby and didn't say anything. Finally I did. "How come you eat so much chocolate?" I said. She smiled at me like she'd known me ages and said, "Because I used to drink, but now I eat a lot of chocolate instead." She told me about A.A. and made it sound fun. She had red cheeks and a laugh snappy as apples. I liked her.

Letty was pretty well fixed. She had her Hewlett-Packard wage plus a pension from her time in the Air Force, and she had this cabin, though she didn't mention that right off. When finally she did, she hardly looked at me. She was spooning herself yogurt at the time. "My husband and I bought it. For six hundred down. Then when the marriage fritzed he took the Corvette and I got the cabin. I thought I would use it more, but I don't."

A guy that would take a car over a cabin interested me. I asked about him. She shrugged. "Before we were married he acted like a human being and afterwards he didn't." Period.

"So how come you don't go up to your cabin more?" I said, getting back to that.

Letty was scraping her yogurt carton, making a real project of it. In a slow careful way she said, "Because the only person I'd want to go with wouldn't want to."

"Who?" I said, because I was really curious, but she wouldn't say, so I said, "Anyhow I'll bet you're wrong. Any man'd be a fool to say no to you." And then, without a thought, I said that I'd be happy to stand in for whoever it was she wasn't asking.

That first weekend Letty had us right off the bat down to the lake fishing out of a rowboat. I'd never fished before but by the end of the day I was a fishing fool. It was September. Sticks and leaves and shadows floated on the water. As Letty rowed us in that Sunday afternoon, they curled around the boat and closed after. She lifted the oars and for a long moment let us coast quietly ahead. I took a deep breath. There was something about the world around Letty that allowed you to nestle down into it and feel the kind of peacefulness I'd spent years trying to learn to live without.

We began spending all our weekends and holidays there. For Christmas, Letty gave me a black silk blouse in a box that said Bullocks Wilshire. "Came from there too," Letty said. When I put it on, she laughed her snappy laugh and said it was what I'd catch my next man in. I wore it New Year's Eve to the Antlers. That was where at about midnight we began to plot an early retirement so we could move up here permanent.

It only took us five years. That's what Letty said when we unlocked the front door with Mr. Finny at our feet and the car in the driveway full of everything in the world we owned.

"It only took us five years." We were real good friends by then, without any secrets I knew about. The idea was to add a bedroom when we could swing it. But in time I got afraid of trying to sleep without Letty breathing beside me, and the extra room never did get built.

I slept poorly the night of the fracas, so when Letty packed up for fishing that afternoon I begged off in favor of a nap. She got Mr. Finny's leash but didn't leave. "I'm going to say just one thing," she said, "and it's about those rummies next door. They're like a wave, a huge gigantic wave, and if we hold fast it'll pass by and we'll still be here. But if we let go and swim for it, we're goners." She gave me a long look. "You see what I mean?" I do now but didn't then, even though I nodded like I did.

After she left, I lay down to think what I was going to do, but my ideas went off in ten different directions. Outside, a scraping sound began repeating itself, so I looked out the window and there was the crooner out back, sharpening a knife. I watched him for quite a while. He was the not-ugly one, which for some reason made me think he was the less mean of the two, so I changed my blouse and went over there. The idea was to tell him that Letty and I were just two regular people who lived together under one roof just like him and his buddy did, nothing more or less, and that we all ought to let bygones be bygones.

When I got there though I just stood behind him and said, "Hi."

He glanced at me once and didn't say a word, merely kept sweeping the knife over the hone. Finally he held up the knife and in a friendly enough way said, "What kinda knife you think this is?"

"Arkansas toothpick?" I said, trying for humor.

He didn't even smile. "Randall-made Smithsonian Bowie," he said. "Cost me three C-notes and I had to wait two years to get it."

On the breeze was a faint odor I couldn't place.

"Ever see *The Iron Mistress,*" he said, "with Alan Ladd as Jim Bowie?—The knife he uses is this knife. The Smithsonian Bowie."

He straightened his back then squatted again. He hunched forward. I couldn't see the black briefs anywhere in the gap between his pants and his back. I was feeling a little giddy. "I always liked Alan Ladd," I said. "Only he hardly ever smiled."

The crooner smiled, just barely, but a smile all the same. He spat on a second hone of finer grit and began again to work the knife.

"Where's your buddy?" I said.

He glanced up. "We're alone if that's what you mean."

"Except for your girlfriend," I said.

This time his look had an edge to it, but then he relaxed himself. "Yeah," he said, "except for my girlfriend."

"She sick?"

He thought about it. "A little."

He switched sides of the blade with each sweep, slow and steady and almost hypnotizing. There was nothing but the sound of the air moving through the tall pines, and a truck in the distance changing gears, and the even sound of the blade on the stone. Except for the bad smell in the air, everything was nice, and all of a sudden he was looking at me while he worked. In his eyes was this calmness that affected me. He looked at me up and down, in and out of my blouse. It was the silk one Letty gave me, I probably should've mentioned that, and it always made me skittish. I don't know what I was considering. It could've been anything. But suddenly the scraping stopped and I heard him saying, "So speaking of best girls, where's yours?" and whatever I was considering changed.

"Fishing," I said, "and she's not my best girl." It didn't come out like I meant it, but I couldn't think of what to say next. That made me cranky, and so did the goon's beginning to polish his knife with a special little cloth he took out of a special little pouch. "Tell me if it's none of my business," I said, "but do you two have a line of work?"

The goon, like he was filling up with importance, raised from his squat. "Bounty hunters," he said, real solemn, and motioned me toward the tin shed they'd built out back.

The shed, it turned out, was where the bad smell was coming from. He opened the door and it got worse. I looked inside. There were furs stretched and tacked on boards and there were dog-shaped slabs of red meat with a sickening glisten to them.

"Coyotes," he said. "Thirty dollars per from a private party. Cash. Been averaging ten . . . *units* a day." He was grinning and putting his calm clammy eyes on me. "Your little mountain resort is just chock-full of unafraid coyotes."

I looked at them again. Even their legs were skinned.

He slid his knife along a curve of slick meat, then wiped it on his special little cloth. "So," he said, "how'd you come to find out about my girlfriend?"

"Grapevine," I said. A lie, and my face shows lies, so I threw in some truth. "And we saw you carrying her the night you moved in."

He looked surprised and then he didn't. We were looking at each other like something significant was on the line. I didn't blink. There were footsteps behind me and I still didn't blink.

"The night the deputy visited us he was real interested in the girlfriend," he said. "Which means whoever called in the sheriff's let what they knew of the girlfriend be known." He glanced over my shoulder then back to me. "And here in idle conversation I come to find out you two magnolias know plenty about the girlfriend."

"So guess who we have to feel called the deputy?" the other goon said, joining in from behind me.

"This isn't what I wanted to talk about," I said, turning round. What I remember about the second goon is the togetherness of his eyes. They made him look deficient. "I came to straighten things out," I said, swinging back to the crooner. "We've tried to be neighborly, but when you popped off last night you hurt Letty's feelings."

The crooner smiled. "Those weren't exactly shots in the dark. That was good information. From one of your neighborly neighbors."

I was wondering just who that would have been when the crooner's smile stretched wider. "Here's what I don't get. How a pretty little unit like you gets hooked up with someone shaggy as her."

"Like who?" I said, but the ugly one leaned in and took me out of my thoughts. His jaw worked, his eyes squinched littler and I thought, Here's the guy who can do the worst thing you can think of, and he did.

"What we want to know is who does what?" he said, which I didn't get, but then the one who I'd wanted to think was nice jumped in and said, "Who does the diddling and who does the giggling?"

My face had frozen up but the rest of me was moving. I felt like I was walking underwater. It took me ages to get to the house. In the kitchen I had to hold my hands one in the other to take the shake out of them. I don't know when I'd felt that scared or after I was through being scared that mad. I felt slapped and wanted to slap back. I couldn't help it, I just stepped out the front door and even though I couldn't see them anywhere I took a speaking position at the gate.

"I've seen you two before," I said in a voice as normal as I could make it. "It was when me and my husband Cy went to Key West, Florida, and stumbled into a hotel swarming with these men," I said and felt my voice rising, "young pretty-looking men in little black swimsuits like the kind you two are always sashaying around in as if your parts are a present to see!"

That was the whole spiel. It was plenty.

Letty came home that afternoon hauling a big cardboard box. "Fishing was bad," she said, "so we hunted bargains." She'd found a garage sale, and had bought a whole set of willowware, which she was spreading out on the table. I wouldn't say anything about them so finally Letty said, "I know what you're thinking. You're thinking, What would the two of us want with a whole set of willowware." That made me feel pretty funny. It was almost exactly what I'd been thinking. I wasn't talking, however. Letty studied me, then went back to her dishes. "So," she said without looking up, "what did you do all afternoon?"

"Nothing," I said, too quickly, and tried to patch it. "Slept."

Letty held a plate to the light. "Why the blouse?"

I'd forgotten to change. My face was getting hot and I needed to give it a reason. "For you," I said.

I could feel Letty peering into me. It was like she'd taken the lid off and was looking inside.

I said, "I thought you might like seeing me in it tonight after last night." This was a black lie, but once you've stopped telling the truth it's a hard thing to get turned around.

Letty believed me. She wanted to, so she did. She stared out the window toward the goons's cabin. "I was thinking about them today," she said. "I guess I don't have to tell you that whatever they think or say doesn't mean beans."

"Who said it did?" I said.

Letty kept looking out. It was getting dark. "There's something I'm ashamed of," she said. She took a deep breath. "It's that I thought you might've gone over there today. I thought it once while I was out and then again for a minute just now." Her face was changing. She looked at me and made an awful smile to keep from crying. "You didn't though, did you?"

"No," I said, "why would I?" and before she could answer turned on the set and began a silence between us that lasted till supper.

Just to put the record straight, Letty was never overly familiar with me. Sometimes in the night she'd cover my breast with her hand, but softly, I would compare it to a whisper. I won't say my nipples never perked, but that was just natural, and if it gave Letty thoughts she never showed it. So I can say to whoever might wonder what went on between us that the answer is almost nothing. But love can take a lot of funny forms. In fact, you could talk me into thinking that it takes nothing but. In my years with Letty, for example, I moved within it, room to room, not giving it a thought until one night two boys called it what it wasn't and gave me doubts.

Mr. Finny had his own doggy door, so he could go out to the yard, which was fenced, whenever he felt like taking care of business. That night we used the willowware for the only time we ever did, and then, while we were watching a movie on the cable, Mr. Finny went out for the last time. A half hour passed before Letty realized he hadn't come in, so she went out to call.

Nothing.

I got the flashlight out. The front gate was ajar. We began to walk, then to drive. We would shut off the motor and stand outside listening for the clinking of his chain or his particular bark. This went on for three days. Letty was miserable and, I'll tell you the truth, I wanted him back alive but a couple of times I was so tired I thought it might be a relief to find him a goner on the road just so we could go home and go to bed knowing what the final score was.

On the third night I said, "Letty, do you remember how the other day I said I just napped? I was fibbing. I went over to the goons's to be nice and straighten things out but they just thought I was silly." I looked at Letty. "I said some things. I think I might've gotten their goat."

The dashboard threw a pale green light and made Letty's eyes look like little caves. I knew something was going on—sadness I thought—but when I put my hand on her arm she pushed it away and in a cold un-Letty-like voice said, "I knew it."

The next day Letty watched the two goons drive off and we walked over there and tried the door. It was open.

"Anybody home?" Letty called when we stepped in. I guess she was thinking about the girl, but nobody answered.

We began to nose around. Letty went back to the freezer. I went into the bedrooms. They were both a mess. There were sheets over the windows and their clothes were in cardboard boxes. Somebody had been busy on the only dresser—there was what looked like gunpowder and stuffing and that sort of thing. In the second closet I found the girl they'd carried in. She was the store-window kind. They had her in a blonde wig, khaki pants, and no shirt. There were these huge coconut halves cupped over her breasts with red Christmas bulbs for nipples. I took her over to a socket and plugged her in. One didn't work but the other one did. It was a blinker. I headed off to the kitchen with the so-called corpse over my shoulder, thinking somehow that it'd put Letty in a calmer frame of mind.

She was standing in the kitchen holding Mr. Finny frozen dead.

"Letty," I said.

She sat down.

Ten minutes went by and I said, "Maybe we should be going."

But Letty set Mr. Finny down, went like a zombie to the freezer and came back with the buffalo gun and a box of shells. She loaded two and stood four more in a row on the table in front of her.

I picked up the box. Hi-Power, it said. Triple-wadding, denser patterns, fewer strays. "Letty," I said, "let's leave now."

She wasn't talking. I looked at her and knew she was way past all the regular things people feel. Maybe thirty minutes passed before we heard them at the front door. Letty got her hands around the gun and leaned forward. The goons came in together and made a quick read of things—the dog dead and Letty grim and the shells set out in a row. They began moving inchmeal away from each other, fanning out. Letty pointed the gun and they stopped. "Let me explain," the crooner said, "I can explain. The dog got into one of our traps is what happened. What you've got is just a part-picture."

It sounded lame and anyhow Letty wasn't ready to listen to anything. They could see that. She was pointing the gun and looking harder and harder at the two goons and in return they were looking worse and worse. "Stand close," she said, and when they did she said, "Close your eyes," and they did that too.

The first shot exploded and the crooning goon's legs crumpled him to his knees, but there was no blood, that was the first clue. The second goon was looking whitefaced at his buddy when the gun went off again and his body just froze there.

After a still moment they began feeling themselves.

I grabbed for the other shells lined up there, and for the box, too, I don't know why. The second goon was looking confused at Letty, as if he couldn't understand how she could've missed.

"Letty, please," I said, but I don't think she heard.

The crooning goon tried to push himself up. "You stay sat," Letty said, and he slithered back down. Letty was looking around for the box of shells like she didn't see me take them. The second goon was staring above him at the wall where the shots went.

Letty kept the gun on them. "All I care about now is making you two die in a way that suits you," she said, "something real agonizing." She was looking so weird and serious you had to believe her. "You'll think of killing me first but you can't because I'm already dead," she said. "A vapor. Know what I mean by that?" They were listening carefully. One of them was even nodding. Letty asked me to get a sack for Mr. Finny and I did and then she put the gun down and we walked out of there and buried Mr. Finny behind the cabin, deep in the ground, beyond predators.

That night, while Letty slept, I watched the goons move. They worked fast and kept it quiet. Dark, too. They threw their stuff in the back of their van, then coasted it down the driveway and past Earl's before they fired it up, turned on their headlights and, after lobbing a couple of bottles onto the pavement and letting out a few last whoops, drove off toward somebody else's neighborhood.

I went in to Letty and whispered, "They're gone for good," but she was out like a light. For dinner I'd made her some soup, which she wouldn't take, and then some thick hot chocolate laced with Nytols, which she did.

Word of what happened travelled fast. By nine the next morning Anne Feenstra, who worked years for See's, brought us a platter of homemade coconut creams, maybe two dozen of them. Letty ate them all by noon, and a couple of Baby Ruths besides. Earl came by and cleaned up the last of Mr. Finny's business in the front yard and raked pine needles and without saying anything made himself helpful. Letty avoided me. If I was inside she went out. If I came outside she went in. Her eyes were half-open and wherever she went she stood half-staring off at who knew what. In the afternoon I found my black silk blouse wadded up in the trash under the sink, and I noticed the beer we kept on hand for Earl was gone from the refrigerator.

"We've got us," I said to myself out loud, just to hear it, though I knew when I said it that when it had been true I hadn't really believed it, and now that I did believe it I could see it wasn't true anymore. That night I stayed awake all night with my arm around Letty, but the next night I couldn't stay awake and somehow or other she got away. I woke up and she was gone.

The only word I got was a note in Letty's hand that went, *Car's at the bus depot in San Berdoo. Keep busy. Love, Letty.* The envelope was postmarked Amarillo. Amarillo, I thought. Amarillo made no sense at all. Neither did keep busy.

Earl took me down to get the car, but before heading back up the hill we went to Danuvios for Mexican, and after two glasses of beer. Earl, who can be sly, said, "How about before calling it a day I run you by the pound?" As soon as I got out of the car and heard them all yapping I knew I'd been had. I took one who was supposed to be part Shih Tzu. She had a caved-in face and not a lot of pep, but she wouldn't take her eyes off me.

A day or two later Sally Ann Newville came over with a couple of romance novels she said she thought I might like. I doubted that but I was just sitting with Earl over coffee, so I asked her in for a cup.

"I'd take some Lipton's tea if you had some," she said to me and gave Earl a big smile. I wondered what Earl looked like to her. Anymore all I see when I look at Earl is his Dumbo-sized ears.

"Cookies?" I said.

"Maybe just one." She was looking at my dog with suspicion.

"Her name's Paula," I said. "I don't know why the name. It just came to me." I scooted Sally Ann her tea and cookies.

"Well," Sally Ann said, still looking at the dog, "fleas can't live up at this altitude. That's one good thing."

That got me, that the best thing she could think of to say about my new dog was that fleas couldn't live on her. I went into a slow burn. Said nothing. Earl, how ever, was taking up the slack. He was being quite a talker. I remember him telling a joke about a wart and a frog that I didn't laugh at. Sally Ann did, extra loud, and afterwards said, "Earl, you're an original!" which of course stoked Earl completely. He kept talking and talking. While she listened Sally Ann took the string from her teabag and began to floss with it. Finally Earl wound down and I said, "Sally Ann, did you ever get a letter about being a space alien?"

Sally Ann said she didn't remember anything like that.

"Letty and I sent it."

Sally Ann got prim and looked at her lap. "I knew that."

I said, "How would you have known that?"

Sally Ann shrugged. Her face was bland as bland can be. It was like a mask of her face. I went fishing. I said, "Those two goons said you talked to them a couple of times."

You should've seen her real face arrive. "Only once."

"They said you said we were dykes." This was a lie, but it didn't really sound like one.

"I didn't say that word," Sally Ann said. "I've never said that word. And I'm not used to hearing that word while I'm a guest in someone's home."

Oh yeah?

"*Dyke!*" I heard myself yell. "*Dyke!Dyke!Dyke!Dyke! Dyke!*"—like I was a needle stitching it into her. "There! Now you're used to it."

After she left, Earl, who'd sat sipping coffee through all this, smiled and said, "Well, I guess it's safe to say you overreacted."

I said, "Well, that was for Letty." And it was. It was for you, Letty.

Earl went to the stove and poured himself a refill. He put in the condensed milk first, then the coffee, so it never even began black. Letty always began with it black. With one hand she'd start her coffee into a nice easy swirl and then with the other she'd slowly pour in the lightener.

"Cold enough to snow," Earl said, and began picking through the newspaper. He was right. It did snow. It's been snowing. The new dog and I go walking in it. It's a deep dry snow, with a waiting stillness to it, soft and quiet to be in.

RICK DEMARINIS

UNDER THE WHEAT

Down in D-3 I watch the sky gunning through the aperture ninety-odd feet above my head. The missiles are ten months away, and I am lying on my back listening to the sump. From the bottom of a hole, where the weather is always the same cool sixty-four degrees, plus or minus two, I like to relax and watch the clouds slide through the circle of blue light. I have plenty of time to kill. The aperture is about fifteen feet wide. About the size of a silver dollar from here. A hawk just drifted by. Eagle. Crow. Small cumulus. Nothing. Nothing. Wrapper.

Hot again today, and the sky is drifting across the hole, left to right, a slow thick wind that doesn't gust. When it gusts, it's usually from Canada. Fierce, with hail the size of eyeballs. I've seen wheat go down. Acres and acres of useless straw.

But sometimes it comes out of the southeast, from Bismarck, bringing ten-mile-high anvils with it, and you find yourself looking for funnels. This is not tornado country to speak of. The tornado path is to the south and west of here. They walk up from Bismarck and farther south and peter out on the Montana border, rarely touching ground anywhere near this latitude. Still, you keep an eye peeled. I've seen them put down gray fingers to the west, not quite touching but close enough to make you want to find a hole. They say it sounds like freight trains in your yard. I wouldn't know. We are from the coast, where the weather is stable and always predictable because of the ocean. We are trying to adjust.

I make five hundred a week doing this, driving a company pickup from hole to hole, checking out the sump pumps. I've found only one failure in two months. Twenty feet of black water in the hole and rising. It's the company's biggest headache. The high water table of North Dakota. You can dig twelve feet in any field and have yourself a well. You can dig yourself a shallow hole, come back in a few days and drink. That's why the farmers here have it made. Except for hail. Mostly they are Russians, these farmers.

Karen wants to go back. I have to remind her it's only for one year. Ten more months. Five hundred a week for a year. But she misses things. The city, her music lessons, movies, the beach, excitement. We live fairly close to a town, but it's one you will never hear of unless a local goes wild and chainsaws all six members of his family. The movie theater has shown *Bush Pilot, Red Skies of Montana, Ice Palace,* and *Kon Tiki* so far. These are movies we would not ordinarily pay money to see. She has taken to long walks in the evenings to work out her moods, which are getting harder and harder for me to pretend aren't there. I get time and a half on Saturdays, double time Sundays and holidays, and thirteen dollars per diem for the inconvenience of relocating all the way from Oxnard, California. That comes to a lot. You don't walk away from a gold mine like that. I try to tell Karen she has to make the effort, adjust. North Dakota isn't all that bad. As a matter of fact, I sort of enjoy the area. Maybe I am more adaptable. We live close to a large brown lake, an earthfill dam loaded with northern pike. I bought myself a little boat and often go out to troll a bit before the car pool comes by. The freezer is crammed with fish, not one under five pounds.

There's a ghost town on the other side of the lake. The houses were built for the men who worked on the dam. That was years ago. They are paintless now, weeds up to the rotten sills. No glass in the windows, but here and there a rag of drape. Sometimes I take my boat across the lake to the ghost town. I walk the overgrown streets and look into the windows. Sometimes something moves. Rats. Gophers. Wind. Loose boards. Sometimes nothing.

When the weather is out of Canada you can watch it move south, coming like a giant roll of silver dough on the horizon. It gets bigger fast and then you'd better find cover. If the cloud is curdled underneath, you know it means hail. The wind can gust to one hundred knots. It scares Karen. I tell her there's nothing to worry about. Our trailer is on a good foundation and tied down tight. But she has this dream of being uprooted and of flying away in such a wind. She sees her broken body caught in a tree, magpies picking at it. I tell her the trailer will definitely not budge. Still, she gets wild-eyed and can't light a cigarette.

We're sitting at the dinette table looking out the window, watching the front arrive. You can feel the trailer bucking like a boat at its moorings. Lightning is stroking the blond fields a mile away. To the southeast, I can see a gray finger reaching down. This is unusual, I admit. But I say nothing to Karen. It looks like the two fronts are going to butt heads straight over the trailer park. It's getting dark fast. Something splits the sky behind the trailer and big hail pours out. The streets of the park are white and jumping under the black sky. Karen has her hands up to her ears. There's a stampede on our tin roof. Two TV antennas fold at the same time in a dead faint. A jagged Y of lightning strikes so close you can smell it. Electric steam. Karen is wild, screaming. I can't hear her. Our garbage cans are rising. They are floating past the windows into a flattened wheat field. This is something. Karen's face is closed. She doesn't enjoy it at all, not at all.

I'm tooling around in third on the usual bad road, enjoying the lurches, rolls, and twists. I would not do this to my own truck. The fields I'm driving through are wasted. Head-on with the sky and the sky never loses. I've passed a few unhappy-looking farmers standing in their fields with their hands in their pockets, faces frozen in an expression of disgust, spitting. Toward D-8, just over a rise and down into a narrow gulch, I found a true glacier. It was made out of hail stones welded together by their own impact. It hadn't begun to melt yet. Four feet thick and maybe thirty feet long. You can stand on it and shade your eyes from the white glare. You could tell yourself you are inside the Arctic Circle. What is this, the return of the Ice Age?

Karen did not cook tonight. Another "mood." I poke around in the fridge. I don't know what to say to her anymore. I know it's hard. I can understand that. This is not Oxnard. I'll give her that. I'm the first to admit it. I pop a beer and sit down at the table opposite her. Our eyes don't meet. They haven't for weeks. We are like two magnetic north poles, repelling each other for invisible reasons. Last night in bed I touched her. She went stiff. She didn't have to say a word. I took my hand back. I got the message. There was the hum of the air conditioner and nothing else. The world could have been filled with dead bodies. I turned on the lights. She got up and lit a cigarette after two tries. Nerves. "I'm going for a walk, Lloyd," she said, checking the sky. "Maybe we should have a baby?" I said. "I'm making plenty of money." But she looked at me as if I had picked up an ax.

I would like to know where she finds to go and what she finds to do there. She hates the town worse than the trailer park. The trailer park has a rec hall and a social club for the wives. But she won't take advantage of that. I know the neighbors are talking. They think she's a snob. They think I spoil her. After she left I went out on the porch and drank eleven beers. Let them talk.

Three farm kids. Just standing outside the locked gate of D-4. "What do you kids want?" I know what they want. A "look-see." Security measures are in effect, but what the hell. There is nothing here yet but a ninety-foot hole with a tarp on it and a sump pump in the bottom. They are excited when I open the access hatch and invite them to climb down the narrow steel ladder to the bottom. They want to know what ICBM stands for. What is a warhead? How fast is it? How do you know if it's really going to smear the right town? What if it went straight up and came straight down? Can you hit the moon? "Look at the sky up there, kids," I tell them. "Lie on your backs, like this, and after a while you sort of get the feeling you're looking *down,* from on top of it." The kids lie down on the concrete. Kids have a way of giving all their attention to something interesting. I swear them to secrecy, not for my protection, because who cares, but because it will make their day. They will run home, busting with secret info. I drive off to D-9, where the sump trouble was.

Caught three lunkers this morning. All over twenty-four inches. It's 7:00 A.M. now and I'm on Ruby Street, the ghost town. The streets are all named after stones. Why I don't know. This is nothing like anything we have on the coast. Karen doesn't like the climate or the people and the flat sky presses down on her from all sides and gives her bad dreams, sleeping and awake. But what can I *do?*

I'm on Onyx Street, number 49, a two-bedroom bungalow with a few pieces of furniture left in it. There is a chest of drawers in the bedroom, a bed with a rotten gray mattress. There is a closet with a raggedy slip in it. The slip has brown water stains on it that look like burns. In the bottom of the chest is a magazine, yellow with age. *Secret Confessions.* I can imagine the woman who lived here with her husband. Not much like Karen at all. But what did she do while her husband was off working on the dam? Did she stand at this window in her slip and wish she were back in Oxnard? Did she cry her eyes out on this bed and think crazy thoughts? Where is she now? Does she think, "This is July 15, 1962, and I am glad I am not in North Dakota anymore"? Did she take long walks at night and not cook? I have an impulse to do something odd, and do it.

When a thunderhead passes over a cyclone fence that surrounds a site, such as the one passing over D-6 now, you can hear the wire hiss with nervous electrons. It scares me because the fence is a perfect lightning rod, a good conductor. But I stay on my toes. Sometimes, when a big cumulus is overhead stroking the area and roaring, I'll just stay put in my truck until it's had its fun.

Because this is Sunday, I am making better than twelve dollars an hour. I'm driving through a small farming community called Spacebow. A Russian word, I think, because you're supposed to pronounce the *e*. No one I know does. Shade trees on every street. A Russian church here, grain elevator there. No wind. Hot for 9:00 A.M.. Men dressed in Sunday black. Ladies in their best. Kids looking uncomfortable and controlled. Even the dogs are behaving. There is a woman, manless I think, because I've seen her before, always alone on her porch, eyes on something far away. A "thinker." Before today I've only waved hello. First one finger off the wheel, nod, then around the block once again and the whole hand out the window and a smile. That was last week. After the first turn past her place today she waves back. A weak hand at first, as if she's not sure that's what I meant. But after a few times around the block she knows that's what I meant. And so I'm stopping. I'm going to ask for a cup of cold water. I'm thirsty anyway. Maybe all this sounds hokey to you if you are from some big town like Oxnard, but this is not a big town like Oxnard.

Her name is Myrna Dan. That last name must be a pruned-down version of Danielovitch or something because the people here are mostly Russians. She is thirty- two, a widow, one brat. A two-year-old named "Piper," crusty with food. She owns a small farm here but there is no one to work it. She has a decent allotment from the U.S. government and a vegetable garden. If you are from the coast you would not stop what you were doing to look at her. Her hands are square and the fingers stubby, made for rough wooden handles. Hips like gateposts.

No supper again. Karen left a note. "Lloyd, I am going for a walk. There are some cold cuts in the fridge." It wasn't even signed. Just like that. One of these days on one of her walks she is going to get caught by the sky which can change on you in a minute.

Bill Finkel made a remark on the way in to the dispatch center. It was a little personal and coming from anybody else I would have called him on it. But he is the lead engineer, the boss. A few of the other guys grinned behind their hands. How do I know where she goes or why? I am not a swami. If it settles her nerves, why should I push it? I've thought of sending her to Ventura to live with her mother for a while, but her mother is getting senile and has taken to writing mean letters. I tell Karen the old lady is around the bend, don't take those letters too seriously. But what's the use when the letters come in like clockwork, once a week, page after page of nasty accusations in a big, inch-high scrawl, like a kid's, naming things that never happened. Karen takes it hard, no matter what I say, as if what the old lady says is true.

Spacebow looks deserted. It isn't. The men are off in the fields, the women are inside working toward evening. Too hot outside even for the dogs who are sleeping under the porches. Ninety-nine. I stopped for water at Myrna's. Do you want to see a missile silo? Sure, she said, goddamn right, just like that. I have an extra hard hat in the truck but she doesn't have to wear it if she doesn't want to. Regulations at this stage of the program are a little pointless. Just a hole with a sump in it. Of course you can fall into it and get yourself killed. That's about the only danger. But there are no regulations that can save you from your own stupidity. Last winter when these holes were being dug, a kid walked out on a tarp. The tarp was covered with light snow and he couldn't tell where the ground ended and the hole began. He dropped the whole ninety feet and his hard hat did not save his ass. Myrna is impressed with this story. She is very anxious to see one. D-7 is closest to Spacebow, only a mile out of town. It isn't on my schedule today, but so what. I hand her the orange hat. She has trouble with the chin strap. I help her cinch it. Piper wants to wear it too and grabs at the straps, whining. Myrna has big jaws. Strong. But not in an ugly way.

I tell her the story about Jack Stern, the Jewish quality control man from St. Louis who took flying lessons because he wanted to be able to get to a decent-sized city in a hurry whenever he felt the need. This flat empty farmland made his ulcer flare. He didn't know how to drive a car, and yet there he was, tearing around the sky in a Bonanza. One day he flew into a giant hammerhead— thinking, I guess, that a cloud like that is nothing but a lot of water vapor, no matter what shape it has or how big—and was never heard from again. That cloud ate him and the Bonanza. At the airport up in Minot they picked up two words on the emergency frequency, "Oh no," then static.

I tell her the story about the motor pool secretary who shot her husband once in the neck and twice in the foot with a target pistol while he slept. Both of them pulling down good money, too. I tell her the one about the one that got away. A northern as big as a shark. Pulled me and my boat a mile before my twelve-pound test monofilament snapped. She gives me a sidelong glance and makes a buzzing sound as if to say, *That* one takes the cake, Mister! We are on the bottom of D-7, watching the circle of sky, lying on our backs.

The trailer *stinks.* I could smell it from the street as soon as I got out of Bill Finkel's car. Fish heads. *Heads!* I guess they've been sitting there like that most of the afternoon. Just the big alligator jaws of my big beautiful pikes, but not the bodies. A platter of them, uncooked, drying out, and getting high. Knife, fork, napkin, glass. I'd like to know what goes on inside her head, what passes for thinking in there. The note: "Lloyd, eat your fill." Not signed. Is this supposed to be humor? I fail to get the point of it. I have to carry the mess to the garbage cans without breathing. A wind has come up. From the southeast. A big white fire is blazing in the sky over my shoulder. You can hear the far-off rumble, like a whale grunting. I squint west, checking for funnels.

Trouble in D-7. Busted sump. I pick up Myrna and Piper and head for the hole. It's a nice day for a drive. It could be a bearing seizure, but that's only a percentage guess. I unlock the gate and we drive to the edge of it. Space- age artillery, I explain, as we stand on the lip of D-7, feeling the vertigo. The tarp is off for maintenance and the hole is solid black. If you let your imagination run, you might see it as bottomless. The "Pit" itself. Myrna is holding Piper back. Piper is whining, she wants to see the hole. Myrna has to slap her away, scolding. I drain my beer and let the can drop. I don't hear it hit. Not even a splash. I grab the fussing kid and hold her out over the hole. "Have yourself a *good* look, brat," I say. I hold her by the ankle with one hand. She is paralyzed. Myrna goes so white I have to smile.

"Oh wait," she says. "Please, Lloyd. No." As if I ever would.

Myrna wants to see the D-flight control center. I ask her if she has claustrophobia. She laughs, but it's no joke. That far below the surface inside that capsule behind an eight-ton door can be upsetting if you're susceptible to confinement. The elevator is slow and heavy, designed to haul equipment. The door opens on a dimly lit room. Spooky. There's crated gear scattered around. And there is the door, one yard thick to withstand the shock waves from the Bomb. I wheel it open. Piper whines, her big eyes distrustful. There is a musty smell in the dank air. The lights and blower are on now, but it will take a while for the air to freshen itself up. I wheel the big door shut. It can't latch yet, but Myrna is impressed. I explain to her what goes on in here. We sit down at the console. I show her where the launch enabling switches will be and why it will take two people together to launch an attack, the chairs fifteen feet apart and both switches turned for a several-second count before the firing sequence can start, in case one guy goes berserk and decides to end the world because his old lady has been holding out on him, or just for the hell of it, given human nature. I show her the escape hole. It's loaded with ordinary sand. You pull this chain and the sand dumps into the capsule. Then you climb up the tube that held the sand into someone's wheat field. I show her the toilet and the little kitchen. I can see there is something on her mind. Isolated places make you think of weird things. It's happened to me more than once. Not here, but in the ghost town on the other side of the lake.

Topside the weather has changed. The sky is the color of pikebelly, wind rising from the southeast. To the west I can see stubby funnels pushing down from the overcast, but only so far. It looks like the clouds are growing roots. We have to run back to the truck in the rain, Piper screaming on Myrna's hip. A heavy bolt strikes less than a mile away. A blue fireball sizzles where it hits. Smell the ozone. It makes me sneeze.

This is the second day she's been gone. I don't know where or how. All her clothes are here. She doesn't have any money. I don't know what to do. There is no police station. Do I call her mother? Do I notify the FBI? The highway patrol? Bill Finkel?

Everybody in the car pool knows but won't say a word, out of respect for my feelings. Bill Finkel has other things on his mind. He is worried about rumored economy measures in the assembly and check-out program next year. It has nothing to do with me. My job ends before that phase begins. I guess she went back to Oxnard, or maybe Ventura. But how?

We are in the D-flight control center. Myrna, with her hard hat cocked to one side, wants to fool around with the incomplete equipment. Piper is with her grandma. We are seated at the control console and she is pretending to work her switch. She has me pretend to work my switch. She wants to launch the entire flight of missiles, D-1 through D-10, at Cuba or Panama. Why Cuba and Panama? I ask. What about Russia? Why not Cuba or Panama? she says. Besides, I have Russian blood. Everyone around here has Russian blood. No, it's Cuba and Panama. Just think of the looks on their faces. All those people lying in the sun on the decks of those big white holiday boats, the coolies out in the cane fields, the tinhorn generals, the whole shiteree. They'll look up trying to shade their eyes but they won't be able to. What in hell is this all about, they'll say, then *zap,* poof, *gone.*

I feel it too, craziness like hers. What if I couldn't get that eight-ton door open, Myrna? I see her hard hat wobble, her lip drop. What if? Just what *if?* She puts her arms around me and our hard hats click. She is one strong woman.

Lloyd, Lloyd, she says.

Yo.

Jesus.

Easy.

Lloyd!

Bingo.

It's good down here—no *rules*—and she goes berserk. But later she is calm and up to mischief again. I recognize the look now. Okay, I tell her. What *next,* Myrna? She wants to do something halfway nasty. This, believe me, doesn't surprise me at all.

I'm sitting on the steel floor listening to the blower and waiting for Myrna to finish her business. I'm trying hard to picture what the weather is doing topside. It's not easy to do. It could be clear and calm and blue or it could be wild. There could be a high, thin overcast or there could be nothing. You just can't know when you're this far under the wheat. I can hear her trying to work the little chrome lever, even though I told her there's no plumbing yet. Some maintenance yokel is going to find Myrna's "surprise." She comes out, pretending to be sheepish, but I can see that the little joke tickles her.

Something takes my hook and strips off ten yards of line then stops dead. Snag. I reel in. The pole is bent double and the line is singing. Then something lets go but it isn't the line because I'm still snagged. It breaks the surface, a lady's shoe. It's brown and white with a short heel. I toss it into the bottom of the boat. The water is shallow here, and clear. There's something dark and wide under me like a shadow on the water. An old farmhouse, submerged when the dam filled. There's a deep current around the structure. I can see fence, tires, an old truck, feed pens. There is a fat farmer in the yard staring up at me, checking the weather, and I jump away from him, almost tipping the boat. My heart feels tangled in my ribs. But it's only a stump with arms.

The current takes my boat in easy circles. A swimmer would be in serious trouble. I crank up the engine and head back. No fish today. So be it. Sometimes you come home empty-handed. The shoe is new, stylish, and was made in Spain.

I'm standing on the buckled porch of 49 Onyx Street. Myrna is inside reading *Secret Confessions:* "What My Don Must Never Know." The sky is bad. The lake is bad. It will be a while before we can cross back. I knock on the door, as we planned. Myrna is on the bed in the stained, raggedy slip, giggling. "Listen to this dogshit, Lloyd," she says. But I'm not in the mood for weird stories. "I brought you something, honey," I say. She looks at the soggy shoe. "That?" But she agrees to try it on, anyway. I feel like my own ghost, bumping into the familiar but run-down walls of my old house in the middle of nowhere, and I remember my hatred of it. "Hurry up," I say, my voice true as a razor.

A thick tube hairy with rain is snaking out of the sky less than a mile away. Is it going to touch? "They never do, Lloyd. This isn't Kansas. Will you please listen to this dogshit?" Something about a pregnant high school girl, Dee, locked in a toilet with a knitting needle. Something about this Don who believes in purity. Something about bright red blood. Something about ministers and mothers and old-fashioned shame. I'm not listening, even when Dee slides the big needle in. I have to keep watch on the sky, because there is a first time for everything, even if this is not Kansas. The wind is stripping shingles from every roof I see. A long board is spinning like a slow propeller. The funnel is behind a bluff, holding back. But I can hear it, the freight trains. Myrna is standing behind me, running a knuckle up and down my back. "Hi, darling," she says. "Want to know what I did while you were out working on the dam today?" The dark tube has begun to move out from behind the bluff, but I'm not sure which way. "Tell me," I say. "Tell me."

WILLIAM KITTREDGE

THE UNDERGROUND RIVER

Red Yount took his time. While the cold November wind was moving like distant water through the tops of yellow-barked ponderosas, Cleve recollected last night's dream, something dreamed so often: a long-haired and ragged old man on a lean gray horse galloping down an undulating grass-covered slope toward the straw-roofed buildings of a creekside village, willow thatch houses behind yellowing grain patches, aspens and evergreens beyond the water. Soundless, framed by fir boughs, shotgun upraised in the man's right hand, forearm corded and hard, the horse galloping endlessly on, seemingly to attack.

"He never *was* sensible when he drank," the deputy said in the midst of saying all the rest. He meant Lonnie; he wasn't talking about Indians in general. Cleve kept staring at his own feet, inch-deep in pumice dust as loose and yellow as corn flour.

The sheriff in Donan had sent Red Yount out here when the word came north from Red Bluff: Lonnie had died the night before in the Tehema County drunk tank, which meant he had managed to live 123 days since coming of legal age and collecting his share of the tribal money. "Leastwise," Red Yount said, "you can afford to bury him." Cleve nodded. The money had led to this: over forty-three thousand dollars which had been seven years drawing interest in a Portland bank. Cleve, who had been resisting two years, since his own twenty-first birthday, had given in to what seemed common sense and taken his own money at the same time, an identical $43,639.42.

"What the hell," the deputy said. His car was a year-old black Plymouth Fury. "Wasn't like a surprise. What do you think? You don't say nothing."

"I was remembering how he acted in jail," Cleve said. "He stayed out a long time."

"He done good that way."

"Yeah," Cleve said. "He done all right. Lasted a number of years." The deputy said the coroner's verdict had been alcohol poisoning. Some balding, half-failed white physician had decided that and scribbled those words on a death certificate, which would later be retyped by some dreaming, erasing girl. "A number of years." Behind the wind's cold sound Cleve could sense the murmuring of the low, dead river below the cut sod bank just back of the house. Lately, since Lonnie left, he had been imagining the water's sound even when he wasn't hearing it. All his life he had gone to bed with that murmur, awakened with it, slept beneath it, lain sleepless listening to Lonnie's tubercular breath and the summer water. His father had built the four-room house in the spring and summer of 1947, when Cleve was two and Lonnie was on his way to being born, with planks and nails bought the fall of 1945 with army mustering-out pay, warped planks and rusted nails by 1947. The building seemed to contain what they were in the way it looked: peeling, never repainted, standing alone above the river in the eddying yellow dust.

"So he finally got away from here," the deputy said. "Anyway, that must have made him happy."

"Probably so."

"We'll get him home," the deputy said. "But you got to do something about having him buried."

"Give me a minute," Cleve said. "I want to get my coat and hook a ride with you"—which he knew was against the rules, probably illegal.

But the near-winter wind was burning from the clear and dry southern sky, and he figured Yount, who had been Indian deputy since before Cleve was born, wouldn't refuse him this time. Yount had come home to this job, a decorated ex-Marine returning from Okinawa in 1945. "Ain't supposed to be giving any rides," the deputy said. "You duck down if we meet somebody. I'll leave you off before we get into town."

"Come on in with me," Cleve said. He was surprised when Yount followed him toward the house, head turned from the wind. The coal-oil lantern on the table was flickering in the drafts, and on a white muslin cloth beside it lay the disassembled parts of a secondhand Remington .30-06 Cleve had been checking and oiling. He had bought the rifle in a Klamath Falls hockshop and wanted to be sure everything was perfect, that nothing was worn and that none of the springs were loose. Around the walls hung his traps and two other rifles in scabbards. Piled in one corner was his saddle and horse gear.

"Money was what did it," the deputy said. "Never was right, giving people all that money."

Cleve dug for his coat in the pile of winter clothes behind the double bed where he slept alone.

"You get a deer?" the deputy asked.

"Yeah, I did." Cleve had killed thirteen, seven bucks and six does. He had sold the bucks to white hunters who had frozen at the moment of kill or had drunk through their sporting trip from Portland or Eugene or wherever it was, and one of the butchered does was hanging now in the back bedroom. The others were in a locker of the Donan cold-storage plant. The room stank of leather and grease and dried blood, of hunting. "I got him hung in the back room," Cleve said. "I'm eating on him."

"You get a tag?" the deputy asked. "You guys got the money now, you got to act like somebody."

"Yeah, I got a tag." Until the reservation dissolved, the tribes hunted freely. Now they were bound by state regulations. Only those who had refused the money had remained free. They could kill as many deer as they wanted without any sort of printed, paid-for permission. Cleve had killed thirteen deer and hadn't bought a tag, and the doe hanging in the back room was illegal. All because he had taken the money, because Lonnie had talked him into the money. He had spent almost none of it because that idea of giving it back had been with him since the beginning.

"I guess maybe you did," the deputy said. "I remember somebody saying you bought a tag." He walked the room slowly, looking at the gear. Cleve buttoned his blanket-lined Levi's jacket. The right sleeve was torn and the lining clotted with cheatgrass stickers. He'd worn it the winter before while feeding cattle, continuing to refuse the money. The front was frayed by alfalfa bales. Lately he had thought of buying a sheepskin-lined leather coat like the ones pictured in the slick-paged New York magazines on the stand in Prince's Tavern.

"You ready?" Cleve asked the deputy.

"I'm looking around. You got some good things. Let me look around." Dust was blowing past the Plymouth, and on the highway three empty cattle trucks passed, each close behind the other. Cleve wished the house was miles into the back-woods, where the river was alone and he wouldn't have to see anything but the water and tree shadows on the ripples and once in a while animals, snow in the winter, with porcupine and maybe traveling deer. He hated the barbed wire and the railroad I-beam cattle guard and the black car waiting for him in the dusty bowl before the house.

Red Yount was fingering the pieces of the .30-06 mechanism spread on the table. Cleve wondered why he had asked him inside. He should never have forgotten the other times, the single jail cell in the basement of the crumbling town hall in Donan. "You're used to it," Red Yount had said, bringing down the first meal, a hamburger and glass of milk from the lunch counter in Prince's. "Ought to be like coming home." Cleve had been in for six months that time, the last time. Car theft. One drunk night in a deer hunter's Jeep station wagon. The deputy laughed and shoved the tray under the bars of the door. Cleve had been there three times before, each time drunk and disorderly, but only for a week or two. Six months was different, sitting in the dampness and dim light, listening to mice and wasting out one of the summers of his life. So far he had never been back. He had run to the forest when they let him go, never drank again. And he wasn't going back.

He wondered how to get Yount away from the illegal doe hanging half-dismembered in the back room, remembered listening for the whistle marking hours from the cupola atop the city hall, asking the deputy what day it was and Yount refusing to tell him, saying, "We'll let you know. Don't worry."

"Ain't no use hanging around here," Cleve said.

"They'll get him here," the deputy said, settling himself in the rocking chair and lighting a filter cigarette. "I give up rolling 'em," he said, dropping his kitchen match to the floor.

"Them roll-your-owns was killing my wind; they do that." Yount began telling about Lonnie, and his speech came in gasps, the years of home-rolled cigarettes and beer fat over his beehive belly seeming to have indeed cost him. The Red Bluff city police found Lonnie passed out on the pedestrian walkway of the highway bridge over the Sacramento River, $3,147 in his wallet and stuffed into his various pockets when they booked his body, alive but unconscious. "They could have pumped his stomach if they'd have knowed," the deputy said. "But you can't think of everything." After the death they found the rest of the money, $27,292, in a box containing a never-worn pair of new Justin boots, the bills in a brown paper bag stuffed into one boot top. Yount ground his cigarette under his heel. "Now," he said. "Before we take off, you want to show me that carcass? I only want to look at the tag."

"No need," Cleve said. "I cut off the head. Buried it. Tag was with it."

"Maybe I'll just look at it anyway."

"Maybe you won't. Lonnie's dead. I better get to town. I better see about all that."

Red Yount stood. "I'm going to see that deer," he said. "Then you and me are going to town." He unsnapped the leather cover over his .38 pistol. "You don't make me any trouble now," he said. "I don't want to have to take you in for resisting."

"Let's go," Cleve said. "Like we was friends. There won't be any trouble at all."

"But I ain't your friend. There's no way we're friends. Which door is that deer behind?"

"Why not just forget it? Go off and leave and forget I ever asked for a ride."

"Just show me that animal." The deputy lifted his .38 from his holster and turned it in his hand. "I got to just take a look."

"OK," Cleve said. "I'll show you." His voice sounded heavy and strange, and he was quickly past the other man. As the deputy passed into the dark room where the carcass hung, Cleve opened his skinning knife.

"Doe," the deputy said. "I knew damned well." Then he cocked the pistol and began to turn, and Cleve slipped the knife just beneath his right ear, and as he did, unable to stop, he saw the puffed and forgotten white face of Red Yount's wife sadly examining a glass of beer on the counter in Prince's Tavern, and twisted the knife and felt the hot splash of blood over his hand and arm, and it was as if the knife were in the face of that stooped, beaten woman.

Red Yount was on the floor, twitching beneath the body of the doe. Wondering if he should be sorry and knowing only that he wasn't, hadn't been since the moment of killing, thinking of that woman, Cleve watched until he was sure it was over. It was only another death. Cleve washed his hands and went outside and drove the Plymouth behind the house, where it couldn't be seen from the road.

Everything was over. Lonnie was dead alone, naked, the crippled left side of his body, wreckage of childbirth, on exhibit: twisted and pretzellike left hand pulled against his chest like the wing of a dressed chicken, bowed left leg no longer covered by the clumping and built-up boot, that maimed side contrasting with the heavily corded right arm built up through years of chinning himself on door frames and the strong right leg of a football kicker and the sullen and fine features of his face, which seemed shrunken and yet resembled the faces of Indians copied on money and stamps.

Cleve walked toward Donan. It was almost evening when he started down the hill behind town, following a logger's skid trail, the blood already stiffened on his coat sleeve. Below, through the tops of the scrub pine regrowth, he could see the tin-sheathed buildings, smoke trailing up from the brick chimney above the shop-built stove at the back of Decker and Preston's garage. Cleve wondered how many of them were gathered there and if someone had gone across to Prince's for a case of beer and if they knew about Lonnie. Wind was blowing down the dusk-filled empty street as he stepped in the back door of the garage and saw only three of them around the stove. Big Jimmy and his running pal, Clarence Dunes, and Lester, the mechanic. The only car inside was Big Jimmy's baby-blue convertible. An open case of Bud sat on the floor by the stove.

Cleve walked slowly to the row where they stood, turned his back to the stove, and stood with them. Lester Braddock was older, around thirty-five, a small and bull-chested man wearing stiff new coveralls. He squatted and opened Cleve a beer. "Drink that," he said. "They're looking for you, man. They found old Yount."

Cleve stood with the cold bottle in his hand. The first sip seemed shockingly bitter and chilled him. "I guess they are," he said, his mind preoccupied with Lonnie. All the walk to town he had thought of the burial. "I'll take off in a minute," he said. "I just want to say how I want him buried."

A half mile below the house the river vanished. Cleve had dreamed of the river, and because of that dream, because Lonnie's death and the dream were all connected with the sound of water falling, he wanted to send Lonnie down through the boulders to the place where the water was sucked into the earth. The water fell between boulders in a long black lava rockslide to resurface at the bottom of the ridge, over a mile away, and the sound of the falling was hollow, as if the water dropped a great distance onto a deadened plate of steel. They had played there as children. Their father had set up a system of net-holding weirs among the boulders, and they had watched him scramble barefoot over the boulders, pulling trout from the nets, secured by a stranded rawhide riata he used for a safety line.

Just at the beginning of the war a child from some other family had fallen and been sucked underground, his body never recovered, and on the flat-surfaced boulders near the water's edge a dim cross had been smeared with greenish house paint, covering more ancient signs and drawings, memorializing that drowned, now-forgotten child. Cleve had dreamed of being that child, of falling.

He and Lonnie had never been allowed near the depressed, cup-shaped saucer of boulders where the water vanished, had played as children on the open ground beneath three huge pines where some rancher's misplaced salt trough had caused the cattle to hole up by the water, beating the pumice ground to dust. From there they threw rocks across toward the painted boulders—the one on which the modern cross dripped over the older marks of ancient tribes, and all of them covered with random-seeming yellow and green lichen-covered inscriptions: simply drawn round-headed snakes with wriggling bodies, and rippling water, and crooked marks that were mountain ranges and indicated days of travel, and the sun surrounded by straight childish rays.

The dream had begun with a thrown rock, a perfect flat skipping stone which fit exactly into his hand, and seemed to have something to do with the act of throwing. Men around him were seated with blankets over their shoulders, resembling schoolbook pictures, and the fire had burned very low, and their faces were aged, corded, and eroded to bone as he approached them, and they were looking at only him, their eyes hooded and gray. He ran to escape by open seawater which resembled pictures of British Columbia, mountains rising from a beach and forested, saw the rider galloping downhill toward the willow-decked village, and then he was on a rock washed by breaking waves and slippery, saw men coming over the sand toward his promontory, tried to run and was trapped.

Again it was night, and the old men were regarding him motionlessly before the same recognizable fire, and it was burning much higher, heaped with brush, and he was kneeling, his hands and feet bound by leather thongs and his face toward the warm flames. A naked cripple approached him from the fire, carrying a ragged stone ax and glistening with sweat—Lonnie, his right arm raised, and then the ax descending on Cleve's exposed neck, and Cleve was awake.

Big Jimmy and Clarence Dunes were looking at him. Lester was older and knew better. Cleve was grateful. They had all been friends, but Lester was the oldest and the only one who'd probably act like he had any sense of how it was to hear your brother was dead. Cleve finished the beer, drinking quickly in the long gulps, and threw the bottle into a rattling empty trash barrel. "Thanks," he said. "You do that for me." He looked at Lester, who was staring at the floor. "I'll see you around." He started to walk from the stove without any further idea of where he was going after the door that led outside, and Big Jimmy hooked him by the shoulder. Jimmy was tall, over six feet, and fat, his belly slouching until only the bottom tip of his silver buckle could be seen. His face was round, always seeming placid, untroubled, even when he was fighting. "They ain't going to go for that," he said. "Some crazy idea like that, no way." He kept his hand on Cleve's shoulder.

"You got to steal him," Cleve said, and he told them how they should put Lonnie on a raft with flowers and torches and send him down the river at night. Jimmy dropped his hand and began to talk like *he* was getting excited, like all he wanted was for somebody to tell him it was possible, that they could make it work. "We could take a case of whiskey and tell everybody and they'll all walk along with all those fires going." Cleve could never remember seeing Jimmy even look excited before.

Not even when Lonnie burned the slaughterhouse. Coming home from the All-Indian Rodeo in McDermit on the Fourth of July 1961, their parents had burned while parked and sleeping alongside the gravel road south of Denio in a six-year-old Chevrolet two-door. When the boys learned of those deaths, Lonnie began a three-day drunk which ended when he opened the door and witnessed the charred interior and fecal stench of the towed-home automobile. That night he carried a five-gallon can of kerosene to the slaughterhouse on the upper edge of the reservation town of Donan and ignited the buildings and hide pile. The next morning the odor of burnt hair and cooking flesh had been mixed with the smoke of blood-impregnated wood hanging in a gray haze. At daybreak Lonnie returned to the house and found police waiting. "How many things do you regret about your life?" The judge had asked him that. "Everything," Lonnie had answered. "Like everybody else, everything. Like you would, if you was anybody." Big Jimmy had sneered at it all. "Just drawed him more time," he had said. "Don't make sense." And now he seemed excited, now that it was too late. Cleve saw Lonnie, the sterile white room, walls, and floor of green ceramic tile, rubber garden hoses curled and hung above faucets, the stiffening body naked on a concrete drainage slab, and the man writing quickly—alcohol poisoning—then dropping the pencil, leaving, distracted by his distaste for the dead object.

Then it was decided, and Cleve was crouched in the trunk of Jimmy's baby-blue Buick convertible and they were heading south, toward Red Bluff. Cleve was curled on burlap sacks around a half-case cold-pack of Olympia, and Lester was driving because Jimmy said he was too stirred up. Cleve could feel each jar of the rough asphalt and at first tried to keep track of the curves, remember the road, and tell where they were. Now he could only tell they were moving fast. Already he had finished one beer and started on another, and he wondered a little about where he was going and really didn't care. He just felt happy and easy to be going. Then the car swerved heavily, throwing him against Jimmy's slick-worn spare, and he heard shouting from the inside and shots, and remembered the burned-out odor of his father's Chevrolet, imagined himself charred, his head filled with that stench while the shots stopped echoing, and then he was against the trunk lid and they were going over.

His head hurt when everything stopped, and he felt something running over the side of his face and wondered if it was blood or beer, and he saw lights through the crack of the now-gaping trunk lid and waited for fire while he heard Jimmy wailing. They were right side up, had rolled completely over, and then the lights were on him when the trunk lid was raised, and he felt himself cornered against a rock pile by dogs and lights and heard Jimmy again crying on and on—*he forced us, he had that gun, he would of killed us*—and then the voice changing, like Jimmy couldn't make up his mind—*they got Lester, he's dead, so get away, he's dead*—and on and on Jimmy wailing, voice changing. Cleve hoped Lester wasn't dead and remembered the .38 pistol and dug it from the pocket of his Levi's jacket, and just as it came free the first shot exploded in his right shoulder, spinning him back into the trunk, and then he had the pistol in his left hand as he fired without aim at the lights twice and dove from the stinking metal cage he was in and heard more shots as the lights scattered.

White-helmeted figures reached at him, belted and booted shadowy men, and then he was past and running toward the darkness hearing more shots, the whine of bullets passing, but at least free of fire, the possibility of fire. He dodged, tried to keep dodging like a coyote, then fell skidding on the asphalt and lay exploring with his fingers the cool granular surface, each embedded stone a mountain he must climb, and it seemed the highway was a river he was flowing down. Jimmy was screaming—*you killed him you sonsabitches*—and he knew he was killed and the wind had stopped and he was going down and down the river with Lonnie toward the place where hooded eyes were capable of infinite resistance.

LAURA HENDRIE

ARMADILLO

Jack says there's nothing out here but a lot of nothing, nothing but a lot of space. He says he likes it that way, all sky and dirt spreading out from one side to the next, with nothing in between but highway and beet fields and arroyos pointing to the little black dots that are us. When we drive, he looks straight ahead. He says you've got to play it as it lays, watch for landmarks, and not want more than what you got to begin with, otherwise you get lost and blow away like dust. He says if you take what's there to begin with, then what happens won't sneak up from behind. That's why he traps the wild dogs that live down in the arroyo. He brings them home and locks them in the old Chevrolet out back. Those dogs are so mean you have to poke food in through a side window with a stick so you don't get your hand bit off. Slobber and dog fur on the windshield so thick sometimes you can't see who's inside, but boy, can you ever hear them when you walk by. Mama Jewell, Tom Go, and the rest, they try to keep the dogs off with guns or poison, but Jack traps them alive. Three years ago, a pack of them broke through Mama Jewell's fence and carried off two pies and her pet chihuahua, but none of them will ever come around our place. They know better than to come sneaking around when they hear their friends yeowling inside the Chevy.

He has always been my father, but I've always called him Jack. I don't know what I called my mother because she left a long time ago with my baby sister, whose name was Luce. Me, I am Reba, and always have been Reba, and probably always will be, because Jack won't let them rename me anything else. They all renamed each other—Tom Go, Mama Jewell, Billy Fiddle, and the rest—but they will never rename me because Jack says that the day they renamed this place Sweetwater, the day the sugar beet plant opened, that was the same day the water started smelling like old farts. Jack says the water will stay that way until they go back to the old name, Platter. Jack says you got to take what's there to begin with because faith is a fool.

But me, I've had dreams about running across the dirt at night, a straight line above the ground, like a light shooting out from behind a just opened door in the dark, streaking out and splitting the dark in two, howling high over beet fields, rock, wire and dirt, out beyond the arroyo and over the lion-lit sky. I've woken up wet, like I'd been running for real, with my legs still twitching in the tangled-up sheet and my hands held out in front and my ears still buzzing. I, Reba, plain Reba have done this: I've woken up and felt watched.

But I know better than to tell Jack.

Tom Go is the one who told me my mother was a beauty. Jack says Tom Go's nothing but a rummy anymore, but I don't mind sitting with him. He told me the whole county fell under a cloud for Jack's sorrow the day she left with my sister, Luce. He said there'd not been a man on this earth with so many tears to cry, not over a woman, not unless it was crocodile tears. Said Jack couldn't even cook anymore, nor take people's money, nor even go to the trouble of locking up at night. "Had to serve ourselves," he said, "cause Jack'd be too busy bawlin' his eyes out." I can't see Jack with such a sorrow as to ever make him cry, but Tom Go says it's true. All I remember is having to go stay with Mama Jewell, who fed me good but wouldn't let Jubilee, my armadillo, stay with me. I don't remember my mother except that she had lot of dark hair, and I don't remember nothing about Luce except a white naked thing that slept in Jack's top dresser drawer.

There's a lot I don't remember or get mixed up when I do. Things come up at you from all sides out here, things you didn't mean to remember, while other things disappear you never meant to lose. I wouldn't tell Jack, but if I could, I'd tell Tom Go what my mother's hair smelled like after she washed it. I'd tell him I remember Jack holding hands with her, or Luce, or me; or Luce smiling, or the four of us going some place, all together, maybe a movie picture or the rodeo in Stygo, all of us laughing.

But what I do remember are the things that last all summer and always come back, so you're never sure if they were then or still are. Like looking out from underneath the porch on a hot afternoon at the highway and the dust and maybe a piece of old laundry soap tangled up in tumble weeds. Or the smell of water down in the arroyo in August, even though there's nothing but sand and cracked mud left by then. Or the smell of empty bottles and rubber out in the heat of the dump.

But at least I do remember Jubilee as she was then, though she's not coming back like those smells do every time we have a drought.

There hasn't been an armadillo in this town since Jubilee, not for hundreds of years. Tom Go got her for me at the Wild Critter Sideshow in Kyle. Jubilee: claws a hold of my T-shirt in her sleep as we lay nose to nose under the porch. She had a smell to her—all armadillos do— but I can't exactly recall it. Black eyes you could see from the inside out, and fur in her ears. She'd cry like a baby when she wasn't allowed to come with me. She could swim underwater, and when she got excited, she'd jump straight up in the air like a popped cork.

Jubilee was around when things were what they were and that was enough, when you didn't have to remember what to remember or forget.

But then my mother took Luce and left, and Jack sent me over to Stygo to Mama Jewell's, and when he told me to come back, he said Jubilee'd run away with another armadillo. And when I found her out in the dump with maggots in her eye holes, when I brought her to Jack, bawling, he went and yelled at me. Said he'd put her in there after she got run over by a truck out on the highway. Said I'd catch disease for touching dead things. Took Jubilee away by the tail and told me to put up or shut up.

And he didn't forgive me either, not for a long time, not till he brought a cardboard box to me and said it was a present. It rattled when he shook it at me. "Come out from under that porch," he said, and when I wouldn't, he shook it at me again. "Take it, Reba. Heed it. I will not have you sad." And then he made me come out and take it, though I didn't want to, though I wanted to hear more first. But his sorrow must have been over by then because I don't remember him saying any more, only flicking off the lid like you might flick a fly off a horse's butt. And there was Jubilee, my Jubilee, with marbles where the maggots had been, with a little pink plastic tongue and all four feet nailed to a board, stiff as popsicle sticks so she could stand up. Jack stood over me, and when I looked up, his head blocked off the sun. He said: "You'll not be sad and soft, Reba, not if you're to stay with me. I'll not account for it."

And it was true, though I didn't think so then. I wanted to be sad a long time, show him I could miss Jubilee forever. Didn't want to call the thing in the box Jubilee either. But Jack took to hunting wild dogs in the arroyo all day, and all night blowing the roof off serving free beer to the beet pickers. Sometimes he didn't even close, and sometimes he'd drag out two dogs and stage a fight so the beet pickers'd have something to stick around for, if there wasn't a fight amongst the pickers themselves first. He hardly took notice of me at all. The beet pickers' wives heard about the betting and threatened to close us down if Jack kept it up; but of course, that came to naught because there isn't another place that makes sweet bacon stew like Jack does, not even if you drive all the way to Kyle.

Then in August, Mama Jewell in all her Godrighteousness came to get me, saying Jack's was no place for the disadvantaged, holding her nose when she said it and looking like a rusty crowbar out in our parking lot in her widow dress with dust to the knees. Jack was down in the arroyo but I was under the porch, and I told her to go to hell in a box first, that if Jack was no good, I wasn't either, that I'd sic the dogs on her if she tried to come get me. I thought for sure she'd keel when I said that—thought I would too—only she left instead, fists clenched, but scared enough to look back to make sure the dogs weren't following. I watched her leave from under the porch, and a hot-cold space pushed under me, making me think of Jubilee, making me want to bust out laughing and bawling at the same time. But I went inside and got the box and set Jubilee out on the counter. Even though the tongue was pink when it should have been purply white, even though the shell was mostly varnish. It seemed to me a right thing to do. I spat on Jack's dish towel and cleaned the dust off the marbles.

And I was right, because that old bag has left us alone ever since, except for what Jack calls pity gifts: Christmas casseroles Jack feeds to the dogs, afghans we use to plug cracks in the windows. Mama Jewell tells Tom Go that Jack and me are animals for doing it, but at least she won't be back. And Jubilee's a big hit with the beet pickers now, more than when she was alive and they said she smelled. They pat her head for luck before they place bets on the dogs.

But me, I still think about the old Jubilee. Sometimes on a day I'll look outside and think I see something skitter under a car or around the corner of the porch or behind the gas pump. At night, just as I'm about to fall asleep, she comes flying up from nowhere. Not sixty yards down the highway, not smacked flat as a hubcap and still rolling, not with the truck already half a mile away and all the little pieces of her popping free. But before all that, when she was just her. I can wake up feeling watched. Sometimes I'll hear the dogs howling out in the Chevy, and other times I'll remember Jubilee's upstairs with all twenty toes nailed to a board. But if I think of these things, I'll fall asleep and find maggots trying to get out behind her eye holes. It doesn't scare me anymore, not much, but I know better than to tell Jack.

There's more tourists now than there was before. I don't stay under the porch as much because the dust gets up my nose when they stop for gas. Last August a big purple car raced in and skidded around the parking lot like a fish, and a piece of gravel nearly put my eye out. Nowadays I sit in the cafe with Tom Go when he comes by to bum a meal and a drink. I can keep cool by the fan and watch out the window.

Usually tourists stay in their car and look at maps while Tom Go cleans crud off their windshields, but sometimes if there's two or more, they'll come inside. They order burgers or beer. I won't talk if I don't have to. Tourists think the world is made for them, and they think it stops when they drive away again. They think I was born just so they'd have something to look at.

That's why it's different when she comes. She's alone for one thing. Tourists are never alone. And she's younger than me, though not by much. And though I know she sees me, she doesn't try to act prissy or pretend I'm not there or stare me down. She doesn't look at me, but she doesn't look away, either. She just sort of stands there in the cafe, standing perfectly, looking at things from the side, like a deer when it's smelled you but hasn't decided what to do yet. I watch her and remember the time a real deer got caught in the cafe. I don't remember how it got there, but before Jack shot it, it busted out every window and broke every chair in the place trying to get back out. I think about that, and I sit on my box waiting to see if she'll do the same thing. Because she *is* like a deer about to bolt, so much like one I'm not sure the story about the real deer isn't made up in my head.

She's wearing a white shirt and white pants and white strap shoes, and there's no dust on any of it. She's got hair down her back like a black river and skin the color of coffee with a lot of cream spooned in. Not yellowish like a Yawktaw, or gray like Jack's brothers, Frank and Tiny, or sun-scarred like Jack and Tom Go and me. Not like anybody around here.

Tom Go comes in, but she doesn't look at him neither, just swishes her hair and holds out her money and says something I can't hear over the fan. I click it off fast, but she's turning her head to follow the point of Tom Go's finger out the window behind me, and I have to look down. I look down. I would slide sideways and cross my ankles if I thought she wouldn't notice. But instead, I have a stare-out with Jubilee, who's lying in my lap on her side, legs out like popsicle sticks. Now that the fan's off, there's a new smell in the room, a smell as dark and thick and sweet as the gardenias beet pickers buy in Kyle for their girls.

And there's something else. Tom Go's a dirty old man when it comes to pretty tourist girls, but he's sure not got a lot to say to her. The screen door squeaks before I can look up again, and then she's standing on the porch, a barrette of silver so bright in her hair it looks scary. Tom Go and I watch her tiptoe off the porch and around the corner. Tom Go, he sinks down on a bar stool. "Holy, holy, holy," he says. "Holy Toledo and back."

He's just talking to himself, so I don't answer.

"If I was a kid, you know, a face like hers could rip my guts out." He chuckles, but he looks hurt. He closes his eyes for a pull of beer. When he opens them, he looks at me. "You think she's pretty, Reba?" he asks.

Me, I can't judge. To say she's pretty is like saying a billion dollars isn't much to ask for. She's beyond all that.

"Well, Jack'd say be glad you don't have to look at her." He turns his back to me and slams down his beer like he's mad or something. "Well, what the hell do we know? Maybe he's right. Maybe I'm just too old to worry about it one way or another." Even so, we're both watching the door after that. It's like waiting down in the arroyo at dawn for the deer to come out of a patch of sand grass.

We hear Jack first, coming around the side of the house, talking about the dogs. Tom Go and I look right into each other just before we hear his boot on the porch, and I see Tom Go's eyebrows shoot up like he's surprised. "Reba?" he says in a funny sort of way, only just then the screen door squeaks. I make sure I'm tucked small and my ankles are crossed.

Jack holds the screen door open for her, but then he thinks better of it and goes first, knocking her with his shoulder. She is maybe just too small to shrink away from him, but I do see her shy, like Jubilee when Jack tried to feed her, and I know it riles Jack. He moves behind the counter and doesn't bother to see if she'll follow. "Come on in then," he says without looking. "Ain't going to bite us, are you?"

And to my surprise, she does come in, and stands directly, perfectly, just like she did before, with that same sideways look. Jack's grinning like a fox. He reaches in the cooler and pulls three beers. He slides one toward her and gives the other to Tom Go, who's gone still as stone in his seat.

"You don't look it, but if I remember right, you're old enough to drink now, right?"

The way Jack grins when he says it, the way Tom Go is not looking at her all of a sudden, the way I suddenly know that nobody's going to look at me if they can help it—something is moving toward something, but I can't figure it yet. And her, who nobody's looking at either, except me that is, she exactly steps to the bar and takes a beer.

I watch the light come through the front window, watch it hit the green bottle and pass through, watch it glint like a steel spark off her silver barrette, watch the cream of her neck take it in when she tilts her head so her hair falls back. She has toes and fingernails painted red. I look down at my hands and then at Jubilee's twenty toes nailed to the board. She holds the bottle in front of her with her painted hands. If I didn't think she'd disappear again, I would close my eyes to shut out her painted hands.

"I'm almost seventeen," she says. It's the first time I've heard her voice, a voice like colors, from light to dark and back again. Even Jack winces.

"So why'd you stop here?" he says.

There *is* something going on now. His voice is poison, enough to stop anybody. But not her. She winds her finger around a strand of hair, winds it until the red is lost in the black. I wonder will she cry or not. Tom Go's trying to suck the bottom out of his beer.

"I came to say hi, that's all I wanted."

But Jack starts laughing like he's choking, and that's when I know what Tom Go's known all long. The word floats up from nowhere. Luce. And I see that I've known it too, all long, known it without thinking it, ever since she walked through that door. Even though I'd planned her to look so much like me that Jack and Tom Go would have to ask which is which, even though I've looked in the mirror sometimes and seen her, even though all of that, now that she's here, I'm hardly surprised. I am Reba and I will always be Reba; and here is Luce, soft and scared and not like me in a million years.

"Remember Jubilee?" I say. But Jack steps in front and blocks off her view, laughing so loud I can't tell if she heard me.

"A sentimental trip, is that it? Is that what you want?" Jack opens his arms and waves them like sticks, trying to catch his breath from laughing. His noises are huge, rising like a howl against her. "It's the grand tour, then? Your mama, that's what she came for. She burned this place alive, she did. I tell you, she set it afire before she left."

"Jack," says Tom Go and he waves his tongue but no words come out. I peek around Jack and see her hair's fallen all around her face like black water so you can't see her eyes.

"Guess you don't have to wait, do you, Luce," says Jack. "A gal like you's got to see the world. Why, we can show you the front yard and the side yard and the back yard, and the dump, of course, and if you stay around long enough, you might even get lucky. . . ." But his voice cuts off when she swings up to look at him straight on. She's not crying neither, though maybe she will in a moment. But when she looks at him, just looks at him, it's like Jack's looking down a gun barrel. Then she looks straight at me and then at Tom Go, and then, maybe in mercy, she turns and looks out the door. No, there's not a word in this world can say what Luce looks like when she looks at you.

Tom Go jumps up. "Lay off her, Jack!" he cries, and his twisted hands shake in fists. "She ain't done nothing wrong. You stop baiting her."

"Baiting her? I ain't baiting her, rummy. I just think if she's come here wanting to change things, she better find out facts first."

"For Chrissakes, she ain't come here to find out nothing or change nothing neither. She's a kid."

"Oh yeah?" Jack's voice rises and cracks like a whip against the smell that is her. "Look at her then, you old fart. Look at her and tell me that!"

Tom Go won't look, but I do. He's right. She's changed everything.

"I'll have no part of this," says Tom Go. "I'm too old and I don't want it." He looks at me once and then he eases by Luce and out the door. Luce looks out the window like there is something to look at. Like a deer she is, her eyes flat with panic and not-knowing. Maybe she'll bolt now. You just can't tell from looking. Jack finally moves a little so I can see without leaning. And though it's her he keeps staring at, somehow I get the feeling it's me he's watching now.

"So what does Luce want first? Want to know how the sun dries you to a little black raisin out there? Want to go see where your mama tried to grow petunias once? Want to know where Jewell's chihuahua is? Or a nice Sunday drive to see what the beet pickers do? Just last week, there was another swarm. Thousands, *billions* of bugs. Think you can handle it with an umbrella and smelling salts? Your mama sure as hell couldn't." He wipes his whole face all of a sudden on his sleeve, so hard his eyeballs roll to white. "Reba can though. Yeah, and what about Reba? You haven't even said hellos yet. In fact if I was her, I might feel insulted, getting overlooked by such a soft pretty thing who calls herself sister. Well, Reba, you better get up and go shake hands with Luce, because she don't look like the type to talk to you. She looks like she'd cut out her own tongue first."

My fingers come up to my face, holding a little bit of fur from Jubilee's ear. "I don't want to, Jack."

Jack breaks out in a grin so wide his jaw could split. His shoulders loosen and he leans back, but his eyes are cold as stone. "Go on," he says. "I'll not have you say I got between you and your sister." He looks at me. "Go."

So I get off my box and try to walk quiet. I would erase her with my eyes, but she will not even look at me, only out the door at all that nothing. I touch her hand. It's cool and light and soft as rain. I would hold it to my neck and eyes. I would hide it underneath my T-shirt to feel its softness there. Luce? I ask. And behind us, there is a funny sort of cry, but when I look around, there is nobody there, only the screen door squeaking closed again.

"Is he gone?"

Oh but her voice is pretty! She looks right at me, and then I follow her, behind, in the smell of her. On the porch, she shades her eyes with one of her painted hands and looks out at all of it and I am beside her. If there was a cloud, if the beets were blooming now, if the sun would go down and turn the sky purple. But there's nothing, nothing but dust and the sign and the gas pump and a car behind it, orange as a tangerine. She's staring at it like she is everywhere else but here. The dogs start up in back and I try to think what to say. Sun burns the skin under my shirt.

"That yours?" Pointing to the car.

"Paulie lent it to me."

I'm afraid to turn sideways and look at her. "Paulie."

"He's my boyfriend."

Boyfriend.

"You getting married?"

"Yeah. Well, not till I'm eighteen. Mama said so."

Mama.

"I'm going to get married."

"You got a boyfriend?" She looks down at my foot.

"Sure I have." The minute it's out, I feel like howling. I look down at Jubilee. "Remember Jubilee?"

"No." She swishes her hair back so I can see her neck. "Why's he keep all those dogs in a car? Jeez, he's gross. If I were you, I'd run away."

"Jack says there's no place to go." We both look down at my foot again. "This here is Jubilee," I say. "Want to pat her for good luck?"

"No." The way she says it, I want to close my eyes and erase her but she steps off the porch. She's craning on her toes, trying to see around the corner, holding back her hair with one hand. "I hate him," she says.

"Sure you don't remember Jubilee?"

"I got to go. Paulie's waiting for his car."

"Wait a minute," I say. "Want to know something? Jubilee used to eat fire ants. That's what armadillos like. I had a time of it catching them for her. But she followed me everywhere and boy could she cry when she was hungry. Only, after you left I had to stay with Mama Jewell who was afraid and said she stunk, but Jack forgot all about her, about Jubilee I mean, so she ran away and got smacked by a truck right out there. And there she was, the best thing I had." I'm out of breath. I touch her arm, I feel it move under her shirt. "She was full of maggots."

Luce turns her eyes on me, blank. I look up and taste gun bluing in the back of my throat. She points with her painted fingernail. "What's wrong with your foot anyway?"

"I was born that way. That's the way it is. That's the way it is and that's the way it is." But she doesn't understand, not her, not in a million years. All at once my eyes do close and my hand is holding Jubilee up, up, up above our heads. And I would smash her on the ground, I would smash them both, but the fingers snap off—pop, pop, pop—and my legs run north while my ears fly south and my arms fall apart like pieces of doll, and me looking up at the lion-lit sky, turning round and round in a body that is not, until the sky and dirt slap shut again, until the thread that holds me together snaps, until I whirl away in space.

Luce!

I am on the ground and she, she is moving to the orange car, moving like a deer and not once looking back. I see her get in and close the door. Are you coming back? I say. Are you coming back, Luce? When she starts the engine, her hair swishes forward, and I can see her neck when she swishes it back. She yells something I can't hear over the engine. Luce! I holler. What about Paulie? Luce, are you coming back? I'm out by the gas pump, but she's already turning onto the highway, and after a while she is nothing but a little orange dot against the dirt, and then she is nothing at all. I sit on the ground again. I forgot to tell her about the dreams at night, about feeling watched, about the dust under the porch on a hot afternoon, about the smell of water in the arroyo when there is nothing there at all. I sit and wait but I know she will not come back.

I stand up and walk around to the back. The sky's starting to cool from white back to blue and soon it will be orange and then it will be black. The dogs in the Chevrolet start growling when they smell me. Jack's stick is lying on the hood, still wet. I tap against the windshield with it, and there's a sort of scream and flash of teeth against the window in answer. I lean over and rest my cheek on the hot window. Until they stop trying to get at me, until it's all quiet except for them panting.

I edge over until I touch the door handle. Hold my breath, undo the wire that holds the door closed, and pull it open. But there's only two, both as sick and torn as hobo-stew dogs. They curl and crouch in the back and watch me. Go on, I whisper, go on.

But they're waiting. I turn my back to the Chevy and hold Jubilee and the door tight against my front and wait too. And at the last minute, when I think maybe it's a mistake after all, that's when they come leaping out, all a hurling ball of legs and fur and teeth and tongues, rolling and flipping and colliding in circles when they touch back down, yipping and yapping and then tearing away, hightailing it under fences and across beet fields, out toward the arroyo without once looking back.

I watch until they disappear, until it's quiet and only killdeers make noise. Then I close the door and tie it together again. Jubilee, I whisper, and hold her up to me, eye to eye.

I go down to my room the back way through the storm cellar, my ears still humming from the quiet, down to the dark cool crowded pantry where my room is, where things are what they are and that is enough. I set Jubilee on the shelf between cases of beer where she can look out in space with her little black eyes. At first it's hard to get used to the quiet, with all its forever no-yeowling that comes in through cracks in the window. But after a while I turn on one side and feel myself going, and then, with my legs still twitching and the heat rising up and my arms already wrapped tight around Paulie's neck, I am there.

RAYMOND CARVER

THE THIRD THING THAT KILLED MY FATHER OFF

I'll tell you what did my father in. The third thing was Dummy, that Dummy died. The first thing was Pearl Harbor. And the second thing was moving to my grandfather's farm near Wenatchee. That's where my father finished out his days, except they were probably finished before that.

My father blamed Dummy's death on Dummy's wife. Then he blamed it on the fish. And finally he blamed himself—because he was the one that showed Dummy the ad in the back of *Field and Stream* for live black bass shipped anywhere in the U.S.

It was after he got the fish that Dummy started acting peculiar. The fish changed Dummy's whole personality. That's what my father said.

I never knew Dummy's real name. If anyone did, I never heard it. Dummy it was then, and it's Dummy I remember him by now. He was a little wrinkled man, bald-headed, short but very powerful in the arms and legs. If he grinned, which was seldom, his lips folded back over brown, broken teeth. It gave him a crafty expression. His watery eyes stayed fastened on your mouth when you were talking—and if you weren't, they'd go to someplace queer on your body.

I don't think he was really deaf. At least not as deaf as he made out. But he sure couldn't talk. That was for certain.

Deaf or no, Dummy'd been on as a common laborer out at the sawmill since the 1920s. This was the Cascade Lumber

Company in Yakima, Washington. The years I knew him, Dummy was working as a cleanup man. And all those years I never saw him with anything different on. Meaning a felt hat, a khaki workshirt, a denim jacket over a pair of coveralls. In his top pockets he carried rolls of toilet paper, as one of his jobs was to clean and supply the toilets. It kept him busy, seeing as how the men on nights used to walk off after their tours with a roll or two in their lunchboxes.

Dummy carried a flashlight, even though he worked days. He also carried wrenches, pliers, screwdrivers, friction tape, all the same things the millwrights carried. Well, it made them kid Dummy, the way he was, always carrying everything. Carl Lowe, Ted Slade, Johnny Wait, they were the worst kidders of the ones that kidded Dummy. But Dummy took it all in stride. I think he'd gotten used to it.

My father never kidded Dummy. Not to my knowledge, anyway. Dad was a big, heavy-shouldered man with a crew-haircut, double chin, and a belly of real size. Dummy was always staring at that belly. He'd come to the filing room where my father worked, and he'd sit on a stool and watch my dad's belly while he used the big emery wheels on the saws.

Dummy had a house as good as anyone's.

It was a tarpaper-covered affair near the river, five or six miles from town. Half a mile behind the house, at the end of a pasture, there lay a big gravel pit that the state had dug when they were paving the roads around there. Three good-sized holes had been scooped out, and over the years they'd filled with water. By and by, the three ponds came together to make one.

It was deep. It had a darkish look to it.

Dummy had a wife as well as a house. She was a woman years younger and said to go around with Mexicans. Father said it was busybodies that said that, men like Lowe and Wait and Slade.

She was a small stout woman with glittery little eyes. The first time I saw her, I saw those eyes. It was when I was with Pete Jensen and we were on our bicycles and we stopped at Dummy's to get a glass of water.

When she opened the door, I told her I was Del Fraser's son. I said, "He works with—" And then I realized. "You know, your husband. We were on our bicycles and thought we could get a drink."

"Wait here," she said.

She came back with a little tin cup of water in each hand. I downed mine in a single gulp.

But she didn't offer us more. She watched us without saying anything. When we started to get on our bicycles, she came over to the edge of the porch.

"You little fellas had a car now, I might catch a ride with you."

She grinned. Her teeth looked too big for her mouth.

"Let's go," Pete said, and we went.

There weren't many places you could fish for bass in our part of the state. There was rainbow mostly, a few brook and Dolly Varden in some of the high mountain streams, and silvers in Blue Lake and Lake Rimrock. That was mostly it, except for the runs of steelhead and salmon in some of the freshwater rivers in late fall. But if you were a fisherman, it was enough to keep you busy. No one fished for bass. A lot of people I knew had never seen a bass except for pictures. But my father had seen plenty of them when he was growing up in Arkansas and Georgia, and he had high hopes to do with Dummy's bass, Dummy being a friend.

The day the fish arrived, I'd gone swimming at the city pool. I remember coming home and going out again to get them since Dad was going to give Dummy a hand—three tanks Parcel Post from Baton Rouge, Louisiana.

We went in Dummy's pickup, Dad and Dummy and me.

These tanks turned out to be barrels, really, the three of them crated in pine lath. They were standing in the shade out back of the train depot, and it took my dad and Dummy both to lift each crate into the truck.

Dummy drove very carefully through town and just as carefully all the way to his house. He went right through his yard without stopping. He went on down to within feet of the pond. By that time it was nearly dark, so he kept his headlights on and took out a hammer and a tire iron from under the seat, and then the two of them lugged the crates up close to the water and started tearing open the first one.

The barrel inside was wrapped in burlap, and there were these nickel-sized holes in the lid. They raised it off and Dummy aimed his flashlight in.

It looked like a million bass fingerlings were finning inside. It was the strangest sight, all those live things busy in there, like a little ocean that had come on the train.

Dummy scooted the barrel to the edge of the water and poured it out. He took his flashlight and shined it into the pond. But there was nothing to be seen anymore. You could hear the frogs going, but you could hear them going anytime it newly got dark.

"Let me get the other crates," my father said, and he reached over as if to take the hammer from Dummy's coveralls. But Dummy pulled back and shook his head.

He undid the other two crates himself, leaving dark drops of blood on the lath where he ripped his hand doing it.

From that night on, Dummy was different.

Dummy wouldn't let anyone come around now anymore. He put up fencing all around the pasture, and then he fenced off the pond with electrical barbed wire. They said it cost him all his savings for that fence.

Of course, my father wouldn't have anything to do with Dummy after that. Not since Dummy ran him off. Not from fishing, mind you, because the bass were just babies still. But even from trying to get a look.

One evening two years after, when Dad was working late and I took him his food and a jar of iced tea, I found him standing talking with Syd Glover, the millwright. Just as I came in, I heard Dad saying, "You'd reckon the fool was married to them fish, the way he acts."

"From what I hear," Syd said, "he'd do better to put that fence round his house."

My father saw me then, and I saw him signal Syd Glover with his eyes.

But a month later my dad finally made Dummy do it. What he did was, he told Dummy how you had to thin out the weak ones on account of keeping things fit for the rest of them. Dummy stood there pulling at his ear and staring at the floor. Dad said, Yeah, he'd be down to do it tomorrow because it had to be done. Dummy never said yes, actually. He just never said no, is all. All he did was pull on his ear some more.

When Dad got home that day, I was ready and waiting. I had his old bass plugs out and was testing the treble hooks with my finger.

"You set?" he called to me, jumping out of the car. "I'll go to the toilet, you put the stuff in. You can drive us out there if you want."

I'd stowed everything in the back seat and was trying out the wheel when he came back out wearing his fishing hat and eating a wedge of cake with both hands.

Mother was standing in the door watching. She was a fair-skinned woman, her blonde hair pulled back in a tight bun and fastened down with a rhinestone clip. I wonder if she ever went around back in those happy days, or what she ever really did.

I let out the handbrake. Mother watched until I'd shifted gears, and then, still unsmiling, she went back inside.

It was a fine afternoon. We had all the windows down to let the air in. We crossed the Moxee Bridge and swung west onto Slater Road. Alfalfa fields stood off to either side, and farther on it was cornfields.

Dad had his hand out the window. He was letting the wind carry it back. He was restless, I could see.

It wasn't long before we pulled up at Dummy's. He came out of the house wearing his hat. His wife was looking out the window.

"You got your frying pan ready?" Dad hollered out to Dummy, but Dummy just stood there eyeing the car. "Hey, Dummy!" Dad yelled. "Hey, Dummy, where's your pole, Dummy?"

Dummy jerked his head back and forth. He moved his weight from one leg to the other and looked at the ground and then at us. His tongue rested on his lower lip, and he began working his foot into the dirt.

I shouldered the creel. I handed Dad his pole and picked up my own.

"We set to go?" Dad said. "Hey, Dummy, we set to go?"

Dummy took off his hat and, with the same hand, he wiped his wrist over his head. He turned abruptly, and we followed him across the spongy pasture. Every twenty feet or so a snipe sprang up from the clumps of grass at the edge of the old furrows.

At the end of the pasture, the ground sloped gently and became dry and rocky, nettle bushes and scrub oaks scattered here and there. We cut to the right, following an old set of car tracks, going through a field of milkweed that came up to our waists, the dry pods at the tops of the stalks rattling angrily as we pushed through. Presently, I saw the sheen of water over Dummy's shoulder, and I heard Dad shout, "Oh, Lord, look at that!"

But Dummy slowed down and kept bringing his hand up and moving his hat back and forth over his head, and then he just stopped flat.

Dad said, "Well, what do you think, Dummy? One place good as another? Where do you say we should come onto it?"

Dummy wet his lower lip.

"What's the matter with you, Dummy?" Dad said. "This your pond, ain't it?"

Dummy looked down and picked an ant off his coveralls.

"Well, hell," Dad said, letting out his breath. He took out his watch. "If it's still all right with you, we'll get to it before it gets too dark."

Dummy stuck his hands in his pockets and turned back to the pond. He started walking again. We trailed along behind. We could see the whole pond now, the water dimpled with rising fish. Every so often a bass would leap clear and come down in a splash.

"Great God," I heard my father say.

We came up to the pond at an open place, a gravel beach kind of.

Dad motioned to me and dropped into a crouch. I dropped too. He was peering into the water in front of us, and when I looked, I saw what had taken him so.

"Honest to God," he whispered.

A school of bass was cruising, twenty, thirty, not one of them under two pounds. They veered off, and then they shifted and came back, so densely spaced they looked like they were bumping up against each other. I could see their big, heavy-lidded eyes watching us as they went by. They flashed away again, and again they came back.

They were asking for it. It didn't make any difference if we stayed squatted or stood up. The fish just didn't think a thing about us. I tell you, it was a sight to behold.

We sat there for quite a while, watching that school of bass go so innocently about their business, Dummy the whole time pulling at his fingers and looking around as if he expected someone to show up. All over the pond the bass were coming up to nuzzle the water, or jumping clear and falling back, or coming up to the surface to swim along with their dorsals sticking out.

Dad signaled, and we got up to cast. I tell you, I was shaky with excitement. I could hardly get the plug loose from the cork handle of my pole. It was while I was trying to get the hooks out that I felt Dummy seize my shoulder with his big fingers. I looked, and in answer Dummy worked his chin in Dad's direction. What he wanted was clear enough, no more than one pole.

Dad took off his hat and then put it back on and then he moved over to where I stood.

"You go on, Jack," he said. "That's all right, son— you do it now."

I looked at Dummy just before I laid out my cast. His face had gone rigid, and there was a thin line of drool on his chin.

"Come back stout on the sucker when he strikes," Dad said. "Sons of bitches got mouths hard as doorknobs."

I flipped off the drag lever and threw back my arm. I sent her out a good forty feet. The water was boiling even before I had time to take up the slack.

"Hit him!" Dad yelled. "Hit the son of a bitch! Hit him good!"

I came back hard, twice. I had him, all right. The rod bowed over and jerked back and forth. Dad kept yelling what to do.

"Let him go, let him go! Let him run! Give him more line! Now wind in! Wind in! No, let him run! Woo-ee! Will you look at that!"

The bass danced around the pond. Every time it came up out of the water, it shook its head so hard you could hear the plug rattle. And then he'd take off again. But by and by I wore him out and had him in up close. He looked enormous, six or seven pounds maybe. He lay on his side, whipped, mouth open, gills working. My knees felt so weak I could hardly stand. But I held the rod up, the line tight.

Dad waded out over his shoes. But when he reached for the fish, Dummy started sputtering, shaking his head, waving his arms.

"Now what the hell's the matter with you, Dummy? The boy's got hold of the biggest bass I ever seen, and he ain't going to throw him back, by God!"

Dummy kept carrying on and gesturing toward the pond.

"I ain't about to let this boy's fish go. You hear me, Dummy? You got another think coming if you think I'm going to do that."

Dummy reached for my line. Meanwhile, the bass had gained some strength back. He turned himself over and started swimming again. I yelled and then I lost my head and slammed down the brake on the reel and started winding. The bass made a last, furious run.

That was that. The line broke. I almost fell over on my back.

"Come on, Jack," Dad said, and I saw him grabbing up his pole. "Come on, goddamn the fool, before I knock the man down."

That February the river flooded.

It had snowed pretty heavy the first weeks of December, and turned real cold before Christmas. The ground froze. The snow stayed where it was. But toward the end of January, the Chinook wind struck. I woke up one morning to hear the house getting buffeted and the steady drizzle of water running off the roof.

It blew for five days, and on the third day the river began to rise.

"She's up to fifteen feet," my father said one evening, looking over his newspaper. "Which is three feet over what you need to flood. Old Dummy going to lose his darlings."

I wanted to go down to the Moxee Bridge to see how high the water was running. But my dad wouldn't let me. He said a flood was nothing to see.

Two days later the river crested, and after that the water began to subside.

Orin Marshall and Danny Owens and I bicycled out to Dummy's one morning a week after. We parked our bicycles and walked across the pasture that bordered Dummy's property.

It was a wet, blustery day, the clouds dark and broken, moving fast across the sky. The ground was soppy wet and we kept coming to puddles in the thick grass. Danny was just learning how to cuss, and he filled the air with the best he had every time he stepped in over his shoes. We could see the swollen river at the end of the pasture. The water was still high and out of its channel, surging around the trunks of trees and eating away at the edge of the land. Out toward the middle, the current moved heavy and swift, and now and then a bush floated by, or a tree with its branches sticking up.

We came to Dummy's fence and found a cow wedged in up against the wire. She was bloated and her skin was shiny-looking and gray. It was the first dead thing of any size I'd ever seen. I remember Orin took a stick and touched the open eyes.

We moved on down the fence, toward the river. We were afraid to go near the wire because we thought it might still have electricity in it. But at the edge of what looked like a deep canal, the fence came to an end. The ground had simply dropped into the water here, and the fence along with it.

We crossed over and followed the new channel that cut directly into Dummy's land and headed straight for his pond, going into it lengthwise and forcing an outlet for itself at the other end, then twisting off until it joined up with the river farther on.

You didn't doubt that most of Dummy's fish had been carried off. But those that hadn't been were free to come and go.

Then I caught sight of Dummy. It scared me, seeing him. I motioned to the other fellows, and we all got down.

Dummy was standing at the far side of the pond near where the water was rushing out. He was just standing there, the saddest man I ever saw.

"I sure do feel sorry for old Dummy, though," my father said at supper a few weeks after. "Mind, the poor devil brought it on himself. But you can't help but be troubled for him."

Dad went on to say George Laycock saw Dummy's wife sitting in the Sportsman's Club with a big Mexican fellow.

"And that ain't the half of it—"

Mother looked up at him sharply and then at me. But I just went on eating like I hadn't heard a thing.

Dad said, "Damn it to hell, Bea, the boy's old enough!"

He'd changed a lot, Dummy had. He was never around any of the men anymore, not if he could help it. No one felt like joking with him either, not since he'd chased Carl Lowe with a two-by-four stud after Carl tipped Dummy's hat off. But the worst of it was that Dummy was missing from work a day or two a week on the average now, and there was some talk of his being laid off.

"The man's going off the deep end," Dad said. "Clear crazy if he don't watch out."

Then on a Sunday afternoon just before my birthday, Dad and I were cleaning the garage. It was a warm, drifty day. You could see the dust hanging in the air. Mother came to the back door and said, "Del, it's for you. I think it's Vern."

I followed Dad in to wash up. When he was through talking, he put the phone down and turned to us.

"It's Dummy," he said. "Did in his wife with a hammer and drowned himself. Vern just heard it in town."

When we got out there, cars were parked all around. The gate to the pasture stood open, and I could see tire marks that led on to the pond.

The screen door was propped ajar with a box, and there was this lean, pock-faced man in slacks and sports shirt and wearing a shoulder holster. He watched Dad and me get out of the car.

"I was his friend," Dad said to the man.

The man shook his head. "Don't care who you are. Clear off unless you got business here."

"Did they find him?" Dad said.

"They're dragging," the man said, and adjusted the fit of his gun.

"All right if we walk down? I knew him pretty well."

The man said, "Take your chances. They chase you off, don't say you wasn't warned."

We went on across the pasture, taking pretty much the same route we had the day we tried fishing. There were motorboats going on the pond, dirty fluffs of exhaust hanging over it. You could see where the high water had cut away the ground and carried off trees and rocks. The two boats had uniformed men in them, and they were going back and forth, one man steering and the other man handling the rope and hooks.

An ambulance waited on the gravel beach where we'd set ourselves to cast for Dummy's bass. Two men in white lounged against the back, smoking cigarettes.

One of the motorboats cut off. We all looked up. The man in back stood up and started heaving on his rope. After a time, an arm came out of the water. It looked like the hooks had gotten Dummy in the side. The arm went back down and then it came out again, along with a bundle of something.

It's not him, I thought. It's something else that has been in there for years.

The man in the front of the boat moved to the back, and together the two men hauled the dripping thing over the side.

I looked at Dad. His face was funny the way it was set.

"Women," he said. He said, "That's what the wrong kind of woman can do to you, Jack."

But I don't think Dad really believed it. I think he just didn't know who to blame or what to say.

It seemed to me everything took a bad turn for my father after that. Just like Dummy, he wasn't the same man anymore. That arm coming up and going back down in the water, it was like so long to good times and hello to bad. Because it was nothing but that all the years after Dummy drowned himself in that dark water.

Is that what happens when a friend dies? Bad luck for the pals he left behind?

But as I said, Pearl Harbor and having to move back to his dad's place didn't do my dad one bit of good, either.

DAN O'BRIEN

CROSSING SPIDER CREEK

Here is a seriously injured man and a frightened horse.

They are high in the Rocky Mountains at the junction of the Roosevelt Trail and Spider Creek. Tom has tried to coax the horse into the freezing water twice before. Both times the horse started to cross then lost its nerve, swung around violently, and lunged back up the bank. The pivot and surge of power had been nearly too much for Tom. Both times he almost lost his grip on the saddlehorn and fell into the boulders of the creek bank. Both times, when it seemed his hold would fail, he had thought of his wife, Carol. He will try the crossing once more. It will take all the strength he has left.

This is not the Old West. It is nineteen eighty-seven, autumn, a nice day near the beginning of elk season. Two days ago, Tom led the horse, his camp packed in panniers hung over the saddle, up this same trail. He had some trouble getting the horse to cross the creek but it hadn't been bad. This was a colt. Carol's colt and well broke to lead. It had come across without much fuss. But that was before the nice weather had swelled Spider Creek with runoff and of course the colt had not had the smell of blood in his nostrils.

Tom's injury is a compound fracture of the right femur. He has wrapped it tightly with an extra cotton shirt but he can not stop the bleeding. The blood covers the right shoulder of the horse, the rifle scabbard, and the saddle from the seat to the stirrup. Tom knows that it is the loss of blood that is making him so weak. He wonders if that is why his thoughts keep wandering from what he is trying to do here, with the horse, to Carol. From time to time, over the years, she has complained that he takes her for granted. He has always known that is not true. But still it seems vaguely funny to him that now she is all he wants to think about. He wishes she could know that, hopes he will have a chance to tell her.

Perhaps it is being on this particular horse, he thinks, the one Carol likes better than any of the others. Maybe Carol has spent enough time with this horse to have become part of it.

The horse moves nervously under him as he reins it around to face the water again. Tom wishes there were a way to ease the animal through this. But there is not, and there is clearly little time. There is just this one last chance.

They begin to move slowly down the bank again. It will be all or nothing. If the horse makes it across Spider Creek they will simply ride down the trail, be at a campground in twenty minutes. There are other hunters there. They will get him to a hospital. If the horse refuses and spins in fear, Tom will fall. The horse will clamber up the bank and stand aloof, quaking with terror and forever out of reach. Tom sees himself bleeding to death, alone, by the cascading icy water.

As the horse stretches out its nose to sniff at the water, Tom thinks that there might be time, if he falls, to grab at the rifle and drag it from the scabbard as he goes down. He clucks to the horse and it moves forward. Though he would hate to, it might be possible to shoot the horse from where he would fall. With luck he would have the strength to crawl to it and hold its warm head for a few moments before it died.

Here is a seriously injured man on a frightened horse. They are standing at the edge of Spider Creek, the horse's trembling front feet in the water and the man's spurs held an inch from the horse's flanks.

DAVID KRANES

THE PHANTOM MERCURY OF NEVADA

This is not science fiction. This is real! I swear. Real as light spreading over the desert, real as thunder in the Tuscaroras. Real as friendship: me and Ross and LaVelle. Real as any Mercury that ever grew to being in Detroit, its ignition firing, its spoked wheels making a blur; its radio blaring an all-night station miles away. Real as losing a nickel in a slot machine, or a dog under the wheels of a backing Bronco. *Real*—and such a mystery!

Still, I vowed I would keep it to myself. And I made LaVelle swear. I said: "LaVelle—whatever happens; if you and I get married or don't get married; if you decide to go off to Winnemucca and sing with that group at the Star; or if you go with Mr. Forbes to Dallas—whatever. Please! Don't tell!" I had taken her on my trail bike up Mount Lewis and we had spent the night there, "engaged." The sun, blood-red, was just climbing in the east, beyond Dunphy, and reaching toward our own streets in Battle Mountain. I took a bluish-veined rock and nearly crushed my left pinkie finger to impress upon LaVelle that I meant what I said. *It was real! Ross Haine was missing.* That was all we knew or should ever say. He'd gone *off.* Maybe he'd gone to be a busboy, down at Stockman's in Elko like he sometimes said he would. But we should never breathe a word about what we felt had happened to Ross with the Phantom Mercury. Who knew? And LaVelle cried. And she sucked away the blood from my struck pinkie. And she said, "Yes, Jason! I promise! Yes!" But now LaVelle's gone. And my dreams are just about exploding. So . . .

My parents own the Owl Motel on Front Street. I live in unit 23; my younger brother, Richie, lives in unit 17; and my parents room behind the office. We're never full, but the motel, I guess, makes money; I've never heard anyone complain. I clerk seven to midnight, Mondays, Wednesdays, and Fridays; Richie, Tuesdays and Thursdays. And when my Grandfather Tombes comes up to visit from Arizona, *he* always clerks. We chip in. It really used to be fun. I could watch the Zenith or have Ross Haine over and we could both watch the Zenith. And checking people in, that was interesting. One time a man had driven all the way without stopping from Guatemala, Central America. "Is this *the* Battle Mountain?" he asked; "Battle Mountain turquoise?" And I told him: Yes, it was; and he just lit up. And then I told him that I cut stones myself, that I had some really nice green and brown spider-webbed pieces and a brand new diamond micro drill and a MT-4S compact tumbler; and we talked rocks. He was a dark man. But now, of course, my shift is terrible. All the stuff on the Zenith is about Death. And Ross is gone. And now LaVelle. And so about all there is to do is sit there, scared really, wondering if the Phantom Mercury is going to come down again out of the Tuscarora Mountains.

I never want to drive. It sounds funny to say that, because I always wanted to. I mean, I'd be going to bed in my unit at maybe one A.M., and a guest would pull his Pontiac or Chevy in and the lights would burn through my curtains, and I'd think, "God! Three more years!" Then: Two more! Then: A year and a half! Then: November! And I'd actually *dream* about this one particular Torino, three lanes wide, with its high beams on, climbing through the Humboldts toward Sparks. But now—Jeez!

Some cattle went. That was first. A family named Pollito had a small range on the Dunphy side of Battle Mountain up Rock Creek. And they started missing head. Their son, Lyle, knew Richie and Richie told me.

"How many are gone?" I asked.

"Six."

The next day Richie said: Eight. And the next: Eleven. I talked to Ross Haines, and he and I took our bikes up to Pollitos' land. It was early September, dry, the north creek barely running. Everything seemed brittle. And there was a flinty smell in the air.

We parked. Ross had gotten a quart of beer and we opened that. We sat down by some yews. We knew something was going to happen. We didn't say anything to each other before, but we talked about it afterward—and we *knew.* We picked yewberries, rolled them around between our fingers and tossed them, and watched the sun fall somewhere beyond Reno.

"Would you ever shoot anyone?" Ross asked me.

The insects and the tree frogs had started up. I didn't say anything; I just threw about three yewberries into where it was dark.

"I hope I get to be in a war," Ross went on. He said it felt like he and I were on sentry duty. We'd both shot chukar and grouse. I wasn't sure what made him think of it.

But then . . . both of us leaned forward and looked up. Neither talked. There was something . . . I don't even know if I can describe it any better than that; something high and far away in the Tuscaroras. And it was coming down. And it was coming down . . . and it was coming down . . . and it was coming down. And we were both leaning forward straining for it. And whatever it was—we never knew what that night—*increased;* that was the word we could both agree on; it *increased.* And it increased enough so that at one point we weren't looking up and away any more; we were looking all around us. "Shit! I wish I'd brought my gun!" I heard Ross whisper. And then we found ourselves looking up again—because, whatever it was, it was going home, up, away, *decreasing* now, ridge to ridge, canyon to canyon.

The next day Richie told me that three more of the Pollitos' steers had gone, and I didn't say anything to him about our being up there. I just found Ross.

We tried to agree. We tried to write down some things that both of us could say we'd seen or felt, or that had happened. We made a list. *Rumbling* was on the list, slight rumbling; we thought a while about the word *vibration,* but *rumbling* won. I was near a slide once, a rock slide close to Tonopah, and it was like that. And there was a . . . we hit up on the word *fluorescent:* a *fluorescent* glow. It wasn't bright. We argued that it could have been just kind of the after-sunset glow, but then we had to say that it wasn't; it was whiter, greener, like the light in Mr. Iatammi's welding shop, seen maybe a mile away. And there was a chemical smell, just *slight.* All of these things were just slight; it took us nearly three hours just to get the four of them down, to agree. But we'd both coughed at least once. So Ross wrote *sulphur.* And the last item was the weirdest of all. I mentioned it kind of as a joke, but then Ross agreed and said that, right, his teeth had hurt him too—when whatever-it-was was the closest. So that was it: a rumbling, a fluorescent glow, sulphur, and our teeth hurt.

LaVelle and I were friends. It hadn't gotten physical yet, except, I know, in my head. Some of the kids called her Frenchie—LaVelle Barrett—which was kind of exciting anyway; but she had a really nice singing voice and played O.K. on the guitar. We joked. She kept asking when I was going to take her to my motel, and I'd say something back and we'd laugh. But we also talked about serious things. Her father had shot a man, and the man had died, and so her father was serving out a term for it in the Wyoming state prison. LaVelle opened up to me about it one day when we were walking by the Reese River, and she cried, and I just held her and let her, and I guess that was the main reason for our friendship. Her mother was strict. She made LaVelle keep pretty exact hours. Her mother dealt at the Owl Club Casino (no relationship to our Owl Motel), but she always checked on her. Anyway, after Ross and I experienced what we experienced that first night, I told LaVelle.

"*Take* me!"

"Well . . . "

"I'd like to see!"

I spoke to Ross. He said sure; but let's the three of us keep it at that. So we decided upon the following Thursday night.

We went up at just the same time. LaVelle had a horse named Tar (she was supposed to just be out riding), and we met her at a certain place, east on I-80; and then the three of us, on Tar—poor Tar! It was crowded—rode on up.

It wasn't quite sundown, so we investigated. "What if Mr. Pollito sees us and shoots us?" LaVelle asked. I said: "I'll just tell him I'm Richie's brother and that we're trying to catch his rustlers. He'll be grateful." Then LaVelle found a rock with a long white-silver scrape mark along it.

"That's paint!" Ross said.

"No," I disagreed. "That's just bruised quartz crystals in the rock."

"The hell you say!" Ross, for some reason, got angry. "That's paint!"

At sunset we all gathered back at the same yew bushes. Ross pointed high to the north. "It'll start up there," he told LaVelle. LaVelle looked at me. She started stroking Tar's neck. She fed him a piece of sugar. Then it began, just like the time before—everything on our list, *everything:* rumbling, fluorescent glow, sulphur, our teeth hurt. Tar spooked. We thought he was going to run off for a minute. He shook his head. It must have hurt *his* teeth. LaVelle had taken my hand. It made me sweat a little. "Gol! What was that?" she asked.

The next day, Richie told me: "Another steer!"

We knew we were on to something. Ross, LaVelle, and I talked. We wanted to see whether we could add anything else to our list. "Did it trace a path?" I asked them, because I sort of had that in my mind.

"Yeah!" Ross said. His eyes just got *large.*

"Yes," LaVelle nodded.

"Coming down—and going up!" Ross moved his hand in a kind of oval.

So that was the fifth thing on our list: *an oval path.*

We tried to decide whether we should tell Mr. Pollito what we were up to, so that he wouldn't pick us off by accident; you know, shoot us. But LaVelle was concerned about her mother. So we agreed that we would just all try very hard to be careful. I went walking with LaVelle after our discussion that day, and we wandered into the woods and stood for a while and kissed. It was the very first time. I was very aware of birds there, for some reason, and I asked LaVelle later if she was. "Not particularly," she said.

Our next trip to Pollitos', we decided to locate a little more north and west. It was closer to the grazing areas, where the cattle were. LaVelle was worried about Tar. He had shied the last mile and a half at least; he had tried very much to get his own head and lead us totally someplace else. "Look at his flanks," LaVelle pointed. His flanks were jumping. "And his mane!" She said the hair was taller than usual there, stiffer. But I couldn't see it.

"Why don't we ride him back a ways?" I suggested. "Where he's more relaxed. Tie him. Then you and I can jog on back to here. We've got another half-hour or so—before dark."

So we did. We tied him and left him where he could reach a good amount of grass. I kissed LaVelle again. She was kind of against a tree, and she pressed herself, it seemed really hard, against me and I let one hand slip down from her shoulder, and she made a sound which I had never heard. But then we ran together, holding hands, back to where Ross was, anxious. "Hurry!" he said when he saw us.

That night everything happened—and *more.* To our list we added: *always just after sunset* (which we could have added after the second time), *heat* (we all agreed we'd felt a rise in heat), and—LaVelle was the one who pointed this out, but when she said it, both Ross and I had to go along—music; there was some kind of tinny or metal or something *music.* And that was the night of the first really great discovery: *tire tracks.* There were tire tracks in a meadow nearby where some steers still were. LaVelle suggested that they belonged to Mr. Pollito's pickup maybe, but working in a motel and being as interested in driving as I was, I knew they were not pickup tracks; they were *car* tracks. And they were fresh. And they were *real.* Again, I tell you this is not science fiction. Somehow a car had come down through that meadow. And not long ago! Also, Ross thought he saw something: "I saw something, I *know* it!" he said; "kind of a *car* or something like that shape!" But neither LaVelle or I could honestly go along with it, so we didn't write it down.

The next day, trying to be casual, I said: "Hey, Rich! How're Pollitos doing with their stock?"

"Weirdest thing!" he said to me. "Last night . . . !"

"Lose more?"

"No, but they found one this morning—*weird*—dead! Lyle said it looked as if it had been hit by a huge rock. Or a *car.*"

Oh, and one more kind of connected thing happened before the *true* time, before the time when we actually stood there in the yellow-and-almost-black light, stood with no breath in us at all and actually *saw* the Phantom Mercury. A Mr. Forbes came into town from Dallas. He stayed at the Big Chief Motel and not the Owl, and so I hardly saw him. But his reason for coming to Battle Mountain was LaVelle. He found her and told her that he had promised her father—who he knew very well and respected—that he would do all that he could to bring her back with him from Battle Mountain to Dallas. He told her that there were quite a few what he called "peripheral circumstances" connected with her father's shooting and killing of the other man. And that he felt that it would really be "to her best advantage" (LaVelle's, that is) to get what she could get out of the house here and return there, to Dallas, with him. They talked for several days, and she would report it back to me. She told him that what she wanted, she thought, was to be a lead singer with a group; and he had told her that that was fine; that was a good ambition; and that he would do all that he could for her. At first she thought the whole thing was just ridiculous, but after a couple days, she began to look on it, kind of, as a dilemma.

Ross got a gun. It was a .45 pistol, made in Peru, he said, but he wouldn't tell us where he got it: "Guns are available." That was it! He nailed a Clorox jug to a stump near the Reese River and marked it up worse than a Keno card with shots. I asked him what he thought he would shoot at when whatever-it-was went by the next time. He said he didn't know.

Meanwhile, LaVelle and I got on. She asked me to listen to her sing. She'd bring her guitar, and we'd climb Mt. Lewis, then sit and she'd play "Leavin' on a Jet Plane" or "Killin' Me Softly," and I'd undo the back buttons on her blouse slowly and when she finished, she'd lean forward so that the two halves of her blouse would fall to either side and she'd just stare out toward Winnemucca and Reno, west, and say to me: "Jason? Do you think I'm good enough?" And I'd say, "LaVelle, I don't know." But before I could finish saying that, she'd ask another question, insert it: "What do you think of Mr. Forbes?" And so I'd just have to tell her again: "I don't know, LaVelle. I don't know what to tell you. He seems short." And then I'd look at her, at her undone blouse kind of riffling in the mountain wind. And at about that same time she'd stand up and walk forward and press one cheek against an aspen tree, and then reach in back of her and do her blouse up again. She was making up her mind.

On the final night—I call it *the final night,* although that was true only for Ross, and even then, not exactly true—we all told our parents we were going back to the school auditorium after supper to attend the annual Battle Mountain Gem Show. We lied. We left early. Ross brought his gun. LaVelle was humming. We rode Tar partway, but on the edge of Pollitos' property, left him tied, and hiked.

"I'm planning to stand right where the tire tracks were," Ross told us. "How about you?"

We looked at him. He was carrying his gun. It was a warm night. It felt like summer coming on, sort of, instead of fall. The sky was that color green.

"Have you two gone together yet?" Ross asked us, out of nowhere. LaVelle looked off. I shook my head. "Jeez," he said, "It's just a question!" And he pointed his gun off at an old, gray junked refrigerator door. We heard our boots and LaVelle's clogs especially, pressing down on rocks all along the bed.

When we got there, where the marks had been, we stood. It was . . . I don't know. Except for insects and the diesel sound of a semi down somewhere on I-80 below, it was quiet. Dark was close. And there was the smell—I guess they'd been there earlier—of Pollitos' stock. It made me want to be beside LaVelle, to touch her, even her levis, which I tried but didn't manage too well.

We checked the air. We looked up as far as we could into the Tuscaroras. They seemed to change their shape. I'd heard a story once about a cougar who was supposed to live high up in them, one that nobody had been able, ever, to kill. His fur looked blue. And somebody had started the rumor—maybe it was an Indian; maybe it was a Shoshone story, anyway—that you could bring him down only with an arrowhead chipped out of black matrix Battle Mountain turquoise.

Ross stationed himself in the path. "I'm ready," he said. LaVelle and I stood on either side, a little away from the tracks. The Tuscaroras got dim. The sun set. The tree frogs started. I heard Ross checking the cylinder of his gun. I heard LaVelle and myself, across from each other, breathing.

"We're going to see it," I said. I don't know what, even, brought the words out.

"I know," LaVelle whispered.

"I saw it last time," Ross picked up the low, quiet tone of LaVelle. We were waiting.

Then things began. Way up. No sound, but a greenish-yellow flare, like heat lightning; the first time, not so bright; the second time, much brighter.

We were quiet.

Then the heat lightning or whatever it was flared again, this time down a ways, closer in. "I know," both Ross and I said together. Ross called out: "Touch the stones!" We saw him in the shadows reaching down and touching the stones in the creek bed. So we both reached down and touched the stones ourselves, and when we did, we could feel them shaking. "Gol!" LaVelle said. It was like the stones had little motors.

Then it flashed a fourth time. It was down now, coming down, increasing. And there was that chemical smell that we had all agreed on—but not just slight. I heard LaVelle say: "Jason!" I said, "It's all right." But Ross didn't say anything. I touched my jaw. I could taste my fillings along with the chemical smell all along the top of my mouth and in my nose. Everything grew. I heard LaVelle making sounds, halfway between crying and the sounds she'd made the night I touched her against the tree. "Get down," I said. "Tar!" she called out. "Tar!" And then: "Jason!" Ross was keeping quiet. It got warmer. Then warmer still.

The glow was coming. LaVelle fell down. It was sort of that welding light. And I could barely stand up myself because of the shaking in the stones. There was an engine sound—and then another sound: like the sound of guitar music turned way up late at night, coming from far away, from some place like Maine or West Virginia on a car radio. "*It's a car!*" I called out. "*You bet it is!*" Ross called back. We could see the shape. The shape was coming down the creek bed, glowing, rumbling, giving off showered light, then crossing the meadow just above us. Ross started piling stones up in a dam. The shape went out of sight behind some trees. "Look out!" I called. He said, "Don't worry!" LaVelle was screaming. Then it broke through the trees where we were. "Get back!" I cried. LaVelle was screaming with every breath. "It's a Mercury!" I yelled to Ross. I recognized its grill. God, it was traveling! Then Ross's gun started, again and again, exploding! I smelled gunpowder and hot rubber and transmission oil all at once, and my own body, and, I swear, LaVelle's. I saw the Mercury go by us down the creek bed and it was all silver and dented white, pitted all over like the moon. *God, it was real!* Ross's gun rang out, then stopped. The Mercury revved once, then entered some trees just below. *It was huge, man!* It was the hugest Mercury, I know, I've ever seen. It was more huge than a Lincoln, even, or a Pontiac!

It was dark. I was sweating. The radio music was in the air, moving, traveling always with the Phantom Mercury. LaVelle was stretched out, rocking, making a kind of sob. There was no moon visible. And I couldn't see Ross. "Ross! It's turned!" I called out. "Ross!" But he didn't answer. I saw the light, saw it turn its oval and start up, north, through a meadow, then begin to climb. "It's going back!" I shouted. LaVelle seemed in pain. I went to her. I knelt. She grabbed hold of me and held me; she was strong. She smelled like Tar. She tried to but couldn't form any words. I said, "That's all right," and I kissed her. She was full of sounds.

I turned my head to one side and called out "Ross!" again. But nothing came. Everything was fading. The light was flickering up into the Tuscaroras. I could see it. And it didn't look huge any more. It just looked like some backpackers with a Coleman lamp. And the stones were nearly still. And the air tasted burnt. That remained most, and the heat. My skin was dry in places, and wet in others. LaVelle calmed down. The first words she said to me, looking up, were, ". . . the music!" I didn't know what she meant; I didn't know what to say. I kissed her on the mouth again. We held it. Then I heard a stone turn, down from us, and I tried again: "Hey, Ross . . . ?"

Someone was standing in the dark. I helped LaVelle and we walked along the dry and now-empty creek bed where the Mercury had come. And Ross was there. He was standing in it, staring up through the night.

"Hi," I said. I squeezed LaVelle. I wanted her to feel that I was there.

Ross nodded.

"You O.K.?" I asked.

He was quiet. He picked up a stone and threw it. It was a white stone and I could see it leaving his hand for just a second or two. But then it went out, like a candle. And we heard it land maybe a hundred feet away. "I shot the driver," Ross told us.

"Are you serious?" LaVelle asked.

"I shot him." He was straight-faced. "That driver's got to be dead." He picked up another stone and threw it; this one was dark.

We hiked to Tar. We didn't talk. He seemed happy to see us. We mounted him and rode him down back into town. It was maybe nine o'clock.

What happened next was chance. We hadn't planned it, but none of us really wanted to go on along to our places and go to bed, so we decided to go to the Cascade Bowling Alleys and Roller Skating Rink and skate a bit. So we did. LaVelle took Tar home. She said her mother probably would be mad, but that it didn't matter. Ross and I understood.

Inside the Cascade it was pretty wonderful, in fact. It's nice to go around in what's not really dark, but not really light either, with one of those mirror-balls in the middle tossing off spots of colored light. It's nice to skate. It's nice just to have records on, too, and to be going around, just be going around and around and around *together,* with your girl in the middle and your very best friend from all your years in school on the other side. And to not be touching the ground! Do you know what I mean? Do you know what I'm talking about? I mean, to be circling and floating there in the Cascade Bowling Alleys and Roller Skating Rink with just *ball bearings* under your toes and heels, is *nice.*

We went outside after ten and just stood together. I'll always remember our feet on the ground again in the dark. It had gotten cool. Ross was quietest. We said: *See you in school tomorrow,* all of us. I remember. *See you in school;* each one; and then, each one: *Yeah . . . Yeah . . . Right . . . See you.* Then Ross turned away. And we watched him. His levi jacket looked like it had been chipped from stone. I hugged LaVelle, sort of. *Why weren't we talking? Any of us? Why?* And then I walked her home. The next day Ross wasn't in school or anywhere. Then, four months later . . . LaVelle.

I know the Mercury got them. Ross especially. I see that heat lightning high in the Tuscaroras now at dusk, and I think: *Maybe he's driving it!* That could be. *Maybe he's the driver now.* And if I go up to Pollitos' meadow at the end of some afternoon and wait—for the rumbling to start and the welding light and for my teeth to hurt—then Ross will come! And LaVelle! And we can all drive the Phantom Mercury down to the Cascade and skate. And Ross will be wearing his chiseled levi jacket. And LaVelle's voice and guitar will be in the air. And I can touch LaVelle again. And taste her. And be Ross's friend. It would be better than seeing Mr. Forbes eating broasted chicken in the Miner's Room at the Owl Club all by himself. Or waking up at headlights.

In fact, I'm sorry that I was ever curious, actually. About the world and about the real things that are in it. I mean . . . why do people disappear?

PAUL RUFFIN

THE MAN WHO WOULD BE GOD

Against the western sky the towering white house seemed as anomalous to the two cowboys as the moon sometimes did hovering in its distant beauty and peace above land that, though they would never think of leaving it, was as austere as anyone could imagine. On the catwalk that ran along the ridge of the second story, widening to an observation platform at one gable, a solitary figure in white eased along until, having come at last to the point where he stopped every rainless day they could remember over the past four years, he stood long and stared at the sparse rangeland, scattered with sage and mesquite, that stretched out to the darkening hills.

"There's Jehovah, right on schedule," one of the cowboys said, not exactly to the other one, but as much in his direction as any; he punctuated the statement with a sigh and squirt of tobacco juice that was drawn into the dust almost before it had finished splattering at his feet.

"Yep. Looking over Paradise one more time before he puts the world to bed again."

"You know, Earl," the first one confided, leaning his chair toward his listener, "there was a time I might have felt sorry for that poor son of a bitch, crazy as he is, lonely as he is—but not no more. He chose it that way."

"Yep. He chose it."

To have passed Bob Billings on the streets of any of the nearby one-horse West Texas towns in the days when he was growing into his father's vast holdings in land, oil, and banking, a stranger would have thought him merely an odd-shaped little man destined to do no more or less in this life than get by. He was short, slender, red-faced, his eyes a moody brown, and the hump in his back already—though he was still a young man—swelling out the back of his shirt. Rich as the family was, beyond all imagining in a land where oil and gas had made many a man wealthy, Billings dressed in the same dark suit each day until it frayed and tattered to the point that apparently he felt it necessary to buy a new one, exactly like the old, from a J.C. Penney store in San Antonio. Or so the story went, one of the many about Bob Billings, who, since he came out with his mother only after the old man had built his dynasty, seemed not to have any origins at all: he was simply there one day in his father's bank in Divot, a taciturn young man with no social life who occupied space for a few hours and was gone.

Whether by choice or under the direct orders of his father, himself eccentric and notoriously silent, the son served as a junior bank officer and general flunky to the old man until the senior Billings died, whereupon he sold the bank and other family enterprises in nearby towns and retreated to the great white house that sat on the Double Star, one of the many cattle spreads—bought or foreclosed on or won in a card game—that his father had owned. From there he ran the family empire, the mother long since having died and Bob an only child. What his total holdings were, no one around Divot knew; or if anyone knew, he had no proof, though wild were the figures that the old men threw around at twilight sitting along Main Street waiting for night to fall and the card games to begin. It was a standard joke that he could buy Texas itself and have enough left over to put a down payment on Europe. Whatever the worth of his inherited wealth, Bob Billings kept it to himself in his lonely castle at the Double Star.

After his father's death, Billings lived alone out there, apparently neither needing nor wanting friends or lovers. He kept one Mexican woman to do the cooking and washing and a handful of cowboys, who lived in a long bunkhouse a few hundred yards from the main house. His father had left a capable cadre of lawyers and financiers to advise his son, and speculation was that Billings had simply accepted them as they were and the empire continued to operate smoothly, as if nothing had changed. An occasional official-looking car boiled up the dirt driveway to the house, sat not even long enough for the engine to cool, then boiled back out again. The Mexican housekeeper never left the house and might as well have been mute for all the light she shed on the mystery of Billings; and the cowboys, who saw him very seldom, then only at a distance, were instructed by a foreman from another of the ranches, a man who, if he knew much about what went on at the house, was reluctant to talk about it with them. How *he* got instructions was not clear.

It was one of the cowboys, Nathan Warwick, who finally, in a late-night poker game after he had lost all he had brought to town with him and was close to slobbering drunk, let slip the seed of a story that would swell to the dimension of legend over the next few years. Fluent enough in Spanish and more than capable with women, Nathan had yielded at last to the gnawing in his loins and talked the Mexican housekeeper into bedding with him. She was not a pretty woman, was in fact short and heavy and not so very young, but she was "at hand," as Nathan put it, available, and she did have what all women, he thanked the Lord, had—and after much entreaty, she agreed to share it with him.

After a few weeks of lovemaking Nathan and Rosanna reached an agreement whereby she would leave the back door unlocked and Nathan would ease in through the mudroom, through the kitchen, and into Rosanna's room, on the bottom floor adjoining the kitchen. He always waited an hour after he saw the lights go out on the second floor, usually somewhere between ten and eleven. By then the other cowboys were asleep or off in town. Not that he cared what *they* might think—not one of them would refuse to fuck Rosanna or the mule she rode in on—but Nathan wanted to take no chances on Billings finding out about the affair.

Sometimes after making love, especially if there were no range work the next day and Nathan could sleep late, they lay and talked long into the night. He tried a couple of times to get her to talk about "The Man," as she called him, but Rosanna steadfastly refused to bring Billings into their conversations, preferring instead to dwell on her childhood days in Fuente. Her stories were good ones, nostalgic and pleasant to the ear, so Nathan did not push: he knew that sooner or later she would talk about him.

"He said *what?*" Hands fell to the table in unison when Nathan blurted it out. Jimmy Scarr was leaning across with his mouth open in front of Nathan's stubble-shadowed face.

"That's what she said. When she finally started talking to me about him."

"He wants to be *God?*" Scarr took another long swig from his beer. "He told some Meskins that he wants to be their *God?*"

"Yeah, Jimmy, their God." Nathan took another shot. "But look, I ought not to be talking about this. I reckon I better get on back out there."

"Bullshit," Walter Benson shouted, rising to his feet. "Here we been wondering about that crazy son of a bitch for years and we find out somebody knows something about him—you figger we gon' let you get out of here without telling us?" He reached over and pushed Nathan down in his chair. The other members of the game nodded. "We ain't being unreasonable, Nathan. We let you walk away from this table lots of times with winnings that we never had no chance to take back, but you ain't taking *this* pot out with you. You ain't got to work tomorrow, so set here and share it with us."

So with the cluster of men gathered around him and the night wearing away to morning, Nathan slugged down shot after shot of whiskey and told Rosanna's story.

"That particular night the moon was out real bright and we decided that we'd go walking. . . ."

"This was after you'd buggered the old whale, huh?"

"Jimmy, you shut up," someone shot back. "Get on with it, Nathan."

"Well, we slipped out the back door and walked out to the tank by the windmill—you know where it's at—and set down awhile and watched the shadows of the blades turning in the dust."

"This old boy's a poet."

"Jimmy," a voice said from the smoke of the table, "you been told to shut up. Now if you don't want to find out how quick that beer bottle of yours can get from your asshole with teeth in it to the one that ain't got teeth, you better shut the one *with* teeth."

"Well," Nathan continued, "the next morning being Sunday and neither one of us having to get up early, we set there a couple of hours talking about nothing in particular when I just out and asked her what was going on at the main house. There'd been a steady stream of Mexicans coming to the back door lately, knocking and going in and coming back out, sometimes with stuff in their arms, sometimes not. They'd get back on their jackasses and head over toward that squatter settlement—you know where it is—down on the river."

"You mean that wetback camp?" somebody asked.

"Well," Nathan answered, taking a slug from the bottle that sat beside his glass, "it's more than that. Lots of them folks has been out there for years, families of 'em, but we got ideas that they let wetbacks stay there on their way over to San Antonio."

"We don't care about that damned wetback camp, Nathan," Jimmy Scarr snapped. "Get on with the story about Billings wanting to play God."

"Aw-right, aw-right. Them Mexicans had been coming around the house a good bit lately and I just wondered what was happening, so I asked her. Well, I could tell right off that it was something that she didn't particularly want to talk about, but the moon was nice and we was nipping from some tequila and the next day being Sunday, we could sleep late. I leaned over and nuzzled on her ear some, and she broke down and told the story." He lifted the bottle again and drank deeply, winced, belched, and stared across that table into the haze. "You sure you got time for this tonight? I'm awful tired, and I'm getting fuzzy-headed."

"We got the time, Nathan," a voice came back. "You just tell the story. Somebody get him another bottle. It's on me."

"O.K. Here she goes. Now Billings, who hadn't said a word to Rosanna except for telling her to find his boots or get his brace—bet y'all didn't even know the little fart wears a back brace—all the time his daddy was alive and not much more since he died, come to her room one night. She sleeps real light anyway, so she heard his feet hit the floor and the boards creak all the way as he come from his room down to hers. He knocked and called out to her, asking if she was asleep, which she pretended to be for a while—hell, she was afraid that he'd been so pussy-starved for so long that he finally couldn't stand it no longer and had come down for the only human female flesh within twenty miles, except for what was out at the settlement.

"But he wouldn't go away, just kept on knocking and calling for her until finally she acted like she had woke up and she told him to come in. She never got up, never turned on the light, so he groped into the room and over to her bed and set down beside her, not saying nothing, just breathing real deep like something was troubling him. And when he started talking to her, Spanish, of course, since she don't know enough English to call a dog, in a low, mournful, faraway voice, she just figgered he was having a heart attack or something, and his daddy not dead a year yet. He pulled his legs up on the bed and laid down beside her and put one of his hands on her shoulder. Well, she had it figgered where the next hand was going, so she tightened herself up like an armadillo and waited. But it never come. He just went on talking and rubbing her shoulder.

"He talked about how his life had been, how he had always been lonely and unloved, how people feared and respected him because of his father's wealth, and now because of his own. He talked about how he could buy airplanes or boats and crews to run them and go anywhere in the world and buy anything he wanted, exotic islands, even small nations, if he wanted to. Told about how miserable he was with all that wealth, and—"

"God," Jimmy Scarr said, "I sure would hate to have to suffer like that, but, as the saying goes, somebody's got to do it."

"—and how all he really wanted was to be on the Double Star and have his own people to love and to love him. And that's where he told her that he wanted to be God, not to everybody—any fool knew that wouldn't work—but to a few simple, hard-working, deserving people, like those out at the settlement."

"Well I'll be damned," a voice sighed from the smoke.

So the story went round as the sun rose on Divot that day—intruding into every corner, every household, like a fresh burst of gospel that, though it might not promise an everlasting life of happiness, at least offered some reprieve from the doldrums of the present one—how Bob Billings proposed to serve as God to a settlement of poor Mexican farmers on the backside of the Double Star.

Rarely numbering more than six families, some twenty-five to thirty people ranging in age from a couple of months to over seventy, the inhabitants of the Mexican settlement, which was known by no name other than The Settlement to outsiders, stopped in a bend of the Frio River one evening after the long trek from the Mexican border, and, finding themselves too tired to move on, simply stayed. Poor and uneducated, but determined to make some sort of go of it in the U.S., they elected to enjoy the relative security of the river, where they found that if they kept a low profile no one would trouble them, if indeed anyone ever found them there. They knew from the fences they had crossed and the occasional signs along the way that they were on someone's property, as if any of them could have doubted that anyway, this being America, but the fact that there were no roads near and no railroad tracks and power poles offered the promise of relative isolation. They were farmers by chance and choice and had never known anything but subsistence, had never expected more. There was water to be had for the carrying, and they could manage to feed themselves; each family had set aside a few pesos and dollar bills for the few trips to small towns nearby, reached by circuitous routes so that no one would know exactly where they had come from.

Here, if they could remain unmolested, the farmers might go on growing a few things and running the handful of scrub cattle they had found along the way, their wives and younger children helping with the farming and the older children making their way, if they wished, to San Antonio or Austin or Houston, where there were jobs to be had that would put something in their pockets as well as their stomachs. They knew that word would get back that the settlement was there, that cousins and friends and dark strangers would be dropping in to spend the night or eat a meal, and they knew as well that Anglos would learn of the place and, sooner or later, the landowner. But until they were found out and made to move, they would live out their simple lives in the little settlement by the river.

The shacks, five in number, were constructed of discarded materials that they had carried or dragged in behind burros from wherever they had found them: mostly tin and barn timbers and fence posts from abandoned buildings and fence lines between the Mexican border and the Double Star. They had no real windows, only openings in the tin sides over which flaps of tin could be dropped when the weather was cold or wet enough to require it; the doors were likewise made of sheets of tin framed with planks. Dreadfully hot in the summer and miserably cold in the winter, the shacks were at best, as Rosanna told Nathan, fit for pigs to live in.

It was an impoverished existence, yet no worse, certainly, than they had had it back in Mexico, and at least here they had the opportunity to raise their children with the promise that they could, if they wished, move on to better things, and here what they did earn they kept, untaxed by any government or landowner. They lived an isolated, somnolent life, the Mexican squatters, where they had food and water and independence. They did not enjoy much surplus—neither did they starve.

These, then, were Bob Billings' chosen people: poor, ignorant, isolated from any church, and already dependent on his good graces for the land they lived on. As he told Rosanna deep in that night of revelation, they would be the recipients of his beneficence and love; in return they would worship him as they would any god in whose hand they were held.

When Billings made his first trip out there, he was received with suspicion and distrust, as he expected. No truck had been to the settlement before, since no roads ran to it, and this one had an Anglo in it, beside him a heavy Mexican woman; and though the bed was filled to overflowing with boxes of fruit and canned meat and dry goods, the squatters had little reason to believe that any of it was for them. They stood by their shacks as the little man, with a slight hump already rising from his far from aged back, crawled up into the bed of the truck to address them.

Billings told them that he owned the land they were living on, for as far and farther than they could see in any direction, owned miles and miles of it, its water and soil and sky, that he owned millions of dollars and had hundreds of people working for him, that he was the richest man they would ever see. To emphasize his great wealth, he told them that he owned and lived in the big white house of the Double Star, a revelation to which they responded with a murmur of disbelief, all having heard of it or seen it.

After distributing the contents of the truck bed among the families and erecting metal signs at each end of the village with the words Nuevo Cielo in white against a green background, Billings met with the elders of the settlement in private; and though Rosanna did not hear exactly what transpired between the landowner and farmers, she learned later from one of the old men who was in the meeting that Billings had made his proposal of divine ascension. He would, over the next two years, erect permanent housing for the inhabitants of Nuevo Cielo, a name which the farmers were mirthful over at first, though they tried not to show it and offend the landowner. He would see to it that the inhabitants were clothed, fed, and given adequate medical attention. On the river a powerful pumping station was to be built to provide them with filtered water for personal use and unfiltered water for irrigation. Most importantly, Billings would supervise the construction of a church.

In return the people of Nuevo Cielo must eschew all prior religious commitments and devote themselves entirely to him, using the new church as the shrine in which they would worship him. They must pray only to him, tithe (as they could afford it) to prove their devotion, come only to him for their needs, and teach their children that Billings was the only true God there was.

There was an immediate uproar from the cluster of men—this Rosanna *did* hear—and a few minutes of extreme agitation before Billings got them quieted down enough to continue. He knew, he said, that they had always worshipped the God of the Catholic faith and followed the tenets of Catholicism and that this was doubtless catching them by surprise. He pointed out to them, though, where their old god had left them: poor, uneducated, isolated in the desert. He motioned to the shacks behind them. Their god had given them hovels unfit for animals to live in and forced them to walk nearly half a mile for water, which must be carried in buckets. He had not even provided them with a place to worship.

He, Billings, on the other hand, would deliver them from their misery and allow them for the first time in their lives to enjoy surplus, asking in return little by way of material reward. They would be the recipients of his generosity, he the object of their love and devotion. He told them that he would leave them to make their decision. "I will be at the big white house over there." He pointed to the north. "When you have weighed this matter and come to the answer that will mean deliverance from misery for yourselves and your children, send someone to let me know."

The people of Nuevo Cielo accepted Bob Billings' offer and he became their God. True to his word, he had a new village built, with concrete-block, tin-roofed houses, brought in electricity, and constructed a waterworks, which delivered running water to the village. Throngs of cowboys, brought in from several ranches, laid an irrigation system, built two enormous barns, and fenced in over five hundred acres for cattle pastures, which, with water, would become highly productive in a year. A social hall was added for their amusement, and a general store, from which they could purchase whatever commodities they needed at a cost that outsiders came to envy. A church with ornate external trim and elegant furnishings rose on a high point over the river, its doors facing the white house of the Double Star. In short, Nuevo Cielo became a small town, joined to a farm-to-market highway by a caliche road, a town where Bob Billings was builder, provider, and God.

"Have y'all been out there?" Nathan Warwick was drunk again and losing and eager to turn the attention of the table to something besides cards.

A murmur came from the smoke.

"Well, you ought to go. Over a hundred Mexicans live in the village now—we throwed up another couple of houses just last week. They running so many cows that we fenced in another five hundred acres and laid in some more pipes for irrigation. Hell, they got real grass growing around them houses and enough growing in the pastures that we been having to *hay* the stuff and store it."

"He's got y'all haying for them Meskins?" someone asked.

"All we do is help them pick it up and store it. He's got folks coming in from Pearsall to do the cutting and baling. The traffic on that little old road has picked up so much that Billings is talking about blacktopping it."

"He got y'all working the cows?"

"Well, we built some real good working pens out there, and the Mexicans can do a pretty good job theirselves, but if they need us we have to go."

"Hell of a note," Jimmy Scarr said, "whites working for them Meskins."

"Yeah," a voice came back from the smoke, "but they God's *chosen* Meskins."

"I don't reckon it matters," Nathan continued, "long's we're paid, *who* we work for. Them's good people, best I can tell, and they living up to their end of the bargain; hell, that place is beginning to look like it's going to be worthy of its name."

"But what about the worship part?" another cowboy asked.

"Far's I can tell, they doing that all right too. They go to the church ever' Sunday and worship Billings, even made up some songs about him, hymns and such, tithe regularly, and teach their children that he's their God. When new ones come in, and, boy, the word has got out that Nuevo Cielo is there, they are made to do the same or told to move on. That's what Rosanna tells me. When them new wetbacks see what that village has got to offer, they forget purty quick about the god they left back in Mexico and take whatever the new one has to offer. If Billings don't put some controls on things out there, he's going to have a city on his hands."

Jimmy Scarr leaned his face out of the smoke. "Nathan, what they use for a Bible?" The group fell silent at the question.

"Well." Nathan took a long swallow from his bottle, which the men had gladly provided to keep the story going. "Rosanna says that Billings is writing his own."

"Jesus Christ!" someone muttered.

"Writing his own Word. Rosanna says that except for them evening trips onto the roof, wearing his white robe, he stays in that room, just stays cloistered up there—that's the way she puts it, *cloistered* like a monk of old—working on a Gospel for his people."

"She know what it says?" a tired voice asked.

"Naw. Can't get near that room. He won't even let her in to change the sheets, just throws them out the door once a week, and she just sets his meals down outside the door and goes and picks up the dishes later. If y'all thought he was weird before, you ain't seen nothing yet."

Someone asked what Billings did if there was trouble in the village. Nathan laughed and answered, "Trouble ain't likely out there. Them old boys got too much to lose. They got their own little police force to take care of things so that Billings not only don't have to come out to see about it—he don't ever know that it happened. I tell you, they're a purty peaceful and productive lot."

Nuevo Cielo continued to prosper over the next two years, burgeoning into a virtual paradise in the desert. Its reputation spread as a place of peace and prosperity, an oasis where hungry wetbacks could spend a few days recovering from the rigors of their journey north and, if they wished, settle into the community for good. When there was trouble, it was handled quickly and resolutely, with minor offenders being reprimanded and put on a probationary status, and those accused of serious crimes banished utterly from the village and told never to return.

Whether Nuevo Cielo operated at a profit or not, no one but Billings and the elders knew, but word was that within three years of its naming, the village had a positive cash flow from the sale of truck crops, hay, and cattle. A few pickups and flatbeds began showing up beside the houses, gifts from Billings, it was assumed, though outsiders did not know for certain. Even Nathan Warwick's dependable Rosanna could not determine, no matter how enthusiastic her efforts, precisely how much money Nuevo Cielo and its inhabitants were making, or losing, and how much Billings was continuing to sink into his personal town. Rosanna did say that the long black cars had come more frequently after the village was rebuilt and the phone had rung more often, but beyond that she knew—or would say—nothing about financial matters involving Billings and the Mexicans.

Indeed, Rosanna now had little contact with the village, the early stream of peasants bearing fruit and vegetables having dried up when their tithing turned to a cash basis as Nuevo Cielo grew and prospered. The money was collected weekly and delivered by one of the elders of the church, with whom she could not seem to find common ground for communication.

He brought the money to the back door in a leather bag every Monday morning just before noon and left it on the mudporch. When the Mexican was out of sight Rosanna took the bag up to Billings' room and left it outside the door. What became of the money she was not certain, though she assumed that it was carried off to a bank by one of the men from the many black cars that came odd hours. These silent men, dressed in dark suits and sparing not even a nod of greeting, came in without knocking, went directly to Billings' room, and after a short while came back down, got in their long black cars, and left, boiling out the dirt drive toward the highway—where they came from and where they went, she had no idea.

"He come to her room again." The table fell silent as Nathan reached for his bottle. The night was wearing on, he was almost drunk, and the game had, as usual, been going against him.

"The first time since—" someone started.

"Yeah, the first time since the first time. Scared the hell out of her too. She was laying there looking out the window—the moon was real bright, the way it was that first night—when she heard him come down the stairs. She thought maybe he was going to the kitchen for something, since she'd heard him do that before."

"You mean even God gets hungry?" a voice asked from the smoke.

"Yep. That one does. Only this time he come to her room. He knocked real light and asked whether she was asleep. Well, hell, she didn't know what to do, so she said no, and he asked whether he could come in and talk to her. Rosanna got up and turned on the light and eased the door open. He told her to turn off the light, which she done, and he stepped through. He was dressed in that long white robe, which she said glowed like a ghost in the light from the window. It was spooky. And he was talking or singing, just a whisper, in something that wasn't English or Spanish either, some language she had never heard before, and holding a box out in front of him about this big." Nathan described a shape about the size of a boot box with his hands.

"He walked over and set down on the bed, laid the box down beside him. Rosanna was standing by the window wondering what to do. She said she was scareder this time than the first, what with the white robe and strange tongue and all. Then he leaned and put out his hand and blessed her, telling her that she was one of his chosen children too and that he loved her like the others. His hand was cold as ice where he touched her on the arm, like she'd been touched by something that wasn't even living. Then he pulled her onto the bed with him.

"He told her that he was finished with the Gospel—that it was in the box—and he was going to deliver it unto his people next Sunday on his return to Nuevo Cielo."

"You talking about—"

"Yeah, day after tomorrow," Nathan answered. He squinted at his watch. "Day after today. Hell, tomorrow, Sunday."

"Wouldn't mind being there for that," Jimmy Scarr said.

"That ain't all. He said he was going to walk out there, beginning at sunup."

"Bullshit!" came a voice from the smoke. "That's ten miles if it's a foot."

"Naw it ain't," Nathan corrected him, "it's eight and a half. He can do it in three hours easy."

"He going straight across or by the trail?" someone asked.

"One thing's sure," another voice answered: "He ain't going to walk on *water*."

"Rosanna never said nothing about which way he was going, only that he was going to walk, beginning at sunup. He ought to be there in time for services." He shrugged that that was all and the game broke up, with much discussion and more than one pledging that he intended to be there to witness the return of God to Nuevo Cielo.

Sunday dawned like most other deep-summer mornings on the Double Star, brightening quickly before the sun broke; a cool wind played up from Mexico to the southwest, rocking the sage and whirling the blades of the windmill. Not wishing to miss the first leg of God's trek across the desert, the men in the pickups parked on the highway were there much earlier, arriving while even the great white house itself was barely visible. They sat and drank coffee and smoked. One or two remarked that the cowboys were already up.

"Hell, I always said that it would take the Second Coming to get them up by dawn on a Sunday," an old rancher said and cackled. The joke spread from truck to truck until the whole caravan was laughing about it.

Just as the sun broke the surface of the hills, casting a rib of sun onto the peak of Billings' house, a figure in white appeared on the roofline, eased along the catwalk, and stood on the observation platform looking off toward the village.

"That's him, that's him!" Like a jolt of electricity the word spread from truck to truck. The cowboys on the steps of the bunkhouse saw too and stood, though they, like most of the men on the road, had seen him many times on the roof at dusk. This was different—almost, as Nathan Warwick put it as he stood with his fellow cowboys by the bunkhouse steps, a religious moment: the stark white figure against the brightening sky ready to descend and walk across the desert to his people, in his hands the Gospel they must live by.

Bob Billings, if it was Bob Billings in the robe that day, disappeared into the house, reappeared at the back door, and walked off toward the Mexican village. The men in the trucks sat silently and watched, along with the cowboys before the bunkhouse, as he shrank to a white dot at the edge of the hills, then vanished into them. When he disappeared, the caravan, now joined by three other trucks from town and the cowboys in another pickup, headed off to Nuevo Cielo, just over twenty miles by road, to await his emergence on the other side.

He never came out. The Mexicans, lined up in expectation outside their church, stood in abject silence looking off to the north as the morning sun mounted to noon and the desert hills became one vast shimmer. The men from town sat in their trucks talking quietly among themselves, drinking beer and smoking and waiting.

God never returned to Nuevo Cielo. Some said that the men who managed the family fortune grew displeased with the way Billings had plowed money into the village and sent out their footmen in the long black cars to abduct and murder him, while others argued that it was Mexican farmers who felt that they had lived beneath this blasphemous human god too long who slew him in the desert and buried his body. Still others believed that Mexican bandits killed him for the money they thought he might have in the box, while some contended that Billings left the country and is living even now on an exotic island somewhere in a corner of the world where he is God to other dark people. No evidence of foul play was ever discovered, though baffled townspeople scoured the hills for days, some using metal detectors to search the sand for Billings' brace.

Sheets of the Gospel were found hither and thither in the desert over the next year or two, blown from the boot box that the sheriff from Divot discovered on a rock in the hills the afternoon of Billings' disappearance. Pieces of the handwritten lined paper may still be found in curiosity shops as far away as Dallas, selling as slivers of the ark might, and in a display case in the library in Divot, guarded rigorously by a sharp-eyed curator, is a quarter-inch-thick portion of the manuscript, and beside it a piece of white cloth that a young cowboy declared he found not a mile from the box a week after the disappearance.

The houses of Nuevo Cielo are shacks again, the green grass gone, the waterworks a wreck, and the church has been stripped to a shell of concrete blocks and tin. Only a few old farmers remain to work with their families' small vegetable patches at the edge of the harsh sand. They work, they wait, and daily they look toward the hills to the north for the God in white who will come to deliver them once again into the world of plenty. The cowboys, those remaining on the dying Double Star, sit evenings on the bunkhouse steps and watch the outline of the great house, not so much believing that a white figure will emerge against the sky as hoping that it might and fearing that they will not be there when it does.

ALICE ADAMS

THE OASIS

In Palm Springs the poor are as dry as old brown leaves, blown in from the desert—wispily thin and almost invisible. Perhaps they are embarrassed at finding themselves among so much opulence (indeed, why are they there at all? why not somewhere else?), among such soaring, thick-trunked palms, such gleamingly white, palatial hotels.

And actually, poor people are only seen in the more or less outlying areas, the stretch of North Canyon Drive, for example, where even the stores are full of sleazy, cut-rate goods, and the pastel stucco hotels are small, one story, and a little seedy, with small, shallow, too-bright blue pools. The poor are not seen in those stores, though, and certainly not in even the tawdriest motels; they stick to the street; for the most part they keep moving. A hunched-up, rag-bound man with his swollen bundle (of what? impossible to guess) might lean against a sturdy palm tree, so much fatter and stronger than he is—but only for a moment, and he would be looking around, aware of himself as displaced. And on one of the city benches a poor woman with her plastic splintered bag looks perched there, an uneasy, watchful bird, with sharp, fierce, wary eyes.

A visibly rich person would look quite odd there too, in that nebulous, interim area, unless he or she were just hurrying through—maybe running, in smart, pale jogging clothes, or briskly stepping along toward the new decorator showrooms just springing up on the outskirts of town. In any case, rich people, except in cars, are seen in that particular area of Palm Springs quite as infrequently as the very poor are.

However, on a strange day in early April—so cold, such a biting wind, in a place where bad weather is almost unheard of and could be illegal—on that day a woman all wrapped in fine, pale Italian wool and French silk, with fine, perfect champagne hair and an expensive color on her mouth—that woman, whose name is Clara Gibson, sits on a bench in what she knows is the wrong part of Palm Springs (she also knows that it is the wrong day for her to be there), and she wonders what on earth to do.

There are certain huge and quite insoluble problems lying always heavily on her mind (is this true of everyone?—she half suspects that it is, but has wondered); these have to do with her husband and her daughter, and with an entity that she vaguely and rather sadly thinks of as herself. But at the moment she can do nothing about any of these three quite problematic people. And so she concentrates on what is immediate, the fact that she has a billfold full of credit cards and almost no cash: a ten, two ones, not even much change. And her cards are not coded for sidewalk cash withdrawal from banks because her husband, Bradley, believes that this is dangerous. Also: today is Tuesday, and because she confused the dates (or something) she will be here alone until Thursday, when Bradley arrives. The confusion itself is suspicious, so unlike her; was she anxious to get away from her daughter, Jennifer, whom she was just visiting in San Francisco? Or, did she wish to curtail Bradley's time alone at his meetings in Chicago? However, this is not the time for such imponderables. She must simply decide what to do for the rest of the afternoon, and where best to go for dinner—by herself, on a credit card; the hotel in which she is staying (the wrong hotel, another error) does not serve meals.

And she must decide whether or not to give her last ten dollars to the withered, desiccated woman, with such crazed, dark, terrified eyes, whom she has been watching on the bench one down from hers. A woman very possibly her own age, or maybe younger; no one could tell. But: should she give her the money, and if so, how? (It hardly matters whether Clara is left with ten or two.)

And: why has this poor woman come to Palm Springs, of all places? Was it by mistake? Is she poor because a long time ago she made a mistaken, wrong marriage—just as Clara's own was so eminently "right"? (Marriage, for women, has often struck Clara as a sort of horse race.) But now Clara passionately wonders all these things about this woman, and she wonders too if there is a shelter for such people here. From time to time she has given money to some of the various shelter organizations in New York, where she comes from, but she has meant to do more, perhaps to go and work in one. Is there a welfare office with emergency funds available for distribution? Or have all the cuts that one reads about affected everything? Lots of MX missiles, no relief. Is there a free clinic, in case the woman is sick?

Something purple is wound among the other garments around that woman's shoulders: a remnant of a somewhat better life or a handout from someone? But it can't be warm, that purple thing, and the wind is terrible.

If Clara doesn't somehow—soon—give her the money, that woman will be gone, gone scuttering down the street like blown tumbleweed, thinks Clara, who is suddenly sensing the desert that surrounds them as an inimical force. Miles of desert, which she has never seen before, so much vaster than this small, square, green, artificial city.

Clara's plane had arrived promptly at 10:10 this morning, and after her first strange views of gray, crevassed mountains, the airport building was comfortingly small, air-conditioned (unnecessary, as things turned out, in this odd cold weather), with everything near and accessible.

The first thing she found out was that the plane from Chicago, due in at 10:30 (this reunion has been a masterpiece of timing, Clara had thought) would not arrive until 11:04. An easy wait; Clara even welcomed the time, during which she could redo her face (Brad, a surgeon, is a perfectionist in such matters), and reassemble her thoughts about and reactions to their daughter. What to tell Brad and what to relegate to her own private, silent scrutiny.

Should it be upsetting that a daughter in her early thirties earns more money than her father does at almost twice her age, her father the successful surgeon? (Clara has even secretly thought that surgeons quite possibly charge too much: Is it right, really, for operations to impoverish people? Not to mention rumors that some operations are not even necessary?) In any case, Jennifer, a corporation lawyer, is a very rich, very young person. And she is unhappy, and the cause of her discomfort is nothing as simple as not being married—the supposedly classic complaint among young women of her age. Jennifer does not want to get married, yet, although she goes out a great deal with young men. What she seems to want, really, is even more money than she has, and more *things.* She has friends of her own age and education who are earning more money than she is, even, who own more boats and condominiums. This is all very distressing to her mother; the very unfamiliarity of such problems and attitudes is upsetting (plus the hated word Yuppie, which would seem to apply). Resolutely, as she sat there in the waiting room, Clara, with her perfectly made-up face, decided that she would simply say to Brad, "Well, Jennifer's fine. She looks marvelous, she's going out a lot but nothing serious. And she's earning scads of money." (Scads? A word she has not used nor surely heard for many years, not since the days when she seemed to understand so much more than she seems to now.)

Brad, though, was not among the passengers from Chicago who poured through the gate in their inappropriate warm-weather vacation clothes, swinging tennis rackets, sacks of golf clubs.

Clara sat down to think. Out of habit, then, and out of some small nagging suspicion, she checked her small pocket notebook—and indeed it was she who had arrived on the wrong day, Tuesday. Brad would come, presumably, on Thursday.

Just next to her yellow plastic bench was a glassed-in gift shop where she could see a shelf of toy animals, one of which she remarked on as especially appealing: a silky brown dog about the size of some miniature breed. Now, as Clara watched, a woman in a fancy pink pants suit came up to exclaim, to stroke the head of the toy. A man, her companion, did the same, and then another group came over to pet and to exclaim over the adorable small false dog.

Clara found this small tableau unaccountably disturbing, and on a sudden wave of decisiveness she got up and went out to the curb where the taxis and hotel limousines assembled. She asked the snappily-uniformed man about transportation to the Maxwell. Oh yes, he assured her; a limousine. And then, "You know there're two Maxwells?"

No, Clara did not know that.

His agile eyes appraised her hair, her careful face, her clothes. "Well, I'm sure you'd be going to the Maxwell Plaza," he concluded, and he ushered her into a long white stretch Mercedes. In which she was driven for several miles of broad palm-lined streets to a huge but wonderfully low-key hotel, sand-colored—the desert motif continued in cactus plantings, a green display of succulents.

At the desk, though, in that largest and most subdued of lobbies, Clara was gently, firmly informed that she (they) had no reservation. And, "Could Mrs. Gibson just possibly have booked into the Maxwell Oasis by mistake?" This of course was the Maxwell *Plaza.*

Well, indeed it was possible that Clara had made that mistake. However, should anyone, especially her husband, *Doctor* Gibson, call or otherwise try to get in touch with her here, at the Plaza, would they kindly direct him to the Oasis, which is (probably) where Clara would be?

The Maxwell Oasis is out on North Canyon Drive, not far from the bench on which Clara was to sit and to observe the wind-blown man and the fierce-eyed, purple-swathed bag lady.

The Oasis is small, a pink-stucco, peeling, one-story building, with a small blue oblong pool. All shrouded with seedy bougainvillea. And it was there, indeed, that Clara by some chance or mischance had made a reservation. But for Thursday, not Tuesday, not today; however, luckily, they still had a room available.

In the lower-level bar of the Maxwell Plaza, though, the desert has been lavishly romanticized: behind the huge, deep, dark leather armchairs are glassed-in displays of permanently flowering cactus, interesting brown shapes of rocks, and bright polished skulls (not too many skulls, just a tasteful few).

Clara, after her meditative, observant afternoon on the bench, decided that it would make some sort of sense to come to this hotel for a drink and dinner. But just now (so out of character for her) she is engaged in telling a series of quite egregious lies to some people who are perfectly all right, probably, but who have insisted that she join them for a drink. A couple: just plain rich, aging people from Seattle, who assume that a woman alone must be lonely.

"Of course I've always loved the desert," has been Clara's first lie. The desert on closer acquaintance could become acutely terrifying is what she truly thinks.

She has also given them a curious version of her daughter, Jennifer, describing her as a social worker in East Oakland—"not much money but she's *very* happy." And she has been gratified to hear her companions, "Oh, isn't that nice! So many young people these days are so—so materialistic. What is it they call them? Yuppies!" Beaming at Clara, who is not the mother of a Yuppie.

The only excuse that Clara can make for her own preposterousness is that their joining her was almost forcible. She was enjoying her drink alone and her private thoughts. She was recalling what happened earlier that very afternoon, when, just as she was reaching into her purse for the ten-dollar bill which, yes, she would give to the bag lady (who fortunately seemed to have dozed off on her bench) Clara remembered the hundred secreted (always, on Brad's instructions) in the lining of her bag. And so, tiptoeing (feeling foolish, tiptoes on a sidewalk) Clara slipped both bills down into the red plastic bag, out of sight.

She had been imagining, thinking of the woman's discovery of the money—surely she would be pleased? she needed it for something?—at the very moment when these Seattle tourists came and practically sat on top of her.

Clara had also been thinking of how Brad would have objected. But what will that woman do with it, he would have wondered. Suppose she has a drinking problem? Clara recognizes that she herself does not much care what the woman does with her money; she simply wanted to make the gift of it. It will do no harm, she believes—although pitifully little good, so little to assuage the thick, heavy terribleness of that life, of most lives.

And then she heard, "Well, you can't sit there drinking all by yourself? You must let us join you."

Aside from their ill-timed intrusiveness, these people are annoying to Clara because (she has to face this) in certain clear ways they so strongly resemble herself and Brad. The woman's hair is the same improbably fragile pale wine color, her clothes

Italian/French. And the man's clothes are just like Brad's, doctor-banker-lawyer clothes (Nixon-Reagan clothes). The couple effect is markedly similar.

And so, partly to differentiate herself from these honest, upright, upper-middle-class citizens, Clara continues to lie.

"No, my husband isn't coming along on this trip," she tells them. "I like to get away by myself." And she smiles, a bright, independent-woman smile. "My life in New York seems impossible sometimes."

And she thinks, Well, that is at least partially true. And, conceivably, Brad too has confused the dates, and will not show up for some time—another week? I could be here by myself for quite a while, Clara thinks, though she knows this to be unlikely. But I could go somewhere else?

No, she says to the couple from Seattle, she is not going to have dinner in this hotel. She has to meet someone.

Actually Clara on the way here noticed a big, flashy delicatessen, a place that assuredly will take her credit cards. But, a place where a bag lady might possibly go? A bag lady with a little recent cash? Very likely not; still, the very possibility is more interesting than that of dinner with this couple.

Clara stands up, and the gentleman too rises. "Well," says Clara, "I've certainly enjoyed talking to you."

Which she very much hopes will be her last lie for quite some time, even if that will take a certain rearrangement of her life.